Love is Strange

Edited by

Richard Glyn Jones

INDIGO

First published in Great Britain 1998
as an Indigo paperback original

Indigo is an imprint of the Cassell Group
Wellington House, 125 Strand, London WC2R OBB

A catalogue record for this book is
available from the British Library.

ISBN 0 575 40154 0

Photoset by SetSystems Ltd, Saffron Walden, Essex
Printed and bound in Great Britain by
Guernsey Press Co. Ltd, Guernsey, Channel Isles

98 99   10 9 8 7 6 5 4 3 2 1

Contents

Introduction

As Mickey and Sylvia originally informed us, 'Love is Strange', though when their record was topping the charts in 1957 it was difficult to say in print just *how* strange it could be. Only maverick writers like Georges Bataille and Charles Bukowski were attempting to document the wilder extremes of human sexuality, and it got them into a good deal of trouble; Bukowski, to begin with, could only get his stories published in 'underground' magazines, and much of Bataille's work was for many years banned in most countries. These days, after many controversies and court battles, writers wishing to explore adult sexuality can do so freely – indeed, can take this freedom for granted on the printed page, if not on the small or big screen; it's worth reminding ourselves occasionally that now, for the first time in perhaps two hundred years, we can actually be grown-up about what we read and write. And it is possible to gather together a collection of stories about love's stranger manifestations with few holds barred.

Amongst the curious exhibits on display here are a female

contortionist looking for true love, a chemical that makes one person literally irresistible to another, a biting machine, an imaginary affair with Raymond Chandler, and sex with an animal (sort of), a corpse and a ghost, though not all at the same time. It will be seen at once that the stories in this book have a strong vein of fantasy running through them, though it is not the sort of fantasy that fills the readers' letters pages of the top-shelf magazines ('For several months I had been admiring my best friend's wife Karen, a busty blonde of thirty-six, but I never suspected that she was interested in me until one day . . .'), which are in any case mostly made up by bored staff-writers, nor is it the kind of fantasy to be found in run-of-the-mill porno books. In a previous anthology* I complained that most of the stuff currently being peddled as 'erotica' is bad because it is essentially dishonest about the way sex really is – quite apart from being for the most part badly written and poorly plotted, with lamentable characterization and no purpose other than that of temporary arousal. Or, as Fiona Pitt-Kethley put it rather more pithily,

> Sex in a porno book is always good –
> the cocks all stand, the cunts are full of cream.

The fantasies gathered in *Love is Strange* are of a rather different order, as might be expected from the writers involved. As well as Bataille and Bukowski, the pioneers,

* *Naked Graffiti* (Indigo, 1996)

there are established names such as Margaret Atwood, T. Coraghessan Boyle, Poppy Z. Brite, Angela Carter, Yasunari Kawabata (a winner of the Nobel Prize for Literature, no less), Clarice Lispector and Clive Sinclair, as well as such fast-rising talents as Nicola Barker, Lucy Ellmann and the mysterious Harold Jaffe. Male and female voices have equal space here. Using fiction to probe areas often unreachable by other means, such writers may tell us things about ourselves that generic erotica never can, and if this some- times feels dangerous and disturbing as it might in the stories by Charles Bukowski (sex with a drowned body?) and Steven Berkoff (homosexual rape) that is because love and sex can be those things. But they can also be wistful, touching, wildly funny, downright weird, complex – above all, *strange* – and all those things are here too.

In the hands of writers like these, sexual fantasy becomes literature, and the fact that they can write about these things and that we can read them are freedoms to be cherished (such freedoms are hard-won and do not always last long) and, indeed, celebrated.

RICHARD GLYN JONES

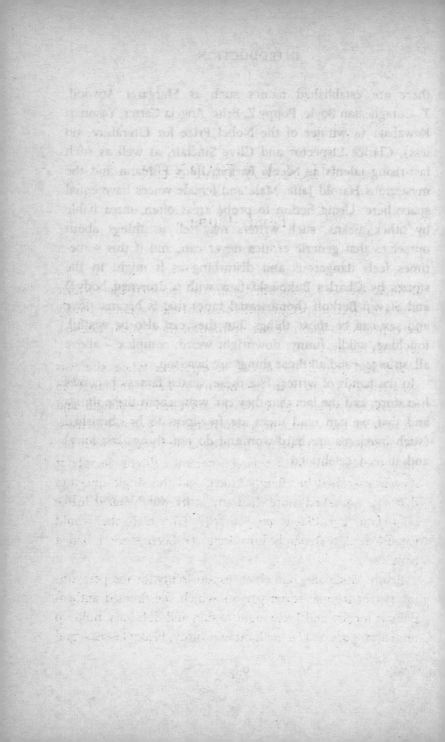

NICOLA BARKER

Bendy-Linda

Belinda was well acquainted with the fact that the tortoise was a protected species, but this information could hardly be expected to improve her opinion of these silent, shelled, sly, *old* creatures.

She had joined the circus at eighteen, when she was awarded an E grade in her history A Level and an F in physics. Six years ago. Now she travelled the length and breadth of the continent, performing her gymnastic feats. She could start off doing a back-bend and end up with her head sticking out from between her own thighs. People at the circus called her Bendy-Linda, and the single question that she was asked more than any other was: *What is it like to perform cunnilingus on yourself?* To which she would usually reply, 'Depends how long it's been since I had a bath.'

Bendy-Linda also had chief responsibility for the performing parrot troupe: seven parrots which she dressed anthropomorphically and had taught to don and doff hats, hold up miniature papers, kiss each other – birdy, beaky kisses – and dance in time to specified tunes. They also talked. They said, 'Hello there', 'Milk and no sugar', 'May I have the pleasure?' and 'Great weather we're having'. She believed that these few sentences and phrases offered the key to a perfect life. A parrot utopia.

Belinda's main problem with the birds was to keep circus people, and others, from using inappropriate language in front of them. One bird had learned how to say 'Bloody Hell' and had been forcibly retired from the troupe as a consequence. Swearwords were like fireworks: much brighter and louder and sparklier than other language. Both children and parrots – those tiny sensualists – were irresistibly drawn to them, couldn't wait to wrap their tongues around them.

There were nine acrobats and tumblers at the circus, all told.

'The turnover of staff in this field has always been rapid.' This was Alberto, circus ring master and manager.

Belinda stared at him, unsmiling. 'I suppose that goes with the territory.'

Alberto nodded, not truly comprehending. *Turnover*, Belinda felt like saying, it's a joke.

Alberto was introducing her to a new tumbler. He was tall, thickset, blond; physically unlike your average acrobat. Alberto said, 'This is Marcus. He's French.'

'Hi.' Belinda offered him her hand. He took it and squeezed it gratefully, but said nothing, only smiled. Belinda smiled back and said, 'We usually all go out for a meal when a new acrobat joins. Pizza or something. It's a tradition. Are you keen?'

He nodded eagerly.

'OK, I'll arrange it.'

The following evening, a large group of them were filling out a significant portion of a local brasserie. Belinda sat to Marcus's left. On her left was Lenny, who in her opinion was a workaholic and a bore. He was analysing one of their routines. 'The first set of tumbles,' he said, his tone rigorous, 'comes from nowhere. It's like the floor exercises in a gymnastic competition, lacking a certain fluidity, a certain finesse. I mean, there are no hard and fast rules in this business.'

Belinda looked at him, her blue eyes sombre and unblinking.

'Anyway, the tempo's all wrong.'

Choosing her moment carefully she said, 'Lenny, let's not talk about work all night, OK?' She turned and took a glass from a tray that was being proffered by a waiter. 'Pernod. Excellent.'

She focused on Marcus. 'How've your first couple of days been? I haven't seen you around much, apart from at practice and the show.' She had seen him at practice in his slinky French lycra garments. At least a foot taller than any of the other men, but gratifyingly agile.

Marcus took so long to respond to her enquiry that she almost came to the conclusion that he spoke no English at all. But eventually he said, 'It was . . . all fine.' He spoke slowly and laboriously. The effort of it brought tiny specks of perspiration to his upper lip. Belinda stared at him, wide-eyed. He's drunk, she thought, and it isn't even an hour since the matinée.

The waiter moved over to Marcus and offered him the tray. Marcus selected a bottle of beer, glad of this distraction, and drank down a hurried swig of it. Belinda said coolly, 'You're unusually tall for a tumbler.'

He nodded. 'Yes . . . I am.' after an inordinately long pause he added, 'Five foot . . . nine.'

He seemed to be relishing his words and observations with a drunk man's delight. Belinda had been tipsy herself on several occasions and was well acquainted with the feeling of intense gratification that the performance of everyday feats accorded one while in this condition. The brain works so slowly, she thought, that opening a door or saying hello are transformed into tasks of terrible complexity.

Marcus put his beer down next to his plate and started to say something else, but before he could complete his sentence, she had turned away, towards Lenny, and had begun to discuss the rudiments of their early tumbling routine with him in some detail.

Later that night, when Belinda attempted to enter her trailer, the door wouldn't slide back smoothly, but jammed when it was half open. She stopped herself from saying anything worse than 'Darn!' adding, 'Needle and thread,' for good measure. (The parrots were tucked up next door, covered for the night but ever vigilant.) She then groped around blindly in the doorway until her hand located a tortoise shell. You little swine! she thought, tucking the tortoise under her arm and reaching inside her pocket for a lighter to ignite one of the lamps.

Once the lamp was lit she kicked the door shut behind her. The tortoise was still under her arm, tucked snugly there, held dispassionately, like a newspaper or a clutch bag. His head and feet were completely drawn in.

This creature had once belonged to her grandmother and was called Smedley. Belinda dumped him down on to the floor again. He scuttled away instantly.

When Belinda had taken possession of Smedley, two years ago, she had been misguidedly under the impression that tortoises were no trouble. They hibernate, she was told. They're one of those creatures that don't need any attention. She couldn't reconcile this description with her own particular specimen. He certainly didn't seem to bother hibernating. In fact he appeared to have difficulty in sleeping at all. Most of his time was spent powering around inside her van, his head fully out, stretching on scaly elephant's skin, his feet working ten to the dozen. He took no interest in things, only walked into them or over them. Even his food.

Belinda's grandmother had owned Smedley for thirty-five years. He had lived in her garden during this time, as happy as Larry. Belinda had been given him, in accordance with the will, and a small financial sum concomitant in quantity with thirty-five more years of carrots and greens. Interest linked.

Twenty-four and thirty-five. She calculated these two numbers every time she caught a glimpse of the tortoise, scuttling from the kitchenette to her bedroom, emerging from under her sofabed. Fifty-nine. I'll be fifty-nine years old, she thought desperately, when that bloody creature finally kicks the bucket. It was as if the tortoise had already stolen those years from her. I'll be sixty, she thought, I'll be retired. I won't even have the parrots any more. I won't be able to do back-flips or walk on my hands. Smedley had taken these things from her, had aged her prematurely, had, inexplicably, made her small trailer smell of Steradent and mothballs.

It had been ten-thirty when she'd returned. At ten-forty someone knocked at her door. She pushed her slippers on, pulled her dressing gown tightly around her and yanked the door open. It was Marcus.

'What do you want?'

She stared into his face, slightly taller than him now, standing, as she was, on her top step. He said nothing, only handed her a note.

'What?' she asked again, taking it.

He bowed, low and formal, then walked off.

Belinda sat down on the top step and unfolded the note. It was written on onion paper. She always found onion paper quite peculiar. So light, so oniony. Very French.

The note said:

Good evening Belinda,
Eugenie told me that you thought I was drunk at dinner. Alas, no. I suffer from a speech impediment, a stammer, which in times of social tension can become terribly

16

pronounced. I apologize if this minor problem irritated you in any way. I can assure you that it irritates me in many ways, but, as they say, such is life. N'est-ce pas?
Marcus

Although the tone of Marcus's note, the night of the dinner out, had been anything but hostile, Belinda spent the following five days trying and failing to apologize to him and to worm her way back into his affections. She found it extremely difficult to talk things over with a person who was virtually monosyllabic.

Because Marcus spoke so very little, he gave the appearance of listening much harder than your average person. Did he listen? Belinda couldn't decide. It felt like he did. She noticed how he became a kind of father confessor to all the tumblers, the acrobats, some of the clowns, the most beautiful tightrope walkers. He didn't strike her as particularly French. His accent – the rare smatterings that she heard – didn't sound especially Gallic.

In fact, both of Marcus's parents were English. They were a couple who had taken advantage of the eighties property slump in France and had emigrated when he was eight. He was now eighteen. His stammer in French was much less pronounced than in English, which struck him as rather strange.

One thing his stammer had taught him, however, was never to waste words. In general he tried only to say things that were incisive and pertinent. He preferred to avoid chit-chat. When others spoke to him, he slashed out gratuitous noises and phrases in his mind, analysed what they said, not with the gentle, non-judgemental sense of a confessor, but with the practised, cool, steady calm of a surgeon. For instance:

Larry says: 'Marcus, tell me straight off if you think I'm out of line here, but I bet you'll find that the double back-flip after the handwalking stuff isn't strictly necessary. I mean, it's great and everything but just a little distracting.'
Marcus hears: 'Don't upstage me, new boy.'

Eugenie says: 'Wow! Those lycra things are fantastic. They look so comfy. They really do. I just love blue. I love that shade. It's my favourite colour. Are they durable? I suppose they must be French. The French are *so* stylish.'
Marcus hears: 'Let me get into your trousers.'

Belinda says: 'You really must come and meet my parrots. How about it? Tonight? After the show. If you're busy though, don't worry or anything. I mean, don't worry if you can't.'
Marcus hears: 'I'm sorry.'

In fact, Marcus was slightly off the mark with his interpretation of Belinda's babblings. The truth of the matter was that Belinda found him to be both aloof and disarming. She, too, wanted to charm the pants right off him.

Marcus had, however, noticed several worrying character-istics in Belinda's behaviour that did little to endear her to him. The first was that she jumped – too easily, too freely – to conclusions. This implied a certain amount of self-righteousness, a nasty, bullying bullishness. Secondly, she completed his sentences, which was something that he especially loathed. He guessed that people who were prone to doing this thought that they were helping him in some way, but it only made him feel useless, gratuitous, inadequate. He'd think: What is the point of *me*, if it's so easy to predict what I want, so easy to complete everything I begin?

The third and final thing that Belinda had done which had both shocked and disturbed Marcus had occurred in the pub several nights after the meal out. Alberto had taken Marcus to one side, late that afternoon, shortly after the matinée, and had raised with him the possibility that he and Belinda might perform together during Belinda's contortionist routine. Since hitherto Belinda had been the only contortionist at the circus, this slot had always been solo. Alberto was keen to have Belinda partnered during this section, and although Marcus was no contortionist himself, Alberto felt that his leonine good looks and strong physique would make him the perfect foil to Belinda's dark skinniness.

That evening, in the pub, Marcus started to mention this new possibility to Belinda as she sipped daintily at her Pernod. He said, 'Can we ... talk about ... your ... contortions ... ?'

Oh yeah? Belinda thought, and what's he up to?

Alberto had said nothing to her about his plans. She was none the wiser.

She stared at Marcus coolly, vaguely disappointed in him

but unsurprised. He was trying to talk again, but she saved him the trouble.

'Cunnilingus,' she said baldly. 'Unfortunately, my tongue is the only part of my body that isn't double-jointed, otherwise I'd dispense with you boys altogether.'

She took another sip of her drink and eyed him over the top of her glass. He blushed. He tried to say something, but it wouldn't come out. He stood up, drank down his drink in one large gulp and left the pub. Now what? She stared after him, profoundly flummoxed.

Eugenie was lounging against Marcus's trailer, waiting for him to return. She was a small, pretty acrobat with long, red ringlets. She was thirty, single, an old hand at the circus, sexually voracious. As Marcus made his way towards her he was thinking: Damn Belinda! Damn her! She's the strangest, coarsest, crudest woman I've ever met. She just seems to enjoy frightening me, on purpose.

'Hello,' Eugenie grinned at him. 'I've come around to borrow a cup of sugar.'

'Sure.'

She wasn't holding a cup. He unlocked his trailer and went inside, then emerged within seconds, holding a teacup full of sweet, white granules. He offered her the cup but she didn't take it.

'You're so literal,' she said, still smiling. 'I like that in a man.'

'Thank . . . you.' He inclined his head graciously. After a pause – not thinking to invite her in – he said, 'Be . . . linda.'

'What about her?'

'She's . . . rude.'

'She is?'

'I find . . . her so.'

Eugenie shrugged. 'You must just bring out the worst in her.'

Marcus considered this and then said, 'You think?'

'Maybe.'

'Why?'

She took the cup of sugar from him and said, 'You want to come and have some tea with me? Or coffee?'

'No . . . I . . .'

His stutter was so pronounced that Eugenie didn't wait around to listen to the reason for his refusal. She didn't mind. 'OK,' she said, phlegmatically, handing him back his cup. 'Some other time.'

Marcus sat down on his top step and stared into the cup. Thousands of grains. Mixed in with the pure, white granules were two extraneous tea leaves. That's me and Belinda, he thought. The world is full of millions of people, all friendly, all benign, the same. Then there's the two of us, destined not to get along. Belinda and Marcus. Both in the circus, this small circus. Both tumblers.

He felt relieved that his early and mid-teens had involved a longstanding but secretive intimacy with American *Playboy*. He was prepared for Belinda's lewdness, her crudeness. His father had kept an entire suitcase full of them in the attic which he had pilfered whenever he felt the inclination. Also, he had taken Latin at school, which in certain situations he found to be an invaluable linguistic tool. *Cunnus* – vulva. *Lingere* – to lick. Like choking on an oyster.

'Hi.'

Marcus looked up and almost dropped his cup. Belinda smiled at him. 'Look, I wanted to apologize. I guess I must've shocked you earlier.'

'No . . .'

'Well . . .' She focused on the strong, firm line of his jaw, its determined progression from behind his ear to the tip of his chin. 'I just saw Alberto.'

'Ah.'

'I don't suppose you want to come and see my parrots?'

'I'm . . .'

'Allergic?'

'No . . . I'm . . .'

'Busy?'

'No.'

'Go on, they're very friendly.'

Inside the parrots' trailer it was cool and dark. Belinda lit a lamp but kept the flame down low. 'It's bed-time for them really. I like them to be well rested. Otherwise they get cross and uncooperative.'

Marcus had seen the parrots already, in the big top. He thought them quaint but unnecessary. One day he hoped to work in a human circus, a wild circus where the performers did stunts on motorbikes and didn't use animals – camels with lopsided humps, sad, fleshy elephants, poodles with full wardrobes. Parrots.

'You like them?'

'I . . .'

'You don't like them?'

'No . . . I . . .'

'You like animals?'

He sighed. 'Yes.'

She said, 'My trailer's adjoining. We could have tea if you like.'

He shrugged.

Belinda opened a door and led him through. Her trailer was identical to his, only full of stuff: posters, trinkets, an extra wardrobe.

'Sit on the bed,' she said. 'I don't ever bother making it into a sofa. Too much trouble. Watch the legs are out properly. It has a tendency to collapse.' She filled the kettle.

Marcus didn't sit down immediately. First he inspected some of the photographs on her pinboard. 'These are . . .'

'Me. Yes. When I was a kid. I got gymnastics medals. I was nearly in the Olympics but I sprained my wrist very badly two weeks before. I cried for a month.'

The pictures were eerie. Belinda at eight, ten, fourteen. Belinda doing headstands, handstands, flying on the high bar. Belinda with no breasts, mosquito bites, breasts like tiny buds under the thin fabric of her leotard.

Little girls; gymnastics. He always found this combination vaguely unsettling. On television, with their stiff backs, pointed toes, determined visages. Obscene. Tumbling was different. Better.

'Coffee or tea?'

'Coffee.'

23

He sat down. The bed collapsed.

'*Merde*!' This word slid out of his mouth as quickly, as smoothly as an angry cat escaping the arms of its owner.

Belinda stopped what she was doing, turned around and then started to laugh at him, at his clumsy disarray. She said, 'You aren't hurt, are you?'

He shook his head and dragged himself up, then tried to rearrange the coverlet and cushions. Belinda turned back, still smirking, to complete her coffee-making.

This bed reminded Marcus in its construction of the deckchairs his parents had used at home; space-efficient but impossible to set up and make secure. He pulled out the metal bar that acted as the front legs and pushed up the springs and mattress. As he lifted he saw the tortoise.

Initially, it looked to him like an exotic seashell, or a lump of wood, centuries old, glossed up by the touch of many fingers, many hands. Then he saw it shudder, noticed a head, four feet. He reached out towards it, expecting a reaction. None came. One of its eyes was open, the other shut. That couldn't be right. He tapped its shell. Nothing.

I'm going to have to tell her now, he thought frantically, that I've killed her tortoise. How will I tell her? After several attempts, he said her name.

'Belinda . . .'

'Yeah?'

She had put two cups on to a tray. She picked up the tray and walked towards him. 'You haven't managed to get the bed up properly yet?'

He stared at her helplessly, as endearing and muddy-eyed

as a golden retriever at tea-time. He pointed towards the tortoise. Her eyes followed the line he was indicating.

'Smedley!'

She quickly slid the tray on top of her dresser and crouched down. 'What's happened to him?'

'The . . . bed . . .'

'He looks all squashed.'

Marcus thought this an exaggeration, but took into account the fact that he hadn't seen the tortoise before its misadventure.

'Is he dead?'

'I . . .'

'He looks dead.' She reached out her hand as if to pick him up but then shuddered and withdrew. 'I can't stand the idea of something being not quite dead.' She added tremulously, 'If he wasn't dead and I touched him and he moved . . .' The thought of this made her feel queasy.

Marcus was staring at her. She saw his face – his expression a mixture of guilt and horror – and realized that these few seconds were crucial.

'He's dead!' she said, and burst into tears.

'I . . . I . . .'

For once he couldn't think of anything to say. Usually he could think of things only couldn't say them. Eventually he said, 'Sorry'.

'Tortoises,' she said, 'are protected. Did you know that? I never really knew what it meant, though. Protected. I never really knew. He was my grandmother's. He lived in her garden for thirty-five years. He was called Smedley. He didn't hibernate, only ran about in my trailer. He wasn't terribly demonstrative, but he seemed . . . happy.'

Marcus stood up. He was eighteen. He didn't feel sufficiently senior, sufficiently adult, experienced enough, loquacious enough, to be able to cope with this situation. He felt like phoning his mother, packing and leaving, joining that other circus, that *human* circus, that un-animalled circus. He could see it already, how good it would be.

Belinda sat down on the bed. It promptly collapsed again. Marcus had only propped up the bottom leg, he hadn't got around to securing it properly. Belinda scrambled up. 'Christ! If he wasn't dead before, he is now. Christ!'

She was still crying, but was already sick of crying. Her tears weren't sufficiently effective. He wasn't hugging her yet, wasn't comforting her. Why am I crying? she thought. To seduce him? That was the sum of it. She wondered idly if you could go to hell for emotional blackmail.

Marcus took a deep breath. 'The tortoise could be hibernating.'

Belinda stopped crying in an instant and said, 'Five words all in a row! Well done! Five words, just like that!' She then burst out laughing. 'Hibernating? *Please!*'

He was mortified by her laughter. She's evil, he thought. Absolutely insincere. Absolutely unprincipled.

He's only eighteen, she thought kindly. Poor bastard.

Marcus turned to leave, so furious now, so angry that he felt like fire, like liquid. 'Your face . . .' he said, struggling, choking, '. . . Chinese Dragon!' Then walked out quickly.

Belinda stopped laughing after he'd gone, stood up,

walked over to the mirror. Her face was still mirthful but tear-smattered. Chinese Dragon?

He was right. She looked like one of those brightly coloured, finely painted Chinese masks, the dragon faces, covered in tears, but grinning, grimacing. A frightening face, apparently, but only, she supposed, if you were Chinese.

Belinda went over to lift her mattress, pulled up the bed and kicked Smedley out from under it. He slid about on the floor like the puck in a game of ice hockey. Click, slither, thud.

Oh, well, she thought, this could've been sad, but I really don't care. I could've shocked myself by caring, but I don't care.

She started to laugh again. Laughing was good for you. A kind of internal aerobics. Then she heard a voice, and it was not her own. '*Merde!*' it said, and cackled. '*Merde! Merde! Merde!*'

Belinda stopped laughing, her eyes tightened, and her mouth – quite spontaneously – performed a sudden, gorgeous, perfectly inadvertent back-bend.

HAROLD JAFFE

Sex Guerrillas

Tough Tiddy Thursday: Wheat toast and coffee followed by hexagonal blue pill with apple juice. Drive to F and Kissinger, Bell-Tel Marriott over there.

Display tag, get admitted. S/he's waiting in lobby, leaning against a Greek Revival pillar, Corinthian, I think, watching animal cartoons on one of the monitors, cracking her gum.

'You humid?' I say.

'I'm always humid,' s/he says.

We skip into the elevator that goes to the 'tower', only get out one floor below. Set the magnet on the door channel to keep it from closing. Coordinate digitals, wait eighty-three seconds, remove the magnet, get back into the elevator, stick gum over the tiny camera head, press T, kick out of our clothes.

Elevator stops at tower but door remains closed. Flashing red warning light goes off. We're nekkid.

My name is Dos. S/he's Una.

S/he: 'You've got a fresh tattoo.'

Me: 'You've got some fresh rings.'

28

S/he: 'I find a hole, I stick a ring through it. I sure like your tattoo.'

Me: 'Wanna lick it, wanna taste it?'

S/he sticks out her tongue, pink, moist, and longer than you'd think.

'Ah, oh, yes, YES, oh, WEE-OO.'

Good, hot sexing.

'Shoot your jizz,' s/he sighs.

Splat, splat, splat ... splat, splat ... splat ... splat, splat ...

Just about all the floor buttons greasy with jizz. I missed # 23, but that's showbiz.

Get dressed, coordinate digitals, remove gum from camera head, press L for lobby. Elevator moves. At the lobby, Bell-Tel security bozos shoot puzzled, angry stares at us. But what can they do, right?

Furry Fisted Friday: Halfbowl of granola, coffee, hexagonal blue pill. Check under the hood. Get in, burn rubber, catch graffiti freeway south.

Una waiting at the ramp, near the pink oleanders, I can see 'her' quarter of a mile away, legs folded under chin, cracking her gum, staring at the tiny TV monitor.

Pull onto the shoulder and s/he slides next to me, touch tongues.

I exit right, re-enter north, graffiti highway, like I said. Acrobatic twelve-year-old guerrillas with spray cans and retractable ladders have done a number on the freeway. Anagrams, ideograms, logos, gang communicadoes, coded shit. One gang sprays on a stanchion, competing gang sprays on a billboard. Media compare them to animals scenting territory. Well, what do you think art is? Plus, they do their shit before dawn, so who's gonna ketch 'em?

We're heading north to Orange, Disney, that deal.

Una has the CD on real loud, Madonna before they offed her.

'You get to sleep last night?' s/he says.

'Not really. You?'

'Not really.'

Traffic building. I'm swerving in and out of lanes. At Zoo Drive, south of Oceanside, I climb onto the median between north and south and Tres pops out, scoots into the front seat. Tres hands Una a pink oleander, me a white one.

Did I say my name is Dos?

Scamper back onto the freeway.

'They're poison – oleanders,' Una says.

'So's the air we breathe,' Tres says.

'So's the water we drink,' I pipe in.

'So's the food we eat,' Tres says.

'So's the puss we lick,' from me.

'Dick too,' from Tres. 'Asshole too.'

'I don't believe it,' Una says. 'How can sweet sex be poison?'

Una's slipped another CD in – Public Enemy before they went MTV.

Tres is slipping out of 'his' clothes.

4:20: brake lights and congestion in Orange County.

4:35: bumper to bumper.

Una and Tres, naked in the backseat, are doin' some shit. Other cars see, point, honk their horns.

Una climbs into the front seat, takes the wheel. I'm naked in the back with Tres, doin' some shit.

Traffic stops dead just south of Anaheim, near the Disneyland exit. Which means Una, Dos, Tres in the backseat doin' some shit: pull-push-slide-slick-lick-bite-slither-spray jizz through the back window, get some on the jacked-up, oversized tires of a GMC longbed pickup. Driver, barechested, tattooed dude with his cap turned back to front, can of Coors in his fist, grins like a fool, flashes us thumbs-up.

Sag Ass Saturday: Wheat toast, coffee, hexagonal blue pill.

Pick up Tres and Quatro. Una has the day off, visiting her grandma in Needles, she's real old.

We drive northwest to one of the biotech complexes. There's a clot of them. Genetic engineering, in vitro micromanipulation, animal experimentation. Plus it's business as usual on Saturdays.

Great spot, this one, on the ocean. Hell, lab techs wouldn't know ocean if it squirted up their colon.

Anyway we park by the ocean and double back. On the northwest side is a double roof, receding superstructure. Boost ourselves up on the lower roof, make our way to the large bay window which looks out to the sea, into the dining hall where techs in their white lab frocks flecked with test-animal blood dine. It's 12:35, the large space is full.

We're in workclothes, carrying implements: shovel, metal

pail, paint rollers. The techs notice us as they eat their institutional quiche or stew or tofu while gazing at the ocean. They look surprised when we lay down our implements, undress, lube each other, commence to tug, suck and fuck. Have you ever seen a biotechnician express surprise? Well, the whole nerdy dining room is watching us in astonishment, some with fork or spoon poised between plate and agape jaws.

The large bay window is noise-proof, but we can tell that no one utters a word. Faint sounds of cutlery, a stray cough, thick breathing.

We paint their window to the ocean with jizz.

Semiotic Sunday: Hexagonal blue pill and juice. No food. Fasting and church on TV. Prayer-packs.

Mambo Hipped Monday: Oatmeal, coffee, hexagonal blue pill. Una, Dos, Tres, Quatro, Cinco, Seis. We're off to the bank. Which one? Wells Fargo. Stagecoach, branding iron, chaps, Indian kills, Duke Wayne, roll-yr-own.

It's noontime, long queues.

Six of us in line, one behind the other, we swap spit, feel each other up a little. Through the clothes.

Draw some nasty looks, sure, but nobody says anything. We know we're on camera, but who ain't?

So we ratchet up a notch, probing hands and fingers under clothes, sucky kisses, earlickings.

Well, the bank guard comes on over, tells us cut it out.

We do, but then start it again, the six of us, changing

partners, dryhumping, sighing, but one behind the other, maintaining the order of the line.

Guard comes over again, threatens to throw us out. Except we wave our checks and money at him.

Quatro says: 'Where in the bank's bylaws does it say anything about sexual conduct while in line?'

Bank guard glares at Quatro.

'You ain't so bad,' Cinco says to the guard. 'Take out your gun, I'll stick a yellow flower in it.'

Guard retreats, glowering.

We start up again. Meanwhile the line is moving and Una is at a window transacting money business. Cinco has tenderly unzipped Tres's organ. Everyone could see it. One of the customers in line actually shouts (which is something you rarely hear in a bank): 'Put that organ back in your pants.'

Instead, the rest of us display *our* organs.

The guard is back with his hand on his holstered Colt.

'This is a b-b-bank,' he sputters.

Tres says: 'Why don't you leave the Colt in the holster and show us your organ.'

Another guard – two more – appear, strong-arm us out of the bank.

'You come in here again, we'll jail your ass,' younger guard shouts at us outside.

Una, who has finished 'her' bank window transaction, comes out at that minute and says: 'You can jail us but you'll never jail our asses.

*

Tuesday Dues Day: Like a rash after eating strawberries, it's another urban uprising, called 'riot'. Broke out suddenly and is radiating out of the inner-city ghettoes.

I said it was a rash, but it's also a tidal wave, tornado, tsunami, earthquake. Has nothing to do with the shit we've been made to swallow from day one, right?

What you have then are enraged folks fucking despite the edicts.

TV claims we're black and brown males, gangbangers, child abusers, drug abusers, but that's a lie. We're females, males, in-betweens, all colors. Moist and soft and hard, sweet-smelling. It's as though someone spiked the water supply with X. Ecstasy to you. The mind police are beside themselves. Cuz we're doing it in the streets, on the roofs, in convenience stores, in municipal offices. *In the banks!* Problem is TV can't report it 'live' because everyone and their mom is nekkid.

Witch Hunt Wednesday: Wheat toast, coffee, hexagonal blue pill.

Was just about to turn off the TV when they kicked the door open, burst in, Uzis, Sig Sauers, clubs, big shined-up shoes. Spread my legs against the wall, hit me hard in the groin, thighs, dragged me out, tossed me in the paddy. Una, Tres and Quatro in there too. Didn't let us talk.

Not jail like we expected but a football stadium is where they took us. Couple thousand of us it looked like standing there on the astroturf. Shitload of TV cameras.

I don't know who gave the signal, or whether anybody

actually did, but we all kicked off our clothes and started touching and playing with each other. But then the guards got into it, clubbing us, kicking.

That night, late, they made us strip and lined us up on the astroturf, two abreast. Then they marched us, twenty or thirty at a time, into the lockers – what used to be the lockers – under the stadium.

Someone cried out: 'Can you smell it? It's gas.'

ANGELA CARTER

The Loves of Lady Purple

Inside the pink-striped booth of the Asiatic Professor only the marvellous existed and there was no such thing as daylight.

The puppet master is always dusted with a little darkness. In direct relation to his skill he propagates the most bewildering enigmas for, the more lifelike his marionettes, the more godlike his manipulations and the more radical the symbiosis between inarticulate doll and articulating fingers. The puppeteer speculates in a no-man's-limbo between the real and that which, although we know very well it is not, nevertheless seems to be real. He is the intermediary between us, his audience, the living, and they, the dolls, the undead, who cannot live at all and yet who mimic the living in every detail since, though they cannot speak or weep, still they project those signals of signification we instantly recognize as language.

The master of marionettes vitalizes inert stuff with the dynamics of his self. The sticks dance, make love, pretend to speak and, finally, personate death; yet, so many Lazaruses out of their graves they spring again in time for the next performance and no worms drip from their noses nor dust clogs their eyes. All complete, they once again offer their brief imitations of men and women with an exquisite precision which is all the more disturbing because we know it to be false; and so this art, if viewed theologically, may, perhaps, be blasphemous.

Although he was only a poor travelling showman, the Asiatic Professor had become a consummate virtuoso of puppetry. He transported his collapsible theatre, the cast of his single drama and a variety of properties in a horse-drawn cart and, after he played his play in many beautiful cities which no longer exist, such as Shanghai, Constantinople and St Petersburg, he and his small entourage arrived at last in a country in Middle Europe where the mountains sprout jags as sharp and unnatural as those a child outlines with his crayon, a dark, superstitious Transylvania where they wreathed suicides with garlic, pierced them through the heart with stakes and buried them at crossroads while warlocks continually practised rites of immemorial beastliness in the forests.

He had only the two assistants, a deaf boy in his teens, his nephew, to whom he taught his craft, and a foundling dumb girl no more than seven or eight they had picked up on their travels. When the Professor spoke, nobody could understand him for he knew only his native tongue, which was an incomprehensible rattle of staccato ks and ts, so he did not speak at all in the ordinary course of things and, if they had taken separate paths to silence, all, in the end, signed a perfect pact with it. But, when the Professor and his nephew sat in the sun outside their booth in the mornings before performances, they held interminable dialogues in sign language punctuated by soft, wordless grunts and whistles so that the choreographed quiet of their discourse was like the mating dance of tropic birds. And this means of communication, so delicately distanced from humanity, was peculiarly apt for the Professor, who had rather the air of a visitant from another world where the mode of being was conducted in nuances rather than affirmatives. This was due partly to his extreme age, for he was very old although he carried his years lightly even if, these days, in this climate, he always felt a little chilly and so wrapped himself always in a moulting, woollen shawl; yet, more so, it was caused by his benign indifference to everything except the simulacra of the living he himself created.

Besides, however far the entourage travelled, not one of its members had ever comprehended to any degree the foreign. They were all natives of the fairground and, after all, all fairs are the same. Perhaps every single fair is no more than a dissociated fragment of one single, great, original fair which was inexplicably scattered long ago in a diaspora of the amazing. Whatever its location, a fair maintains its invariable, self-consistent atmosphere. Hieratic as knights in chess, the painted horses on the roundabouts describe perpetual circles as immutable as those of the planets and as immune to the drab world of here and now whose inmates come to gape at such extraordinariness, such freedom from actuality. The huckster's raucous invitations are made in a language beyond language, or, perhaps, in that ur-language of grunt and bark which lies behind all language. Everywhere, the same old women hawk glutinous candies which seem devised only to make flies drunk on sugar and, though the outward form of such excessive sweets may vary from place to place, their nature, never. A universal cast of two-headed dogs, dwarfs, alligator men, bearded ladies and giants in leopard-skin loin cloths reveal their singularities in the sideshows and, wherever they come from, they share the sullen glamour of deformity, an inter-nationality which acknowledges no geographic boundaries. Here, the grotesque is the order of the day.

The Asiatic Professor picked up the crumbs that fell from this heaping table yet never seemed in the least at home there for his affinities did not lie with its harsh sounds and primary colouring although it was the only home he knew. He had the wistful charm of a Japanese flower which only blossoms when dropped in water for he, too, revealed his passions through a medium other than himself and this was his heroine, the puppet, Lady Purple.

She was the Queen of Night. There were glass rubies in her head for eyes and her ferocious teeth, carved out of mother o' pearl, were always on show for she had a permanent smile. Her face was as white as chalk because it was covered with the skin of supplest white leather which also clothed her torso, joimed limbs and complication of extremities. Her beautiful hands seemed more like weapons because her nails were so long, five inches of pointed tin enamelled scarlet, and she wore a wig of black hair arranged in a chignon more heavily elaborate than any human neck could have endured. This monumental *chevelure* was stuck through with many brilliant pins tipped with pieces of broken mirror so that, every time she moved, she cast a multitude of scintillating reflections which danced about the theatre like mice of light. Her clothes were all of deep, dark, slumbrous colours – profound pinks, crimson and the vibrating purple with which she was synonymous, a purple the colour of blood in a love suicide.

She must have been the masterpiece of a long-dead, anonymous artisan and yet she was nothing but a curious structure until the Professor touched her strings, for it was he who filled her with necromantic vigour. He transmitted to her an abundance of the life he himself seemed to possess so tenuously and, when she moved, she did not seem so much a cunningly simulated woman as a monstrous goddess, at once preposterous and magnificent, who transcended the notion she was dependent on his hands and appeared wholly real and yet entirely other. Her actions were not so much an imitation as a distillation and intensification of those of a born woman and so she could become the quintessence of eroticism, for no woman born would have dared to be so blatantly seductive.

The Professor allowed no one else to touch her. He himself looked after her costumes and jewellery. When the show was over, he placed his marionette in a specially constructed box and carried her back to the lodging house where he and his children shared a room, for she was too precious to be left in the flimsy theatre, and, besides, he could not sleep unless she lay beside him.

The catchpenny title of the vehicle for this remarkable actress was: *The Notorious Amours of Lady Purple, the Shameless Oriental Venus.* Everything in the play was entirely exotic. The incantatory ritual of the drama instantly annihilated the rational and imposed upon the audience a magic alternative in which nothing was in the least familiar. The series of tableaux which illustrated her story were in themselves so filled with meaning that when the Professor chanted her narrative in his impenetrable native tongue, the compulsive strangeness of the spectacle was enhanced rather than diminished. As he crouched above the stage directing his heroine's movements, he recited a verbal recitative in a voice which clanged, rasped and swooped up and down in a weird duet with the stringed instrument from which the dumb girl struck peculiar intervals. But it was impossible to mistake him when the Professor spoke in the character of Lady Purple herself for then his voice modulated to a thick, lascivious murmur like fur soaked in honey which sent unwilling shudders of pleasure down the spines of the watchers. In the iconography of the melodrama, Lady Purple stood for passion, and all her movements were calculations in an angular geometry of sexuality.

The Professor somehow always contrived to have a few handbills printed off in the language of the country where they played. These always gave the title of his play and then they used to read as follows:

Come and see all that remains of Lady Purple, the famous prostitute and wonder of the East!

A unique sensation. See how the unappeasable appetites of Lady Purple turned her at last into the very puppet you see before you, pulled only by the strings of *lust*. Come and see the very doll, the only surviving relic of the shameless Oriental Venus herself.

The bewildering entertainment possessed almost a religious intensity for, since there can be no spontaneity in a puppet drama, it always tends towards the rapt intensity of ritual, and, at its conclusion, as the audience stumbled from the darkened booth, it had almost suspended disbelief and was more than half convinced, as the Professor assured them so eloquently, that the bizarre figure who had dominated the stage was indeed the petrification of a universal whore and had once been a woman in whom too much life had negated life itself, whose kisses had withered like acids and whose embrace blasted like lightning. But the Professor and his assistants immediately dismantled the scenery and put away the dolls who were, after all, only mundane wood and, next day, the play was played again.

This is the story of Lady Purple as performed by the Professor's puppets to the delirious *obbligato* of the dumb girl's samisen and the audible click of the limbs of the actors.

The Notorious Amours of Lady Purple

the Shameless Oriental Venus

When she was only a few days old, her mother wrapped her in a tattered blanket and abandoned her on the doorstep of a prosperous merchant and his barren wife. These respectable bourgeois were to become the siren's first dupes. They lavished upon her all the attentions which love and money could devise and yet they reared a flower which, although perfumed, was carnivorous. At the age of twelve, she seduced her foster father. Utterly besotted with her, he trusted to her the key of the safe where he kept all his money and she immediately robbed it of every farthing.

Packing his treasure in a laundry basket together with the clothes and jewellery he had already given her, she then stabbed her first lover and his wife, her foster mother, in their bellies with a knife used in the kitchen to slice fish. Then she set fire to their house to cover the traces of her guilt. She annihilated her own childhood in the blaze that destroyed her first home and, springing like a corrupt phoenix from the pyre of her crime, she rose again in the pleasure quarters, where she at once hired herself out to the madame of the most imposing brothel.

In the pleasure quarters, life passed entirely in artificial day for the bustling noon of those crowded alleys came at the time of drowsing midnight for those who lived outside that inverted, sinister, abominable world which functioned only to gratify the whims of the senses. Every rococo desire the mind of man might, in its perverse ingenuity, devise found ample gratification here, amongst the halls of mirrors, the flagellation parlours, the cabarets of nature-defying copulations and the ambiguous soirées held by men-women and female men. Flesh was the speciality of every house and it came piping hot, served up with all the garnishes imaginable. The Professor's puppets dryly and perfunctorily performed these tactical manoeuvres like toy soldiers in a mock battle of carnality.

Along the streets, the women for sale, the mannequins of desire, were displayed in wicker cages so that potential customers could saunter past inspecting them at leisure. These exalted prostitutes sat motionless as idols. Upon their real features had been painted symbolic abstractions of the various aspects of allure and the fantastic elaboration of their dress hinted it covered a different kind of skin. The cork heels of their shoes were so high they could not walk but only totter and the sashes round their waists were of brocade so stiff the movements of the arms were cramped and scant so they presented attitudes of physical unease which, though powerfully moving, derived partly, at least, from the deaf assistant's lack of manual dexterity, for his apprenticeship had not as yet reached even the journeyman stage. Therefore the gestures of these *hetaerae* were as stylized as if they had been clockwork. Yet, however fortuitously, all worked out so well it seemed each one was as absolutely circumscribed as a figure in rhetoric, reduced by the rigorous discipline of her vocation to the nameless essence of the idea of woman, a metaphysical abstraction of the female which could, on payment of a specific fee, be instantly translated into an oblivion either sweet or terrible, depending on the nature of her talents.

Lady Purple's talents verged on the unspeakable. Booted, in leather, she became a mistress of the whip before her fifteenth birthday. Subsequently, she graduated in the mysteries of the torture chamber, where she thoroughly researched all manner of ingenious mechanical devices. She utilized a baroque apparatus of funnel, humiliation, syringe, thumbscrew, contempt and spiritual anguish; to her lovers, such severe usage was both bread and wine and a kiss from her cruel mouth was the sacrament of suffering.

Soon she became successful enough to be able to maintain her own establishment. When she was at the height of her fame, her slightest fancy might cost a young man his patrimony and, as soon as she squeezed him dry of fortune, hope and dreams, for she was quite remorseless, she abandoned him; or else she might, perhaps, lock him up in her closet and force him to watch her while she took for nothing to her usually incredibly expensive bed a beggar encountered by chance on the street. She was no malleable, since frigid, substance upon which desires might be executed; she was not a true prostitute for she was the object on which men prostituted themselves. She, the sole perpetrator of desire, proliferated malign fantasies all around her and used her lovers as the canvas on which she executed boudoir masterpieces of destruction. Skins melted in the electricity she generated.

Soon, either to be rid of them or, simply, for pleasure, she took to murdering her lovers. From the leg of a politician she poisoned she cut out the thighbone and took it to a craftsman who made it into a flute for her. She persuaded succeeding lovers to play tunes for her on this instrument and, with the supplest and most serpentine grace, she danced for them to its unearthly music. At this point, the dumb girl put down her samisen and took up a bamboo pipe from which issued weird cadences and, though it was by no means the climax of the play, this dance was the apex of the Professor's performance for, as she stamped, wheeled and fumed to the sound of her malign chamber music, Lady Purple became entirely the image of irresistible evil.

She visited men like a plague, both bane and terrible enlightenment, and she was as contagious as the plague. The final condition of all her lovers was this: they went clothed in rags held together with the discharge of their sores, and their eyes held an awful vacancy, as if their minds had been blown out like candles. A parade of ghastly spectres, they trundled across the stage, their passage implemented by medieval horrors for, here, an arm left its socket and whisked up out of sight into the flies and, there, a nose hung in the air after a gaunt shape that went tottering noseless forward.

So foreclosed Lady Purple's pyrotechnical career, which ended as if it had been indeed a firework display, in ashes, desolation and silence. She became more ghastly than those she had infected. Circe at last became a swine herself and, seared to the bone by her own flame, walked the pavements like a desiccated shadow. Disaster obliterated her. Cast out with stones and oaths by those who had once adulated her, she was reduced to scavenging on the seashore, where she plucked hair from the heads of the drowned to sell to wigmakers who catered to the needs of more fortunate since less diabolic courtesans.

Now her finery, her paste jewels and her enormous superimposition of black hair hung up in the green room and she wore a drab rag of coarse hemp for the final scene of her desperate decline, when, outrageous nymphomaniac, she practised extraordinary necrophilies on the bloated corpses the sea tossed contemptuously at her feet for her dry rapacity had become entirely mechanical and still she repeated her former actions though she herself was utterly other. She abrogated her humanity. She became nothing but wood and hair. She became a marionette herself, herself her own replica, the dead yet moving image of the shameless Oriental Venus.

The Professor was at last beginning to feel the effects of age and travel. Sometimes he complained in noisy silence to his nephew of pains, aches, stiffening muscles, tautening sinews, and shortness of breath. He began to limp a little and left to the boy all the rough work of mantling and dismantling. Yet the balletic mime of Lady Purple grew all the more remarkable with the passage of the years, as though his energy, channelled for so long into a single purpose, refined itself more and more in time and was finally reduced to a single, purified, concentrated essence which was transmitted entirely to the doll; and the Professor's mind attained a condition not unlike that of the swordsman trained in Zen, whose sword is his soul, so that neither sword nor swordsman has meaning without the presence of the other. Such swordsmen, armed, move towards their victims like automata, in a state of perfect emptiness, no longer aware of any distinction between self or weapon. Master and marionette had arrived at this condition.

Age could not touch Lady Purple for, since she had never aspired to mortality, she effortlessly transcended it and, though a man who was less aware of the expertise it needed to make her so much as raise her left hand might, now and then, have grieved to see how she defied ageing, the Professor had no fancies of that kind. Her miraculous inhumanity rendered their friendship entirely free from the anthropomorphic, even on the night of the Feast of All Hallows when, the mountain-dwellers murmured, the dead held masked balls in the graveyards while the devil played the fiddle for them.

The rough audience received their copeck's worth of sensation and filed out into a fairground which still roared like a playful tiger with life. The foundling girl put away her samisen and swept out the booth while the nephew set the stage afresh for the next day's matinée. Then the Professor noticed Lady Purple had ripped a seam in the drab shroud she wore in the final act. Chattering to himself with displeasure, he undressed her as she swung idly, this way and that way, from her anchored strings and then he sat down on a wooden property stool on the stage and plied his needle like a good housewife. The task was more difficult than it seemed at first for the fabric was also torn and required an embroidery of darning so he told his assistants to go home together to the lodging house and let him finish his task alone.

A small oil-lamp hanging from a nail at the side of the stage cast an insufficient but tranquil light. The white puppet glimmered fitfully through the mists which crept into the theatre from the night outside through all the chinks and gaps in the tarpaulin and now began to fold their chiffon drapes around her as if to decorously conceal her or else to render her more translucently enticing. The mist softened her painted smile a little and her head dangled on one side. In the last act, she wore a loose, black wig, the locks of which hung down as far as her softly upholstered flanks, and the ends of her hair flickered with her random movements, creating upon the white blackboard of her back one of those fluctuating optical effects which make us question the veracity of our vision. As he often did when he was alone with her, the Professor chatted to her in his native language, rattling away an intimacy of nothings, of the weather, of his rheumatism, of the unpalatability and expense of the region's coarse, black bread, while the small winds took her as their partner in a scarcely perceptible *valse triste* and the mist grew minute by minute thicker, more pallid and more viscous.

The old man finished his mending. He rose and, with a click or two of his old bones, he went to put the forlorn garment neatly on its green-room hanger beside the glowing, winy purple gown splashed with rosy peonies, sashed with carmine, that she wore for her appalling dance. He was about to lay her, naked, in her coffin-shaped case and carry her back to their chilly bedroom when he paused. He was seized with the childish desire to see her again in all her finery once more that night. He took her dress off its hanger and carried it to where she drifted, at nobody's volition but that of the wind. As he put her clothes on her, he murmured to her as if she were a little girl for the vulnerable flaccidity of her arms and legs made a six-foot baby of her.

'There, there, my pretty; this arm here, that's right! Oops a daisy, easy does it . . .'

Then he tenderly took off her penitential wig and clucked his tongue to see how defencelessly bald she was beneath it. His arms cracked under the weight of her immense chignon and he had to stretch up on tiptoe to set it in place because, since she was as large as life, she was rather taller than he. But then the ritual of apparelling was over and she was complete again.

Now she was dressed and decorated, it seemed her dry wood had all at once put out an entire springtime of blossoms for the old man alone to enjoy. She could have acted as the model for the most beautiful of women, the image of that woman whom only a man's memory and imagination can devise, for the lamp light fell too mildly to sustain her air of arrogance and so gently it made her long nails look as harmless as ten fallen petals. The Professor had a curious habit; he always used to kiss his doll good night.

A child kisses its toy before she pretends it sleeps although, even though she is only a child, she knows its eyes are not constructed to close so it will always be a sleeping beauty no kiss will waken. One in the grip of savage loneliness might kiss the face he sees before him in the mirror for want of any other face to kiss. These are kisses of the same kind; they are the most poignant of caresses, for they are too humble and too despairing to wish or seek for any response.

Yet, in spite of the Professor's sad humility, his chapped and withered mouth opened on hot, wet, palpitating flesh.

The sleeping wood had wakened. Her pearl teeth crashed against his with the sound of cymbals and her warm, fragrant breath blew around him like an Italian gale. Across her suddenly moving face flashed a whole kaleidoscope of expression, as though she were running instantaneously through the entire repertory of human feeling, practising, in an endless moment of time, all the scales of emotion as if they were music. Crushing vines, her arms, curled about the Professor's delicate apparatus of bone and skin with the insistent pressure of an actuality by far more authentically living than that of his own, time-desiccated flesh. Her kiss emanated from the dark country where desire is objectified and lives. She gained entry into the world by a mysterious loophole in its metaphysics and, during her kiss, she sucked his breath from his lungs so that her own bosom heaved with it.

So, unaided, she began her next performance with an apparent improvisation which was, in reality, only a variation upon a theme. She sank her teeth into his throat and drained him. He did not have the time to make a sound. When he was empty, he slipped straight out of her embrace down to her feet with a dry rustle, as of a cast armful of dead leaves, and there he sprawled on the floorboards, as empty, useless and bereft of meaning as his own tumbled shawl.

She tugged impatiently at the strings which moored her and out they came in bunches from her head, her arms and her legs. She stripped them off her fingertips and stretched out her long, white hands, flexing and unflexing them again and again. For the first time for years, or, perhaps, for ever, she closed her blood-stained teeth thankfully, for her cheeks still ached from the smile her maker had carved into the stuff of her former face. She stamped her elegant feet to make the new blood flow more freely there.

Unfurling and unravelling itself, her hair leaped out of its confinements of combs, cords and lacquer to root itself back into her scalp like cut grass bounding out of the stack and back again into the ground. First, she shivered with pleasure to feel the cold, for she realized she was experiencing a physical sensation; then either she remembered or else she believed she remembered that the sensation of cold was not a pleasurable one so she knelt and, drawing off the old man's shawl, wrapped it carefully about herself. Her every motion was instinct with a wonderful, reptilian liquidity. The mist outside now seemed to rush like a tide into the booth and broke against her in white breakers so that she looked like a baroque figurehead, lone survivor of a shipwreck, thrown up on a shore by the tide.

But whether she was renewed or newly born, returning to life or becoming alive, awakening from a dream or coalescing into the form of fantasy generated in her wooden skull by the mere repetition so many times of the same invariable actions, the brain beneath the reviving hair contained only the scantiest notion of the possibilities now open to it. All that had seeped into the wood was the notion that she might perform the forms of life not so much by the skill of another as by her own desire that she did so, and she did not possess enough equipment to comprehend the complex circularity of the logic which inspired her for she had only been a marionette. But, even if she could not perceive it, she could not escape the tautological paradox in which she was trapped; had the marionette all the time parodied the living or was she, now living, to parody her own performance as a marionette? Although she was now manifestly a woman, young and beautiful, the leprous whiteness of her face gave her the appearance of a corpse animated solely by demonic will.

Deliberately, she knocked the lamp down from its hook on the wall. A puddle of oil spread at once on the boards of the stage. A little flame leaped across the fuel and immediately began to eat the curtains. She went down the aisle between the benches to the little ticket booth. Already, the stage was an inferno and the corpse of the Professor tossed this way and that on an uneasy bed of fire. But she did not look behind her after she slipped out into the fairground although soon the theatre was burning like a paper lantern ignited by its own candle.

Now it was so late that the sideshows, gingerbread stalls and liquor booths were locked and shuttered and only the moon, half obscured by drifting cloud, gave out a meagre, dirty light, which sullied and deformed the flimsy pasteboard façades, so the place, deserted, with curds of vomit, the refuse of revelry, underfoot, looked utterly desolate.

She walked rapidly past the silent roundabouts, accompanied only by the fluctuating mists, towards the town, making her way like a homing pigeon, out of logical necessity, to the single brothel it contained.

CLARICE LISPECTOR

Plaza Mauá

The cabaret on Plaza Mauá was called The Erotica. And Luisa's stage name was Carla.

Carla was a dancer at The Erotica. She was married to Joaquim, who was killing himself working as a carpenter. And Carla 'worked' at two jobs: dancing half nude and cheating on her husband.

Carla was beautiful. She had little teeth and a tiny waist. She was delicate throughout. She had scarcely any breasts, but she had well-shaped hips. She took an hour to make herself up: afterward, she seemed a porcelain doll. She was thirty but looked much younger.

There were no children. Joaquim and she couldn't get together. He worked until ten at night. She began work at exactly ten. She slept all day long.

Carla was a lazy Luisa. Arriving at night, when the time came to present herself to the public, she would begin to yawn, wishing she were in her nightgown in bed. This was also due to shyness. Incredible as it might seem, Carla was a timid Luisa. She stripped, yes, but the first moments of the dance, of voluptuous motion, were moments of shame. She only 'warmed up' a few minutes later. Then she unfolded, she undulated, she gave all of herself. She was best at the samba. But a nice, romantic blues also turned her on.

She was asked to drink with the clients. She received a commission per bottle. She always chose the most expensive drinks. And she pretended to drink: but hers wasn't alcohol. The idea was to get the clients drunk and make them spend. It was boring talking with them. They would caress her, passing their hands over her tiny breasts. And she in a scintillating bikini. Beautiful.

Once in a while she would sleep with a client. She would take the money, keep it well hidden in her bra, and the next day she would buy some new clothes. She had clothes without end. She bought blue jeans. And necklaces. A pile of necklaces. And bracelets and rings.

Sometimes, just for variety's sake, she danced in blue jeans and without a bra, her breasts swinging among the flashing necklaces. She wore bangs and, using a black pencil, painted on a beauty mark close to her delicate lips. It was adorable. She wore long pendant earrings, sometimes, pearl, sometimes imitation gold.

In moments of unhappiness, she turned to Celsinho, a man who wasn't a man. They understood each other well. She told him her troubles, complained about Joaquim, complained about inflation. Celsinho, a successful transvestite, listened to it all and gave her advice. They weren't rivals. They each worked their own turf.

Celsinho came from the nobility. He had given up everything for his vocation. He didn't dance. But he did wear lipstick and false eyelashes. The sailors of Plaza Mauá loved him. And he played hard to get. He only gave in at the very end. And he was paid in dollars. After changing the money on the black market, he invested it in the Banco Halles. He was very afraid of growing old, destitute and forsaken. Especially since an old transvestite is a sad thing. He took two envelopes of powdered proteins a day for energy. He had large hips and, from taking so many hormones, he had acquired a facsimile of breasts. Celsinho's stage name was Moleirão.

Moleirão and Carla brought good money to the owner of The Erotica. The smoke-filled atmosphere, the smell of alcohol. And the dance floor. It was tough being forced to dance with a drunken sailor. But what could you do? Everyone has his *métier*.

Celsinho had adopted a little girl of four. He was a real mother to her. He slept very little in order to look after the girl. And she lacked for nothing: she had only the best. Even a Portuguese nanny. On Sundays Celsinho took little Clareta to the zoo at the Quinta de Boa Vista. And they both ate popcorn. And they fed the monkeys. Little Clareta was afraid of the elephants. She asked: 'Why do they have such big noses?'

Celsinho then told her a fantastic tale involving good fairies and bad fairies. Or else he would take her to the circus. And they would suck hard, clicking candies, the two of them. Celsinho wanted a brilliant future for little Clareta: marriage with a man of fortune, children, jewels.

Carla had a Siamese cat who looked at her with hard blue eyes. But Carla scarcely had time to take care of the creature: either she was sleeping, or dancing, or out shopping. The cat was named Leléu. And it drank milk with its delicate little red tongue.

Joaquim hardly saw Luisa. He refused to call her Carla. Joaquim was fat and short, of Italian descent. It had been a Portuguese woman neighbor who had given him the name of Joaquim. His name was Joaquim Fioriti. Fioriti? There was nothing flowerlike about him.

The maid who worked for Joaquim and Luisa was a wily black woman who stole whatever she could. Luisa hardly ate, in order to keep her figure. Joaquim drowned himself in minestrone. The maid knew about everything, but kept her trap shut. It was her job to polish Carla's jewelry with Brasso and Silvo. When Joaquim was sleeping and Carla working, this maid by the name of Silvinha wore her mistress's jewelry. And she was kind of grayish-black in color.

This is how what happened happened.

Carla was confiding in Moleirão when she was asked to dance by a tall man with broad shoulders. Celsinho lusted after him. And he ate his heart out in envy. He was vindictive.

When the dance ended and Carla returned to sit down next to Moleirão, he could hardly hold in his rage. And, Carla, innocent. It wasn't her fault she was attractive. And, in fact, the big man appealed to her. She said to Celsinho:

'I'd go to bed with that one for free.'

Celsinho said nothing. It was almost three in the morning.

58

The Erotica was full of men and women. Many mothers and housewives went there for the fun of it and to earn a bit of pocket money.

Then Carla said:

'It's so good to dance with a real man.'

Celsinho sprang:

'But you're not a real woman!'

'Me? How come I'm not?' said the startled girl, who, dressed that night in black, in a long dress with long sleeves, looked like a nun. She did this on purpose to excite those men who desired a pure woman.

'You,' screamed Celsinho, 'are no woman at all! You don't even know how to fry an egg! And I do! I do! I do!'

Carla turned into Luisa. White, bewildered. She had been struck in her most intimate femininity. Confused, staring at Celsinho who had the face of a witch.

Carla didn't say a word. She stood up, crushed her cigarette in the ashtray, and, without turning to anyone, abandoning the party at its height, she left.

On foot, in black, on the Plaza Mauá at three in the morning. Like the lowest of whores. Alone. Without recourse. It was true: she didn't know how to fry an egg. And Celsinho was more of a woman than she.

The plaza was dark. And Luisa breathed deeply. She looked at the lampposts. The plaza was empty.

And in the sky, the stars.

T. CORAGHESSAN BOYLE

Descent of Man

> I could never have achieved what I have done had I been stubbornly
> set on clinging to my origins ... In fact, to give up being stubborn
> was the supreme commandment I laid upon myself; free ape as I
> was, I submitted myself to that yoke.
>
> Franz Kafka, 'A Report to an Academy'
>
> *Ungowa!*
>
> Johnny Weismuller, *Tarzan Finds a Son*

I was living with a woman who suddenly began to stink. It
was very difficult. The first time I confronted her she merely
smiled. 'Occupational hazard,' she said. The next time she
curled her lip. There were other problems too. Hairs, for
instance. Hairs that began to appear on her clothing, sharp
and black and brutal. Invariably I would awake to find these
hairs in my mouth, or I would glance into the mirror to see
them slashing like razor edges across the collars of my white
shirts. Then too there was the fruit. I began to discover
moldering bits of it about the house – apple and banana most
characteristically – but plum and tangelo or even passion

fruit and yim-yim were not at all anomalous. These fruit fragments occurred principally in the bedroom, on the pillow, surrounded by darkening spots. It was not long before I located their source: they lay hidden like gems in the long wild hanks of her hair. Another occupational hazard.

Jane was in the habit of sitting before the air conditioner when she came home from work, fingering out her hair, drying the sweat from her face and neck in the cool hum of the machine, fruit bits sifting silently to the carpet, black hairs drifting like feathers. On these occasions the room would fill with the stink of her, bestial and fetid. And I would find my eyes watering, my mind imaging the dark rotting trunks of the rain forest, stained sienna and mandalay and Hooker's green with the excrements dropped from above. My ears would keen with the whistling and crawking of the jungle birds, the screechings of the snot-nosed apes in the branches. And then, slack-faced and tight-boweled, I would step into the bathroom and retch, the sweetness of my own intestinal secrets a balm against the potent hairy stench of her.

One evening, just after her bath (the faintest odor lingered, yet still it was so trenchant I had to fight the impulse to get up and urinate on a tree or a post or something), I laid my hand casually across her belly and was suddenly startled to see an insect flit from its cover, skate up the swell of her abdomen, and bury itself in her navel. 'Good Christ,' I said.

'Hm?' she returned, peering over the cover of her Yerkish reader.

'That,' I said. 'That bug, that insect, that vermin.'

She sat up, plucked the thing from its cachette, raised it to her lips and popped it between her front teeth, 'Louse,' she said, sucking. 'Went down to the old age home on Thirteenth Street to pick them up.'

I anticipated her: 'Not for—?'

'Why certainly, potpie – so Konrad can experience a tangible gratification of his social impulses during the grooming ritual. You know: you scratch my back, I scratch yours.'

I lay in bed that night sweating, thinking about Jane and those slippery-fingered monkeys poking away at her, and listening for the lice crawling across her scalp or nestling their bloody little siphons in the tufts under her arms. Finally, about four, I got up and took three Doriden. I woke at two in the afternoon, an insect in my ear. It was only an earwig. I had missed my train, failed to call in at the office. There was a note from Jane: Pick me up at four. Konrad sends love.

The Primate Center stood in the midst of a macadamized acre or two, looking very much like a school building: faded brick, fluted columns, high mesh fences. Finger paintings and mobiles hung in the windows, misshapen ceramics crouched along the sills. A flag raggled at the top of a whitewashed flagpole. I found myself bending to examine the cornerstone: Asa Priff Grammar School, 1939. Inside it was dark and cool, the halls were lined with lockers and

curling watercolors, the linoleum gleamed like a shy smile.
I stepped into the BOYS' ROOM. The urinals were a foot and
a half from the floor. Designed for little people, I mused.
Youngsters. Hardly big enough to hold their little peters
without the teacher's help. I smiled, and situated myself
over one of the toy urinals, the strong honest scent of Pine-
Sol in my nostrils. At that moment the door wheezed open
and a chimpanzee shuffled in. He was dressed in shorts,
shirt and bow tie. He nodded to me, it seemed, and made a
few odd gestures with his hands as he moved up to the
urinal beside mine. Then he opened his fly and pulled out
an enormous slick red organ like a peeled banana. I looked
away, embarrassed, but could hear him urinating mightily.
The stream hissed against the porcelain like a thunderstorm,
rattled the drain as it went down. My own water wouldn't
come. I began to feel foolish. The chimp shook himself
daintily, zippered up, pulled the plunger, crossed to the
sink, washed and dried his hands, and left. I found I no
longer had to go.

Out in the hallway the janitor was leaning on his flathead
broom. The chimp stood before him gesticulating with
manic dexterity: brushing his forehead and tugging his chin,
slapping his hands under his armpits, tapping his wrists, his
tongue, his ear, his lip. The janitor watched intently.
Suddenly – after a particularly virulent flurry – the man
burst into laughter, rich braying globes of it. The chimp
folded his lip and joined in, adding his weird nasal snicker-
ing to the janitor's barrel-laugh. I stood by the door to the
BOYS' ROOM in a quandary. I began to feel that it might be

wiser to wait in the car – but then I didn't want to call attention to myself, darting in and out like that. The janitor might think I was stealing paper towels or something. So I stood there, thinking to have a word with him after the chimp moved on – with the expectation that he could give me some grassroots insight into the nature of Jane's job. But the chimp didn't move on. The two continued laughing, now harder than ever. The janitor's face was tear-streaked. Each time he looked up the chimp produced a gesticular flurry that would stagger him again. Finally the janitor wound down a bit, and still chuckling, held out his hands, palms up. The chimp flung his arms up over his head and then heaved them down again, rhythmically slapping the big palms with his own. 'Right on! Mastuh Konrad,' the janitor said, 'Right on!' The chimp grinned, then hitched up his shorts and sauntered off down the hall. The janitor turned back to his broom, still chuckling.

I cleared my throat. The broom began a geometrically precise course up the hall toward me. It stopped at my toes, the ridge of detritus flush with the pinions of my wingtips. The janitor looked up. The pupil of his right eye was fixed in the corner, beneath the lid, and the white was red. There was an ironic gap between his front teeth. 'Kin ah do sumfin fo yo, mah good man?' he said.

'I'm waiting for Miss Good.'

'Ohhh, Miz *Good*,' he said, nodding his head. 'Fust ah tought yo was thievin paypuh tow-els outen de Boys' Room but den when ah sees yo standin dere rigid as de Venus de Milo ah thinks to mahsef: he is some kinda new sculpture de stoodents done made is what he is.' He was squinting up at me and grinning like we'd just come back from sailing around the world together.

'That's a nice broom,' I said.

He looked at me steadily, grinning still. 'Yo's wonderin what me and Mastuh Konrad was jivin bout up dere, isn't yo? Well, ah tells yo: he was relatin a hoomerous anecdote, de punch line ob which has deep cosmic implications in dat it establishes a common groun between monks and Ho-mo sapiens despite dere divergent ancestries.' He shook his head, chortled. 'Yes, in-deed, dat Mastuh Konrad is quite de wit.'

'You mean to tell me you actually understand all that lip-pulling and finger-waving?' I was beginning to feel a nameless sense of outrage.

'Oh sartinly, mah good man. Dat ASL.'

'What?'

'ASL is what we was talkin. A-merican Sign Language. Developed for de deef n dumb. Yo sees, Mastuh Konrad is sumfin ob a genius round here. He can commoonicate de mos esoteric i-deas in bof ASL and Yerkish, re-spond to and translate English, French, German and Chinese. Fack, it was Miz Good was tellin me dat Konrad is workin right now on a Yerkish translation ob Darwin's *De-scent o Man*. He is mainly into anthro-pology, yo knows, but he has cultivated a in-teress in udder fields too. Dis lass fall he done undertook a Yerkish translation ob Chomsky's *Language and Mind* and Nietzsche's *Jenseits von Gut and Böse*. And dat's some pretty heavy shit, Jackson.'

I was hot with outrage. 'Stuff,' I said. 'Stuff and nonsense.'

'No sense in feelin personally treateed by Mastuh Konrad's chievements, mah good fellow – yo's got to ree-lize dat he is a genius.'

A word came to me: 'Bullhonk,' I said. And turned to leave.

The janitor caught me by the shirtsleeve. 'He is now scorin his turd opera,' he whispered. I tore away from him and stamped out of the building.

Jane was waiting in the car. I climbed in, cranked down the sunroof and opened the air vents.

At home I poured a water glass of gin, held it to my nostrils and inhaled. Jane sat before the air conditioner, her hair like a urinal mop, stinking. Black hairs cut the atmosphere, fruit bits whispered to the carpet. Occasionally the tip of my tongue entered the gin. I sniffed and tasted, thinking of plastic factories and turpentine distilleries and rich sulfurous smoke. On my way to the bedroom I poured a second glass.

In the bedroom I sniffed gin and dressed for dinner. 'Jane?' I called, 'shouldn't you be getting ready?' She appeared in the doorway. She was dressed in her work clothes: jeans and sweatshirt. The sweatshirt was gray and hooded. There were yellow stains on the sleeves. I thought of the lower depths of animal cages, beneath the floor meshing. 'I figured I'd go like this,' she said. I was knotting my tie. 'And I wish you'd stop insisting on baths every night – I'm getting tired of smelling like a coupon in a detergent box. It's unnatural. Unhealthy.'

In the car on the way to the restaurant I lit a cigar, a cheap twisted black thing like half a pepperoni. Jane sat hunched against the door, unwashed. I had never before smoked a cigar. I tried to start a conversation but Jane said she didn't feel like talking: talk seemed so useless, such an anachronism. We drove on in silence. And I reflected that this was not the Jane I knew and loved. Where, I wondered, was the girl who changed wigs three or four times a day and sported nails like a Chinese emperor? – and where was the girl who dressed like an Arabian bazaar and smelled like the trade winds?

She was committed. The project, the study, grants. I could read the signs: she was growing away from me.

The restaurant was dark, a maze of rocky gardens, pancake-leafed vegetation, black fountains. We stood squinting just inside the door. Birds whistled, carp hissed through the pools. Somewhere a monkey screeched. Jane put her hand on my shoulder and whispered in my ear. 'Siamang,' she said. At that moment the leaves parted beside us: a rubbery little fellow emerged and motioned us to sit on a bench beneath a wicker birdcage. He was wearing a soiled loincloth and eight or ten necklaces of yellowed teeth. His hair flamed out like a brushfire. In the dim light from the braziers I noticed his nostrils – both shrunken and pinched, as if once pierced straight through. His face was of course inscrutable. As soon as we were seated he removed my socks and shoes, Jane's sneakers, and wrapped our feet in what I later learned were plantain leaves. I started to object – I bitterly resent anyone looking at my feet – but Jane shushed me. We had waited three months for reservations.

The maitre d' signed for us to follow, and led us through a dripping stone-walled tunnel to an outdoor garden where the flagstones gave way to dirt and we found ourselves on a narrow plant-choked path. He licked along like an iguana and we hurried to keep up. Wet fronds slapped back in my face, creepers snatched at my ankles, mud sucked at the plantain leaves on my feet. The scents of mold and damp and long-lying urine hung in the air, and I thought of the men's room at the subway station. It was dark as a womb. I offered Jane my hand, but she refused it. Her breathing was fast. The monkey chatter was loud as a zoo afire. 'Far out,' she said. I slapped a mosquito on my neck.

A moment later we found ourselves seated at a bamboo table overhung with branch and vine. Across from us sat Dr and Mrs U-Hwak-Lo, director of the Primate Center and wife. A candle guttered between them. I cleared my throat, and then began idly tracing my finger around the circular hole cut in the table's center. The Doctor's ears were the size of peanuts. 'Glad you two could make it,' he said. 'I've long been urging Jane to sample some of our humble island fare.' I smiled, crushed a spider against the back of my chair. The Doctor's English was perfect, pure Martha's Vineyard – he sounded like Ted Kennedy's insurance salesman. His wife's was weak: 'Yes,' she said, 'nussing cook here, all roar.' 'How exciting!' said Jane. And then the conversation turned to primates, and the Center.

Mrs U-Hwak-Lo and I smiled at one another. Jane and the

Doctor were already deeply absorbed in a dialogue concerning the incidence of anal retention in chimps deprived of Frisbee coordination during the sensorimotor period. I gestured toward them with my head and arched my eyebrows wittily. Mrs U-Hwak-Lo giggled. It was then that Jane's proximity began to affect me. The close wet air seemed to concentrate her essence, distill its potency. The U-Hwak-Los seemed unaffected. I began to feel queasy. I reached for the fingerbowl and drank down its contents. Mrs U-Hwak-Lo smiled. It was coconut oil. Just then the waiter appeared carrying a wooden bowl the size of a truck tire. A single string of teeth slapped against his breastbone as he set the bowl down and slipped off into the shadows. The Doctor and Jane were oblivious – they were talking excitedly, occasionally lapsing into what I took to be ASL, ear- and nose- and lip-licking like a manager and his third-base coach. I peered into the bowl: it was filled to the rim with clean-picked chicken bones. Mrs U-Hwak-Lo nodded, grinning: 'No ontray,' she said. 'Appeticer.' At that moment a simian screamed somewhere close, screamed like death itself. Jane looked up. 'Rhesus,' she said.

On my return from the men's room I had some difficulty locating the table in the dark. I had already waded through two murky fountains and was preparing to plunge through my third when I heard Mrs U-Hwak-Lo's voice behind me. 'Here,' she said. 'Make quick, repass now serve.' She took my hand and led me back to the table. 'Oh, they're enormously resourceful,' the Doctor was saying as I stumbled into my chair, pants wet to the knees. 'They first employ a general anesthetic – distillation of the chu-bok root – and then the chef (who logically doubles as village surgeon) makes a circular incision about the macaque's cranium, carefully peeling back the already-shaven scalp, and stanching the blood flow quite effectively with maura-ro, a highly absorbent powder derived from the tamana leaf. He then removes both the frontal and parietal plates to expose the brain . . .' I looked at Jane: she was rapt. I wasn't really listening. My attention was directed toward what I took to be the main course, which had appeared in my absence. An unsteady pinkish mound now occupied the center of the table, completely obscuring the circular hole – it looked like cherry vanilla yogurt, a carton and a half, perhaps two. On closer inspection I noticed several black hairs peeping out from around its flaccid edges. And thought immediately of the bush-headed maitre d'. I pointed to one of the hairs, remarking to Mrs U-Hwak-Lo that the rudiments of culinary hygiene could be a little more rigorously observed among the staff. She smiled. Encouraged, I asked her what exactly the dish was. 'Much delicacy,' she said. 'Very rare find in land of Lincoln.' At that moment the waiter appeared and handed each of us a bamboo stick beaten flat and sharpened at one end.

'. . . then the tribal elders or visiting dignitaries are seated around the table,' the Doctor was saying. 'The chef has previously of course located the macaque beneath the table, the exposed part of the creature's brain protruding from the hole in its center. After the feast, the lower ranks of the village population divide up the remnants. It's really quite efficient.'

'How fascinating!' said Jane. 'Shall we try some?'

'By all means . . . but tell me, how has Konrad been coming with that Yerkish epic he's been working up?'

Jane turned to answer, bamboo stick poised: 'Oh I'm so glad you asked – I'd almost forgotten. He's finished his tenth book and tells me he'll be doing two more – out of deference to the Miltonic tradition. Isn't that a groove?'

'Yes,' said the doctor, gesturing toward the rosy lump in the center of the table. 'Yes it is. He's certainly – and I hope you won't mind the pun – a brainy fellow. Ho-ho.'

'Oh Doctor,' Jane laughed, and plunged her stick into the pink. Beneath the table, in the dark, a tiny fist clutched at my pantleg.

I missed work again the following day. This time it took five Doriden to put me under. I had lain in bed sweating and tossing, listening to Jane's quiet breathing, inhaling her fumes. At dawn I dozed off, dreamed briefly of elementary school cafeterias swarming with knickered chimps and weltered with trays of cherry vanilla yogurt, and woke stale-mouthed. Then I took the pills. It was three-thirty when I woke again. There was a note from Jane: Bringing Konrad home for dinner. Vacuum rug and clean toilet.

Konrad was impeccably dressed – long pants, platform wedgies, cufflinks. He smelled of eau de cologne, Jane of used litter. They arrived during the seven o'clock news. I opened the door for them. 'Hello Jane,' I said. We stood at the door, awkward, silent. 'Well?' she said. 'Aren't you going to greet our guest?' 'Hello Konrad,' I said. And then: 'I believe we met in the boys' room at the Center the other day?' He bowed deeply, straight-faced, his upper lip like a halved cantaloupe. Then he broke into a snicker, turned to Jane and juggled out an impossible series of gestures. Jane laughed. Something caught in my throat. 'Is he trying to say something?' I asked. 'Oh potpie,' she said, 'it was nothing – just a little quote from Yeats.'

'Yeats?'

'Yes, you know: "An aged man is but a paltry thing."'

Jane served watercress sandwiches and animal crackers as hors d'oeuvres. She brought them into the living room on a cut-glass serving tray and set them down before Konrad and me, where we sat on the sofa, watching the news. Then she returned to the kitchen. Konrad plucked up a tiny sandwich and swallowed it like a communion wafer, sucking the tips of his fingers. Then he lifted the tray and offered it to me. I declined. 'No thank you,' I said. Konrad shrugged, set the plate down in his lap and carefully stacked all the sandwiches in its center. I pretended to be absorbed with the news: actually I studied him, half-face. He was filling the gaps in his sandwich-construction with animal crackers. His lower lip protruded, his ears were rubbery, he was balding. With both hands he crushed the heap of crackers and sandwiches together and began kneading it until it took on the consistency of raw dough. Then he lifted the whole thing to his mouth and swallowed it without chewing. There were no whites to his eyes.

Konrad's only reaction to the newscast was a burst of excitement over a war story – the reporter stood against the wasteland of treadless tanks and recoilless guns in Thailand or Syria or Chile: huts were burning, old women weeping. 'Wow-wow! Eeeeeeee! Er-er-er-er,' Konrad said. Jane appeared in the kitchen doorway, hands dripping. 'What is it, Konrad?' she said. He made a series of violent gestures. 'Well?' I asked. She translated: 'Konrad says that "the pig oppressors" genocidal tactics will lead to their mutual extermination and usher in a new golden age . . .' – here she hesitated, looked up at him to continue (he was springing up and down on the couch, flailing his fists as though they held whips and scourges) – '". . . of freedom and equality for all, regardless of race, creed, color – or genus." I wouldn't worry,' she added, 'it's just his daily slice of revolutionary rhetoric. He'll calm down in a minute – he likes to play Che, but he's basically nonviolent.'

Ten minutes later Jane served dinner. Konrad, with remarkable speed and coordination, consumed four cans of fruit cocktail, thirty-two spareribs, half a dozen each of oranges, apples and pomegranates, two cheeseburgers and three quarts of chocolate malted. In the kitchen, clearing up, I commented to Jane about our guest's prodigious appetite. He was sitting in the other room, listening to *Don Giovanni*, sipping brandy. Jane said that he was a big, active male and that she could attest to his need for so many calories. 'How much does he weigh?' I asked. 'Stripped,' she said, 'one eighty-one. When he stands up straight he's four eight and three quarters.' I mulled over this information while I scraped away at the dishes, filed them in the dishwasher, neat ranks of blue china. A few moments later I stepped into the living room to observe Jane stroking Konrad's ears, his head in her lap. I stand five seven, one forty-three.

When I returned from work the following day, Jane was gone. Her dresser drawers were bare, the closet empty. There were white rectangles on the wall where her Rousseau reproductions had hung. The top plank of the bookcase was ribbed with the dust-prints of her Edgar Rice Burroughs collection. Her girls' softball trophy, her natural foods cookbook, her oaken cudgel, her moog, her wok: all gone. There were no notes. A pain jabbed at my sternum, tears started in my eyes. I was alone, deserted, friendless. I began to long even for the stink of her. On the pillow in the bedroom I found a fermenting chunk of pineapple. And sobbed.

By the time I thought of the Primate Center the sun was already on the wane. It was dark when I got there. Loose gravel grated beneath my shoes in the parking lot; the flag snapped at the top of its pole; the lights grinned lickerishly from the Center's windows. Inside the lighting was subdued, the building hushed. I began searching through the rooms, opening and slamming doors. The linoleum glowed all the way up the long corridor. At the far end I heard someone whistling 'My Old Kentucky Home'. It was the janitor.

74

'Howdedo,' he said. 'Wut kin ah do fo yo at such a inauspicious hour ob de night?'

I was candid with him. 'I'm looking for Miss Good.'

'Ohhh, she leave bout fo-turdy evy day – sartinly yo should be well apprised ob dat fack.'

'I thought she might be working late tonight.'

'Noooo, no chance ob dat.' He was staring at the floor.

'Mind if I look for myself?'

'Mah good man, ah trusts yo is not intimatin dat ah would dis-kise de troof . . . far be it fum me to pre-varicate jus to proteck a young lady wet run off fum a man dat doan unnerstan her needs nor 'low her to spress de natchrul inclination ob her soul.'

At that moment a girlish giggle sounded from down the hall. Jane's girlish giggle. The janitor's right hand spread itself across my chest. 'Ah wooden insinooate mahsef in de middle ob a highly sinificant speriment if ah was yo, Jackson,' he said, hissing through the gap in his teeth. I pushed by him and started down the corridor. Jane's laugh leaped out again. From the last door on my left. I hurried. Suddenly the Doctor and his wife stepped from the shadows to block the doorway. 'Mr Horne,' said the Doctor, arms folded against his chest, 'take hold of yourself. We are conducting a series of experiments here that I simply cannot allow you to—'

'A fig for your experiments,' I shouted. 'I want to speak to my, my – roommate.' I could hear the janitor's footsteps behind me. 'Get out of my way, Doctor,' I said. Mrs U-Hwak-Lo smiled. I felt panicky. Thought of the Tong Wars.

'Is dey a problem here, Doc?' the janitor said, his breath hot on the back of my neck. I broke. Grabbed the Doctor by his elbows, wheeled around and shoved him into the janitor. They went down on the linoleum like spastic skaters. I applied my shoulder to the door and battered my way in. Mrs U-Hwak-Lo's shrill in my ear: 'You make big missake, Misser!' Inside I found Jane, legs and arms bare, pinching a lab smock across her chest. She looked puzzled at first, then annoyed. She stepped up to me, made some rude gestures in my face. I could hear scrambling in the hallway behind me. Then I saw Konrad – in a pair of baggy BVDs. I grabbed Jane. But Konrad was there in an instant – he hit me like the grill of a Cadillac and I spun across the room, tumbling desks and chairs as I went. I slumped against the chalkboard. The door slammed: Jane was gone. Konrad swelled his chest, swayed toward me, the fluorescent lights hissing overhead, the chalkboard cold against the back of my neck. And I looked up into the black eyes, teeth, fur, rock-ribbed arms.

MILAN KUNDERA

The Hitchhiking Game

I

The needle on the gas gauge suddenly dipped toward empty and the young driver of the sports car declared that it was maddening how much gas the car ate up. 'See that we don't run out of gas again,' protested the girl (about twenty-two), and reminded the driver of several places where this had already happened to them. The young man replied that he wasn't worried, because whatever he went through with her had the charm of adventure for him. The girl objected; whenever they had run out of gas on the highway it had, she said, always been an adventure only for her. The young man had hidden and she had had to make ill use of her charms by thumbing a ride and letting herself be driven to the nearest gas station, then thumbing a ride back with a can of gas. The young man asked the girl whether the drivers who had given her a ride had been unpleasant, since she spoke as if her task had been a hardship. She replied (with awkward flirtatiousness) that sometimes they had been *very* pleasant

MILAN KUNDERA

but that it hadn't done her any good as she had been burdened with the can and had had to leave them before she could get anything going. 'Pig,' said the young man. The girl protested that she wasn't a pig, but that he really was. God knows how many girls stopped him on the highway, when he was driving the car alone! Still driving, the young man put his arm around the girl's shoulders and kissed her gently on the forehead. He knew that she loved him and that she was jealous. Jealousy isn't a pleasant quality, but if it isn't overdone (and if it's combined with modesty), apart from its inconvenience there's even something touching about it. At least that's what the young man thought. Because he was only twenty-eight, it seemed to him that he was old and knew everything that a man could know about women. In the girl sitting beside him he valued precisely what, until now, he had met with least in women: purity.

The needle was already on empty, when to the right the young man caught sight of a sign, announcing that the station was a quarter of a mile ahead. The girl hardly had time to say how relieved she was before the young man was signaling left and driving into a space in front of the pumps. However, he had to stop a little way off, because beside the pumps was a huge gasoline truck with a large metal tank and a bulky hose, which was refilling the pumps. 'We'll have to wait,' said the young man to the girl and got out of the car. 'How long will it take?' he shouted to the man in overalls. 'Only a moment,' replied the attendant, and the young man said: 'I've heard that one before.' He wanted to go back and sit in the car, but he saw that the girl had gotten out the

78

other side. 'I'll take a little walk in the meantime,' she said. 'Where to?' the young man asked on purpose, wanting to see the girl's embarrassment. He had known her for a year now but she would still get shy in front of him. He enjoyed her moments of shyness, partly because they distinguished her from the women he'd met before, partly because he was aware of the law of universal transience, which made even his girl's shyness a precious thing to him.

II

The girl really didn't like it when during the trip (the young man would drive for several hours without stopping) she had to ask him to stop for a moment somewhere near a clump of trees. She always got angry when, with feigned surprise, he asked her why he should stop. She knew that her shyness was ridiculous and old-fashioned. Many times at work she had noticed that they laughed at her on account of it and deliberately provoked her. She always got shy in advance at the thought of how she was going to get shy. She often longed to feel free and easy about her body, the way most of the women around her did. She had even invented a special course in self-persuasion: she would repeat to herself that at birth every human being received one out of the millions of available bodies, as one would receive an allotted room out of the millions of rooms in an enormous hotel; that, consequently, the body was fortuitous and impersonal, only a ready-made, borrowed thing. She would repeat this to herself in different ways, but she could never manage to feel it. This mind–body dualism was alien to her. She was too much one with her body; that is why she always felt such anxiety about it.

She experienced this same anxiety even in her relations with the young man, whom she had known for a year and with whom she was happy, perhaps because he never separated her body from her soul and she could live with him *wholly*. In this unity there was happiness, but right behind the happiness lurked suspicion, and the girl was full of that. For instance, it often occurred to her that the other women (those who weren't anxious) were more attractive and more seductive and that the young man, who did not conceal the fact that he knew this kind of woman well, would someday leave her for a woman like that. (True, the young man declared that he'd had enough of them to last his whole life, but she knew that he was still much younger than he thought.) She wanted him to be completely hers and she to be completely his, but it often seemed to her that the more she tried to give him everything, the more she denied him something: the very thing that a light and superficial love or a flirtation gives to a person. It worried her that she was not able to combine seriousness with lightheartedness.

But now she wasn't worrying and any such thoughts were far from her mind. She felt good. It was the first day of their vacation (of their two-week vacation, about which she had been dreaming for a whole year), the sky was blue (the whole year she had been worrying about whether the sky would really be blue), and he was beside her. At his, 'Where to?' she blushed, and left the car without a word. She walked around the gas station, which was situated beside the highway in total isolation, surrounded by fields. About a hundred yards away (in the direction in which they were traveling), a wood began. She set off for it, vanished behind a little bush, and gave herself up to her good mood. (In solitude it was possible for her to get the greatest enjoyment from the presence of the man she loved. If his presence had been continuous, it would have kept on disappearing. Only when alone was she able to *hold on* to it.)

When she came out of the wood onto the highway, the gas station was visible. The large gasoline truck was already pulling out and the sports car moved forward toward the red turret of the pump. The girl walked on along the highway and only at times looked back to see if the sports car was coming. At last she caught sight of it. She stopped and began to wave at it like a hitchhiker waving at a stranger's car. The sports car slowed down and stopped close to the girl. The young man leaned toward the window, rolled it down, smiled, and asked, 'Where are you headed, miss?' 'Are you going to Bystritsa?' asked the girl, smiling flirtatiously at him. 'Yes, please get in,' said the young man, opening the door. The girl got in and the car took off.

III

The young man was always glad when his girlfriend was gay. This didn't happen too often; she had a quite tiresome job in an unpleasant environment, many hours of overtime without compensatory leisure and, at home, a sick mother. So she often felt tired. She didn't have either particularly good nerves or self-confidence and easily fell into a state of anxiety and fear. For this reason he welcomed every manifestation of her gaiety with the tender solicitude of a foster parent. He smiled at her and said: 'I'm lucky today. I've been driving for five years, but I've never given a ride to such a pretty hitchhiker.'

The girl was grateful to the young man for every bit of flattery; she wanted to linger for a moment in its warmth and so she said, 'You're very good at lying.'

'Do I look like a liar?'

'You look like you enjoy lying to women,' said the girl, and into her words there crept unawares a touch of the old anxiety, because she really did believe that her young man enjoyed lying to women.

The girl's jealousy often irritated the young man, but this time he could easily overlook it for, after all, her words didn't apply to him but to the unknown driver. And so he just casually inquired, 'Does it bother you?'

'If I were going with you, then it would bother me,' said the girl and her words contained a subtle, instructive message for the young man; but the end of her sentence applied only to the unknown driver, 'but I don't know you, so it doesn't bother me.'

'Things about her own man always bother a woman more than things about a stranger' (this was now the young man's subtle, instructive message to the girl), 'so seeing that we are strangers, we could get on well together.'

The girl purposely didn't want to understand the implied meaning of his message, and so she now addressed the unknown driver exclusively:

'What does it matter, since we'll part company in a little while?'

'Why?' asked the young man.

'Well, I'm getting out at Bystritsa.'

'And what if I get out with you?'

At these words the girl looked up at him and found that he looked exactly as she imagined him in her most agonizing hours of jealousy. She was alarmed at how he was flattering her and flirting with her (an unknown hitchhiker), and *how becoming it was to him*. Therefore she responded with defiant provocativeness, 'What would *you* do with me, I wonder?'

'I wouldn't have to think too hard about what to do with such a beautiful woman,' said the young man gallantly and at this moment he was once again speaking far more to his own girl than to the figure of the hitchhiker.

But this flattering sentence made the girl feel as if she had caught him at something, as if she had wheedled a confession out of him with a fraudulent trick. She felt toward him a brief flash of intense hatred and said, 'Aren't you rather too sure of yourself?'

The young man looked at the girl. Her defiant face appeared to him to be completely convulsed. He felt sorry for her and longed for her usual, familiar expression (which he used to call childish and simple). He leaned toward her, put his arm around her shoulders, and softly spoke the name with which he usually addressed her and with which he now wanted to stop the game.

But the girl released herself and said: 'You're going a bit too fast!'

At this rebuff the young man said: 'Excuse me, miss,' and looked silently in front of him at the highway.

IV

The girl's pitiful jealousy, however, left her as quickly as it had come over her. After all, she was sensible and knew perfectly well that all this was merely a game; now it even struck her as a little ridiculous that she had repulsed her man out of jealous rage; it wouldn't be pleasant for her if he found out why she had done it. Fortunately she had the miraculous ability to change the meaning of her actions after the event. Using this ability, she decided that she had repulsed him not out of anger but so that she could go on with the game, which, with its whimsicality, so well suited the first day of their vacation.

So again she was the hitchhiker, who had just repulsed the overenterprising driver, but only so as to slow down his conquest and make it more exciting. She half turned toward the young man and said caressingly:

'I didn't mean to offend you, mister!'

'Excuse me, I won't touch you again,' said the young man.

He was furious with the girl for not listening to him and refusing to be herself when that was what he wanted. And since the girl insisted on continuing in her role, he transferred his anger to the unknown hitchhiker whom she was portraying. And all at once he discovered the character of his own part: he stopped making the gallant remarks with which he had wanted to flatter his girl in a roundabout way, and began to play the tough guy who treats women to the coarser aspects of his masculinity: wilfulness, sarcasm, self-assurance.

This role was a complete contradiction of the young man's habitually solicitous approach to the girl. True, before he had met her, he had in fact behaved roughly rather than gently toward women. But he had never resembled a heartless tough guy, because he had never demonstrated either a particularly strong will or ruthlessness. However, if he did not resemble such a man, nonetheless he had *longed* to at one time. Of course it was a quite naive desire, but there it was. Childish desires withstand all the snares of the adult mind and often survive into ripe old age. And this childish desire quickly took advantage of the opportunity to embody itself in the proffered role.

The young man's sarcastic reserve suited the girl very well – it freed her from herself. For she herself was, above all, the epitome of jealousy. The moment she stopped seeing the gallantly seductive young man beside her and saw only his inaccessible face, her jealousy subsided. The girl could forget herself and give herself up to her role.

Her role? What was her role? It was a role out of trashy

literature. The hitchhiker stopped the car not to get a ride, but to seduce the man who was driving the car. She was an artful seductress, cleverly knowing how to use her charms. The girl slipped into this silly, romantic part with an ease that astonished her and held her spellbound.

V

There was nothing the young man missed in his life more than lightheartedness. The main road of his life was drawn with implacable precision: his job didn't use up merely eight hours a day, it also infiltrated the remaining time with the compulsory boredom of meetings and home study, and, by means of the attentiveness of his countless male and female colleagues, it infiltrated the wretchedly little time he had left for his private life as well; this private life never remained secret and sometimes even became the subject of gossip and public discussion. Even two weeks' vacation didn't give him a feeling of liberation and adventure; the gray shadow of precise planning lay even here. The scarcity of summer accommodations in our country compelled him to book a room in the Tatras six months in advance, and since for that he needed a recommendation from his office, its omnipresent brain thus did not cease knowing about him even for an instant.

He had become reconciled to all this, yet all the same from time to time the terrible thought of the straight road would overcome him – a road along which he was being pursued, where he was visible to everyone, and from which he could not turn aside. At this moment that thought returned to him. Through an odd and brief conjunction of ideas the figurative road became identified with the real highway along which he was driving – and this led him suddenly to do a crazy thing.

'Where did you say you wanted to go?' he asked the girl.

'To Banska Bystritsa,' she replied.

'And what are you going to do there?'

'I have a date there.'

'Who with?'

'With a certain gentleman.'

The car was just coming to a large crossroads. The driver slowed down so he could read the road signs, then turned off to the right.

'What will happen if you don't arrive for that date?'

'It would be your fault and you would have to take care of me.'

'You obviously didn't notice that I turned off in the direction of Nove Zamky.'

'Is that true? You've gone crazy!'

'Don't be afraid, I'll take care of you,' said the young man.

So they drove and chatted thus – the driver and the hitchhiker who did not know each other.

The game all at once went into a higher gear. The sports car was moving away not only from the imaginary goal of Banska Bystritsa, but also from the real goal, toward which it had been heading in the morning: the Tatras and the room that had been booked. Fiction was suddenly making an assault upon real life. The young man was moving away from himself and from the implacable straight road, from which he had never strayed until now.

'But you said you were going to the Low Tatras!' The girl was surprised.

'I am going, miss, wherever I feel like going. I'm a free man and I do what I want and what it pleases me to do.'

VI

When they drove into Nove Zamky it was already getting dark.

The young man had never been here before and it took him a while to orient himself. Several times he stopped the car and asked the passersby directions to the hotel. Several streets had been dug up, so that the drive to the hotel, even though it was quite close by (as all those who had been asked asserted), necessitated so many detours and round-about routes that it was almost a quarter of an hour before they finally stopped in front of it. The hotel looked unprepossessing, but it was the only one in town and the young man didn't feel like driving on. So he said to the girl, 'Wait here,' and got out of the car.

Out of the car he was, of course, himself again. And it was upsetting for him to find himself in the evening somewhere completely different from his intended destination – the more so because no one had forced him to do it and as a matter of fact he hadn't even really wanted to. He blamed himself for this piece of folly, but then became reconciled to it. The room in the Tatras could wait until tomorrow and it wouldn't do any harm if they celebrated the first day of their vacation with something unexpected.

He walked through the restaurant – smoky, noisy, and crowded – and asked for the reception desk. They sent him to the back of the lobby near the staircase, where behind a glass panel a superannuated blonde was sitting beneath a board full of keys. With difficulty, he obtained the key to the only room left.

The girl, when she found herself alone, also threw off her role. She didn't feel ill-humored, though, at finding herself in an unexpected town. She was so devoted to the young man that she never had doubts about anything he did, and confidently entrusted every moment of her life to him. On the other hand the idea once again popped into her mind that perhaps – just as she was now doing – other women had waited for her man in his car, those women whom he met on business trips. But surprisingly enough this idea didn't upset her at all now; in fact, she smiled at the thought of how nice it was that today she was this other woman, this irresponsible, indecent other woman, one of those women of whom she was so jealous; it seemed to her that she was cutting them all out, that she had learned how to use their weapons; how to give the young man what until now she had not known how to give him: lightheartedness, shamelessness, and dissoluteness; a curious feeling of satisfaction filled her, because she alone had the ability to be all women and in this way (she alone) could completely captivate her lover and hold his interest.

The young man opened the car door and led the girl into the restaurant. Amid the din, the dirt, and the smoke he found a single, unoccupied table in a corner.

VII

'So how are you going to take care of me now?' asked the girl provocatively.

'What would you like for an aperitif?'

The girl wasn't too fond of alcohol, still she drank a little wine and liked vermouth fairly well. Now, however, she purposely said: 'Vodka.'

'Fine,' said the young man. 'I hope you won't get drunk on me.'

'And if I do?' said the girl.

The young man did not reply but called over a waiter and ordered two vodkas and two steak dinners. In a moment the waiter brought a tray with two small glasses and placed it in front of them.

The man raised his glass, 'To you!'

'Can't you think of a wittier toast?'

Something was beginning to irritate him about the girl's game; now sitting face to face with her, he realized that it wasn't just the *words* which were turning her into a stranger, but that her *whole persona* had changed, the movements of her body and her facial expression, and that she unpalatably and faithfully resembled that type of woman whom he knew so well and for whom he felt some aversion.

And so (holding his glass in his raised hand), he corrected his toast: 'OK, then I won't drink to you, but to your kind, in which are combined so successfully the better qualities of the animal and the worse aspects of the human being.'

'By "kind" do you mean all women?' asked the girl.

'No, I mean only those who are like you.'

'Anyway it doesn't seem very witty to me to compare a woman with an animal.'

'OK,' the young man was still holding his glass aloft, 'then I won't drink to your kind, but to your soul. Agreed? To your soul, which lights up when it descends from your head into your belly, and which goes out when it rises back up to your head.'

The girl raised her glass. 'OK, to my soul, which descends into my belly.'

'I'll correct myself once more,' said the young man. 'To your belly, into which your soul descends.'

'To my belly,' said the girl, and her belly (now that they had named it specifically), as it were, responded to the call; she felt every inch of it.

Then the waiter brought their steaks and the young man ordered them another vodka and some soda water (this time they drank to the girl's breasts), and the conversation continued in this peculiar, frivolous tone. It irritated the young man more and more how *well able* the girl was to become the lascivious miss; if she was able to do it so well, he thought, it meant that she really was like that; after all, no alien soul had entered into her from somewhere in space; what she was acting now was she herself, perhaps it was that part of her being which had formerly been locked up

91

and which the pretext of the game had let out of its cage. Perhaps the girl supposed that by means of the game she was *disowning* herself, but wasn't it the other way around? Wasn't she becoming herself only through the game? Wasn't she freeing herself through the game? No, opposite him was not sitting a strange woman in his girl's body; it was his girl, herself, no one else. He looked at her and felt growing aversion toward her.

However, it was not only aversion. The more the girl withdrew from him *psychically*, the more he longed for her *physically*; the alienation of her soul drew attention to her body; yes it turned her body into a body; as if until now it had been hidden from the young man within clouds of compassion, tenderness, concern, love, and emotion, as if it had been lost in these clouds (yes; as if this body had been *lost*!). It seemed to the young man that today he was *seeing* his girl's body for the first time.

After her third vodka and soda the girl got up and said flirtatiously, 'Excuse me.'

The young man said, 'May I ask you where you are going, miss?'

'To piss, if you'll permit me,' said the girl and walked off between the tables back toward the plush screen.

VIII

She was pleased with the way she had astounded the young man with this word, which – in spite of all its innocence –

he had never heard from her; nothing seemed to her truer to the character of the woman she was playing than this flirtatious emphasis placed on the word in question; yes, she was pleased, she was in the best of moods; the game captivated her. It allowed her to feel what she had not felt till now: *a feeling of happy-go-lucky irresponsibility*.

She, who was always uneasy in advance about her every next step, suddenly felt completely relaxed. The alien life in which she had become involved was a life without shame, without biographical specifications, without past or future, without obligations; it was a life that was extraordinarily free. The girl, as a hitchhiker, could do anything: *everything was permitted her*; she could say, do, and feel whatever she liked.

She walked through the room and was aware that people were watching her from all the tables; it was also a new sensation, one she didn't recognize: *indecent joy caused by her body*. Until now she had never been able to get rid of the fourteen-year-old girl within herself who was ashamed of her breasts and had the disagreeable feeling that she was indecent, because they stuck out from her body and were visible. Even though she was proud of being pretty and having a good figure, this feeling of pride was always immediately curtailed by shame; she rightly suspected that feminine beauty functioned above all as sexual provocation and she found this distasteful; she longed for her body to relate only to the man she loved; when men stared at her breasts in the street it seemed to her that they were invading a piece of her most secret privacy which should belong only to herself and her lover. But now she was the hitchhiker, the woman without a destiny. In this role she was relieved of the tender bonds of her love and began to be intensely aware of her body; and her body became more aroused the more alien the eyes watching it.

She was walking past the last table when an intoxicated man, wanting to show off his worldliness, addressed her in French: 'Combien, mademoiselle?'

The girl understood. She thrust out her breasts and fully experienced every movement of her hips, then disappeared behind the screen.

IX

It was a curious game. This curiousness was evidenced, for example, in the fact that the young man, even though he himself was playing the unknown driver remarkably well, did not for a moment stop seeing his girl in the hitchhiker. And it was precisely this that was tormenting; he saw his girl seducing a strange man, and had the bitter privilege of being present, of seeing at close quarters how she looked and of hearing what she said when she was cheating on him (when she had cheated on him, when she would cheat on him); he had the paradoxical honor of being himself the pretext for her unfaithfulness.

This was all the worse because he worshipped rather than loved her; it had always seemed to him that her inward nature was *real* only within the bounds of fidelity and purity, and that beyond these bounds it simply didn't exist;

beyond these bounds she would cease to be herself, as water ceases to be water beyond the boiling point. When he now saw her crossing this horrifying boundary with nonchalant elegance, he was filled with anger.

The girl came back from the rest room and complained: 'A guy over there asked me: *Combien, mademoiselle?*'

'You shouldn't be surprised,' said the young man, 'after all, you look like a whore.'

'Do you know that it doesn't bother me in the least?'

'Then you should go with the gentleman!'

'But I have you.'

'You can go with him after me. Go and work out something with him.'

'I don't find him attractive.'

'But in principle you have nothing against it, having several men in one night.'

'Why not, if they're good-looking.'

'Do you prefer them one after the other or at the same time?'

'Either way,' said the girl.

The conversation was proceeding to still greater extremes of rudeness; it shocked the girl slightly but she couldn't protest. Even in a game there lurks a lack of freedom; even a game is a trap for the players. If this had not been a game and they had really been two strangers, the hitchhiker could long ago have taken offense and left. But there's no escape from a game. A team cannot flee from the playing field before the end of the match, chess pieces cannot desert the chessboard: the boundaries of the playing field are fixed.

The girl knew that she had to accept whatever form the game might take, just because it was a game. She knew that the more extreme the game became, the more it would be a game and the more obediently she would have to play it. And it was futile to evoke good sense and warn her dazed soul that she must keep her distance from the game and not take it seriously. Just because it was only a game her soul was not afraid, did not oppose the game, and narcotically sank deeper into it.

The young man called the waiter and paid. Then he got up and said to the girl, 'We're going.'

'Where to?' The girl feigned surprise.

'Don't ask, just come on,' said the young man.

'What sort of way is that to talk to me?'

'The way I talk to whores,' said the young man.

X

They went up the badly lit staircase. On the landing below the second floor a group of intoxicated men was standing near the rest room. The young man caught hold of the girl from behind so that he was holding her breast with his hand. The men by the rest room saw this and began to call out. The girl wanted to break away, but the young man yelled at her: 'Keep still!' The men greeted this with general ribaldry and addressed several dirty remarks to the girl. The young man and the girl reached the second floor. He opened the door of their room and switched on the light.

It was a narrow room with two beds, a small table, a chair, and a washbasin. The young man locked the door and turned to the girl. She was standing facing him in a defiant pose with insolent sensuality in her eyes. He looked at her and tried to discover behind her lascivious expression the familiar features which he loved tenderly. It was as if he were looking at two images through the same lens, at two images superimposed one upon the other with the one showing through the other. These two images showing through each other were telling him that *everything* was in the girl, that her soul was terrifyingly amorphous, that it held faithfulness and unfaithfulness, treachery and inno-cence, flirtatiousness and chastity. This disorderly jumble seemed disgusting to him, like the variety to be found in a pile of garbage. Both images continued to show through each other and the young man understood that the girl differed only on the surface from other women, but deep down was the same as they: full of all possible thoughts, feelings, and vices, which justified all his secret misgivings and fits of jealousy. The impression that certain outlines delineated her as an individual was only a delusion to which the other person, the one who was looking, was subject – namely himself. It seemed to him that the girl he loved was a creation of his desire, his thoughts, and his faith and that the *real* girl now standing in front of him was hopelessly *alien*, hopelessly *ambiguous*. He hated her.

'What are you waiting for? Strip,' he said.

The girl flirtatiously bent her head and said, 'Is it necessary?'

The tone in which she said this seemed to him very familiar; it seemed to him that once long ago some other woman had said this to him, only he no longer knew which one. He longed to humiliate her. Not the hitchhiker, but his own girl. The game merged with life. The game of humiliating the hitchhiker became only a pretext for humiliating his girl. The young man had forgotten that he was playing a game. He simply hated the woman standing in front of him. He stared at her and took a fifty-crown bill from his wallet. He offered it to the girl. 'Is that enough?'

The girl took the fifty crowns and said: 'You don't think I'm worth much.'

The young man said: 'You aren't worth more.'

The girl nestled up against the young man. 'You can't get around me like that! You must try a different approach, you must work a little!'

She put her arms around him and moved her mouth toward his. He put his fingers on her mouth and gently pushed her away. He said: 'I only kiss women I love.'

'And you don't love me?'

'No.'

'Whom do you love?'

'What's that got to do with you? Strip!'

XI

She had never undressed like this before. The shyness, the feeling of inner panic, the dizziness, all that she had always felt when undressing in front of the young man (and she couldn't hide in the darkness), all this was gone. She was standing in front of him self-confident, insolent, bathed in light, and astonished at where she had all of a sudden discovered the gestures, heretofore unknown to her, of a slow, provocative striptease. She took in his glances, slipping off each piece of clothing with a caressing movement and enjoying each individual stage of this exposure.

But then suddenly she was standing in front of him completely naked and at this moment it flashed through her head that now the whole game would end, that since she had stripped off her clothes, she had also stripped away her dissimulation, and that being naked meant that she was now herself and the young man ought to come up to her now and make a gesture with which he would wipe out everything and after which would follow only their most intimate love-making. So she stood naked in front of the young man and at this moment stopped playing the game. She felt embarrassed and on her face appeared the smile which really belonged to her: a shy and confused smile.

But the young man didn't come to her and didn't end the game. He didn't notice the familiar smile; he saw before him only the beautiful, alien body of his own girl, whom he hated. Hatred cleansed his sensuality of any sentimental coating. She wanted to come to him, but he said: 'Stay where you are, I want to have a good look at you.' Now he longed only to treat her as a whore. But the young man had never had a whore and the ideas he had about them came from literature and hearsay. So he turned to these ideas and the first thing he recalled was the image of a woman in black underwear (and black stockings) dancing on the shiny top of a piano. In the little hotel room there was no piano, there was only a small table covered with a linen cloth leaning against the wall. He ordered the girl to climb up on it. The girl made a pleading gesture, but the young man said, 'You've been paid.'

When she saw the look of unshakable obsession in the young man's eyes, she tried to go on with the game, even though she no longer could and no longer knew how. With tears in her eyes she climbed onto the table. The top was scarcely three feet square and one leg was a little bit shorter than the others so that standing on it the girl felt unsteady.

But the young man was pleased with the naked figure, now towering above him, and the girl's shy insecurity merely inflamed his imperiousness. He wanted to see her body in all positions and from all sides, as he imagined other men had seen it and would see it. He was vulgar and lascivious. He used words that she had never heard from him in her life. She wanted to refuse, she wanted to be released from the game. She called him by his first name, but he immediately yelled at her that she had no right to address him so intimately. And so eventually in confusion and on the verge of tears, she obeyed, she bent forward and squatted according to the young man's wishes, saluted, and then wiggled her hips as she did the Twist for him; during a slightly more violent movement, when the cloth slipped beneath her feet and she nearly fell, the young man caught her and dragged her to the bed.

He had intercourse with her. She was glad that at least now finally the unfortunate game would end and they would again be the two people they had been before and would love each other. She wanted to press her mouth against his. But the young man pushed her head away and repeated that he only kissed women he loved. She burst into loud sobs. But she wasn't even allowed to cry, because the young man's furious passion gradually won over her body, which then silenced the complaint of her soul. On the bed there were soon two bodies in perfect harmony, two sensual bodies, alien to each other. This was exactly what the girl had most dreaded all her life and had scrupulously avoided till now: love-making without emotion or love. She knew that she had crossed the forbidden boundary, but she proceeded across it without objections and as a full participant; only somewhere, far off in a corner of her consciousness, did she feel horror at the thought that she had never known such pleasure, never so much pleasure as at this moment – beyond that boundary.

XII

Then it was all over. The young man got up off the girl and, reaching out for the long cord hanging over the bed, switched off the light. He didn't want to see the girl's face. He knew that the game was over, but didn't feel like returning to their customary relationship; he feared this return. He lay beside the girl in the dark in such a way that their bodies would not touch.

After a moment he heard her sobbing quietly; the girl's hand diffidently, childishly touched his; it touched, withdrew, then touched again, and then a pleading, sobbing voice broke the silence, calling him by his name and saying, 'I am me, I am me . . .'

The young man was silent, he didn't move, and he was aware of the sad emptiness of the girl's assertion, in which the unknown was defined by the same unknown.

And the girl soon passed from sobbing to loud crying and went on endlessly repeating this pitiful tautology: 'I am me, I am me, I am me . . .'

The young man began to call compassion to his aid (he had to call it from afar, because it was nowhere near at hand), so as to be able to calm the girl. There were still thirteen days' vacation before them.

Translated by Suzanne Rappaport

MARGARET ATWOOD

In Love with Raymond Chandler

An affair with Raymond Chandler, what a joy! Not because of the mangled bodies and the marinated cops and hints of eccentric sex, but because of his interest in furniture. He knew that furniture could breathe, could feel, not as we do but in a way more muffled, like the word *upholstery*, with its overtones of mustiness and dust, its bouquet of sunlight on ageing cloth or of scuffed leather on the backs and seats of sleazy office chairs. I think of his sofas, stuffed to roundness, satin-covered, pale-blue like the eyes of his cold blonde unbodied murderous women, beating very slowly, like the hearts of hibernating crocodiles; of his chaises longues, with their malicious pillows. He knew about front lawns too, and greenhouses, and the interiors of cars.

This is how our love affair would go. We would meet at a hotel, or a motel, whether expensive or cheap it wouldn't matter. We would enter the room, lock the door, and begin to explore the furniture, fingering the curtains, running our hands along the spurious gilt frames of the pictures, over the real marble or the chipped enamel of the luxurious or tacky washroom sink, inhaling the odour of the carpets, old cigarette smoke and spilled gin and fast meaningless sex or else the rich abstract scent of the oval transparent soaps imported from England, it wouldn't matter to us; what would matter would be our response to the furniture, and the furniture's response to us. Only after we had sniffed, fingered, rubbed, rolled on and absorbed the furniture of the room would we fall into each other's arms, and onto the bed (king-sized? peach-coloured? creaky? narrow? four-posted? pioneer-quilted? lime-green chenille-covered?), ready at last to do the same things to each other.

CLIVE SINCLAIR

Titillatio

Bedded in her double-divan wedded Bella, miles away, is suddenly robbed of her senses and instinctively buttock-shoves husband Quentin deeper inside of her, responding at last to his pumping with helpless spasms of her own until, with a final cry of 'I'm coming!' she reaches her climax.

'How do you feel?' asks Quentin.

'Good,' says Bella, yawning, and promptly falling asleep. Quentin, too, after wiping himself with a Kleenex, nods off.

Bella, next morning, hears the phone ring. She picks up the receiver.

'What are you doing?' the other end asks.

'I am writing about ethics,' she replies.

'I don't know much about ethics,' the man says, 'but I know what I like.' This remark is somewhat ingenuous, since the speaker (a famous Professor of Philosophy) is in fact the supervisor of Bella's thesis.

'And what do you like?' whispers Bella, assuming a familiar role.

'Bathing you,' he answers, 'feeling your soap-smooth skin, smelling a mixture of you and the talc.'

Bella smiles. He isn't like that, really. And knowing him well as she does, she recognizes that he is excited and that he is, however obscure the origin of his impulse, attempting to involve her in the same experience. She knows exactly what he wants.

'Tonight,' she whispers.

'Tonight,' he agrees.

Do not be misled into thinking that Bella is whispering for the sake of any extraneous erotic effect, on the contrary it is a necessary precaution, because her eldest daughter (aged twelve) is now standing in the doorway behind her, requiring maternal attention.

The husband, as is often the case, knows nothing about the true nature of his wife's relationship with her academic mentor. There is, moreover, an especial irony in his situation; for it was he who finally persuaded Bella to take her Masters degree, and who felt the greatest pride in her achievement when she was invited to complete her doctorate. Such is the bad luck of a husband who encourages his wife to be, simultaneously, a Master of Arts and the mistress of an ageing Professor of Philosophy. But if we say that Quentin is a builder of bridges we are not making fun of the cuckold, we are talking about his occupation. Quentin's achievements at linking opposite banks of a river filled his doting, spoiling mother with a perverse joy; for had her own husband (Quentin's father) not died beside the River Kwai?

This suggestion of son-succeeding-where-father-failed gives Quentin a sense of security (expressed outwardly in the ancient sturdy home that houses his family), and in reflective moments he is wont to view his happy predicament with genial satisfaction. Nor does the smile leave his fond face when his younger daughter (aged eleven) comes in with the news that he has to prepare dinner tonight because Mummy has to go to an important meeting at the university.

Needless to say, the important meeting (if that is what we choose to call it) does not take place at the university, but rather in a flat rented by the prophetic Professor of Philosophy for just such occasions. The apartment is bare; a single large room containing nothing but a double-bed. A key is inserted into a lock, a door opens, our illicit couple enters. Perhaps we may pause to wonder just what there is about this fifty-five-year-old professor that has so captivated his thirty-year-old student. Hair: grey, thick at sides, thin on top. Eyes: also grey, surrounded by laughter lines, underlined by bags.

'Just as a hotel receptionist is suspicious of a guest who arrives without luggage,' says the Professor, 'so you should be wary of a man without bags. He will not stay with you longer than a night.' His mouth, then, is witty and wise. His voice is generally gentle, though it can be stern, whereupon it reveals a continental accent. He has a nose to match; large, slightly curved. His chief vanity is his assumed resemblance to Saul Bellow. We could go on, but will it make Bella's infatuation any easier to understand? Indeed, the whole affair will appear even more improbable when we reveal that, for the past few years, the Professor of Philosophy has been, more or less, impotent.

They have never made love properly. This is what generally happens: Bella undresses and lies supine on the bed, while the Professor touches, strokes her compliant responsive flesh, slowly but clearly exciting her, until she directs his hand herself, moving her pelvis up and down, rubbing herself against his firm fingertip, stimulating her clitoris, ticklish at first, then tenser, till her orgasm comes. While Bella concentrates all of herself to this one end the Professor is, as it were, left alone with his thoughts. He remembers, with a certain degree of embarrassment, Spinoza's 'active emotions' of which joy or *hilaritas* is the chief and most vital expression of the whole personality, whereas sensuous pleasure or *titillatio* is but the automatic reaction to the local stimulation of an organ. Sometimes Bella's transports convince him that she is indeed expressing a joy that comes from her whole being, and then allows her to deal in a like manner with his own out-of-tune organ so that, by dint of prolonged fondling, and perhaps some further oral persuasion, he too has an orgasm.

Tonight, in the flat, the Professor introduces a variation. As he makes his way, in his familiar meticulous fashion, over Bella's naked body, he gives her a running commentary.

'Here's Bella's flat belly, and down this slope, down here, between her thighs, there's a slit, covered with curly hair; you can open it up, and inside are damp, shiny folds of pinkish flesh, and now there's her smell and this little knob – shall I go on?'

'Please.'

'What will happen if I touch just here?'

'Yes, yes, yes, touch.' Bella closes her eyes and awaits the moving finger.

Afterwards, laughing with pleasure and relief, she curls up on the bed, cuddles up against her man, and begins to hum an old song, 'My Heart Belongs to Daddy'.

Bella's own father was the head-waiter in a large hotel on the South Coast of England in the austere but tranquil post-war years. Her late mother, unfortunately, had artistic aspirations, which led her to desert her husband for the fading intellectual blossoms of Bloomsbury, leaving every-thing behind, including her daughter. But poor little Bella was not destined to spend happy hours with Papa either; after just a few months alone together he packed Bella off to London, packed his own belongings and vanished for ever, leaving his daughter with half-remembered memories of sea-side walks and talks on sandy windswept beaches. Very different to serving tea to homosexual authors, wine to artists who sported velvet hats and fucked heiresses for their livelihood, and cigarettes to poets who dedicated their lives to finding a rhyme for Eliot. Quentin's mother appeared at one such soirée, as these gatherings were known, and in time Bella and Quentin were introduced. Quentin was handsome and Bella was young, well-developed, eager to learn the mysterious ways of a man with a maid. She got pregnant at the age of seventeen, and married soon after; but that is just as they wanted it because, have no doubts, they were in love. From the very beginning Quentin was anxious that his new wife should be happy, so he initiated his dangerous policy of allowing her to make most decisions for them both. From a mere indulgence this grew into a way of life that characterized their whole relationship, until Bella became the dominant partner in the marriage, and more and more impatient with Quentin's inability to make up his mind on any subject without first consulting her.

Such is the explanation (for which Quentin searched in vain) of Bella's otherwise inexplicable behaviour on the night of their thirteenth wedding anniversary.

Quentin suggested that they dine out, Bella agreed, a babysitter was obtained to look after the girls. There remained only the decision about the restaurant. Although Bella kept maintaining that she couldn't care less where they ate, she took considerable trouble over her appearance, and finally emerged from the bathroom with false eyelashes, lashings of mascara, rosy cheeks and brand-new lipstick; dressed also in the long gown reserved exclusively for special events. But Quentin had no table booked, and by the time he had decided where to try it was too late to get a table anywhere; so they ended up on their thirteenth anniversary dining in the local pizza parlour. It was there, when Quentin was dallying over the wine list, that Bella had hysterics. Quentin was amazed, he couldn't understand why Bella was so upset. It never occurred to him that sometimes Bella simply wanted to have a fuss made of her, wanted to be taken out for treats; in effect, she wanted all the delights due to a favourite daughter. But this role Bella fancied for herself was constantly undermined by the presence of her own children; frequently she wondered where these two human beings could have come from, it seemed inconceivable that they could have emerged from her womb. When they were born she had refused to breast-feed either one. She was frightened by their dependence upon her; later she came to feel that the whole security of their home was founded upon a lie, for she was too weak to carry the burden of all their lives; secretly Bella longed to be dependent upon someone else. She chose the Professor of Philosophy.

Therefore, one night (soon after that disastrous thirteenth wedding anniversary) the Professor was astonished to have his flirtatious banter returned with a passion that, in a single moment, threw into question thirty-five years of self-doubt. The Professor was even more astonished when he later learned that Quentin was a most competent lover (unlike himself). But it was Quentin's very competence that worked against him; for in his love-making with Bella he neither asked for anything, nor ever needed help, so that the whole became a process of giving, for the benefit of Bella; on the other hand, with the Professor, it was Bella who gave the pleasure, Bella who sometimes made him come. You will observe, then, how unfair are the ways of the heart; for when Bella wanted to be dominated Quentin was passive, but when Quentin was active, under the sheets, between her thighs, was the very time that Bella required a sign of weakness. This is what Bella wanted: she wanted a man who

111

was strong in the eyes of the world, but whose very strength concealed secret fallibilities, which she alone knew, which she alone could overcome.

After a final chorus of 'My Heart Belongs to Daddy' Bella looks up into the face of the Professor and, seeing acquiescence there, begins to kiss his balls and lick his penis, until she can feel upward jerks and the thing beginning to grow beneath her mouth. The Professor gazes with gratitude at this girl who will do anything for him, but he is still wise enough to know that self-gratification is, by itself, a form of bondage.

'When I am driven to an act by external stimuli or by desire, such as I now have, I am not truly free,' he reasons, 'for neither Bella's action nor my desire is rational, and so long as it remains irrational I am a slave to my passions.'

By this time his penis is very big.

'We say that we love one another, yet if love ceases to be an agent of goodness it is surely a false love, and our love threatens the happiness of five other people; no, I am certainly not free,' concludes the Professor. Simultaneously his penis stabs the air and his glans opens releasing little spurts of semen.

'Was it good?' asks Bella.

'I think so,' answers the Professor.

Bella laughs and wipes her mouth with a Kleenex.

'Why am I doing this?' wonders the Professor. 'Why am I allowing it to happen to me?'

Once, when the Professor had actually voiced these doubts to Bella she had said, 'Fuck Spinoza. Listen to Kant.'

The Professor had listened.

'Freedom is the choice you make in deciding whether or not you submit to your passion or submit to your duty,' Bella had said, 'so make up your mind, mister, passion or duty?'

But even as the Professor surrendered to his instincts he tried to discern if his affair with Bella was the result of a unique coincidence of personalities or merely a coincidence of events. Destiny or opportunity? However, none of these worries prevented him from continuing. Despite his wisdom he had no answer to his student's tongue.

'Titillatio.'

'Fellatio.'

'Spinoza.'

'Spermatozoa.'

'Kant.'

'Cunt.' She got him every time. Thus unadulterated pleasure can make a hypocrite and an adulterer of the most ethical of men.

Quentin, as we have noted, considers that he is happy, blessed with a trouble-free life; which just goes to show that men who are accustomed to scrutinizing every detail to ensure that the bridges they build will not topple are not necessarily the best judges when it comes to an assessment of the grounds upon which they base their own existence. He assumes, in his complacency, that he has constructed a secure family unit for himself, supported by foundations that are sunk deep into the love that he and Bella share. And he could have been right, had he not forgotten the simple fact that marriage is a dynamic state, and that fundamentals which were true ten years ago need no longer be in operation a decade later. Both he and Bella have developed as personalities in the time they have lived together, but their relationship has not grown, indeed it has become repressed, smothered by Quentin's feather-brained pillow of easy acquiescence.

We've already made a flippant reference to the beginnings of Quentin's career as a builder of bridges so, in fairness, we should add a few more details. For the truth of the matter is that Quentin had wanted to be an engineer from the moment he received his first Meccano set: and all the troubled years between puberty and manhood were spanned by balsa-wood replicas of the world's greatest bridges. Indeed, so good were some of the models that Quentin still displays them in his private study. He is relaxing in a leather armchair in that very room when Bella returns (so he thinks) from her university meeting.

'Hello,' she says, 'are the children in bed?'

'Hours ago,' replies Quentin, without a trace of sarcasm; although Bella is back late it does not occur to him to be annoyed.

'Did you have a good meeting?' he asks.

'I enjoyed myself,' Bella replies, truthfully.

Although, as we've disclosed, the Professor (*pace* conscience) is content in the progress of his affair with Bella, it would be a mistake to assume that he will be satisfied to let things continue the way they are. He feels, in some odd way, that it would be somehow selfish of him, egocentric, as it were, and that he ought to give pleasure as well as receive it. He is a man after all, and he considers that fifty-five is too early an age to bid farewell to his potency for ever. However, as he does not understand the cause of his own impotence, indeed had been amazed to discover that he was impotent, he is quite powerless to reassert his previous prowess. Is it, he asks himself, some ill-defined punishment on his wife's behalf for all those times he had made loveless love to her, regular as clockwork, with his cock hooded like some thief in the night? Having decided that one unknowable daughter was sufficient. Is it something to do with Kant? If Bella's analysis was correct, and freedom is the choice between passion and duty, and if he had clearly decided to go along with passion, why then was his penis not acting in accordance with his will? Does it mean that he is not a free man after all, that he is, in effect, the captive of a duty he does not comprehend? Is Kant's unanswerable criterion that one should act 'as if the maxim of your actions were to become by your will law universal' putting a block on his animal instincts? The Professor of Philosophy, a rational man, is perplexed. It does not occur to him that there is something darker, less flattering, in his passion; and at the root of his impotence. So we leave him, still in two minds, once more dialling the number of his mistress.

'According to Kinsey,' says Bella to Quentin as the telephone starts to ring, 'some psychoanalysts contend that they have never had a patient who has not had incestuous relationships. Sort of kith and Kinsey. Don't worry, I'll get it.'

'What is the significance of that?' asks Quentin. But Bella is already whispering into the receiver.

'Bet you didn't know,' says Bella, returning to the conversation, 'that if unofficial American estimates are anything to go by seventy-eight per cent of all incestuous relationships are between father and daughter, while only one per cent occur between mother and son. So I'll be keeping an eye on you, Daddy.'

'Don't be daft,' says Quentin.

Over the telephone the Professor of Philosophy had invited Bella to the farewell party of one of his more eccentric graduate students: an American, shortly to be deported for possession of a small amount of cocaine. Bella, who rather liked the American, accepted at once, and now informs her husband that she will have to go out two nights hence.

The party begins quietly, and though that soon changes it does not have much effect upon the Professor and Bella who stand chatting over chalices of Spanish burgundy, that is, until the curly American asks Bella to dance. Actually, Bella's American host was rather glad to see her arrive, gladder still to see her without her husband. Innocent, he assumes that an estrangement has occurred, and that Bella has come round to him for comfort. Needless to say, he is quite ignorant of her affair with the Professor, as his actions will testify; however anarchic, all American graduates have a highly developed sense of academic hierarchy. The music's rocking, Rolling Stones stuff, but still he holds her tight. The Professor, who has never before had any reason to doubt Bella's devotion, is suddenly seized by jealousy, a juvenile luxury, and piqued accepts a stranger's offer of a sniff of cocaine.

'They say it's an aphrodisiac, Prof,' the tempter whispers, 'but I wouldn't know about that.'

However, all that happens to the Professor is that his nose goes numb. Just as well, as it turns out.

Fifteen minutes pass and Bella remains in the American's arms, revolving like a lamb on a spit. The Professor of Philosophy, despite himself, is increasingly tormented; not only by the actual image of Bella in revolution, but also by the fearful illusion that what is being re-enacted in front of him is nothing less than the deflowering of his own daughter, long imagined. Gradually Bella and his daughter become hopelessly confused in his fogged mind and his resentment toward the American grows from simple jealousy into an insane conviction that he is deliberately mocking his quality as a lover and, worse, as a father. In other words, he feels himself provoked, and already driven thus far it only takes a trick of the light (or is he really kissing Bella?) to make him leap upon the astounded American!

'What are you doing? Vot are you doing, you bloody Yank?' screams the Professor, aiming several blows at the American.

The American, not really grasping what is going on, lashes out in self-defence and connects with the Professor's curved beak. The Professor, still in an uncontrollable fury, grabs Bella, too shocked to move of her own accord, and drags her out of the flat.

Nor do they stop until they reach the Professor's private address. Once inside, with the light on, Bella screams. Not because she is scared, but because the Professor's face is covered with blood.

'What's the matter?' asks the Professor. Thanks to the cocaine, which is acting as a sort of anaesthetic, he does not know that the American's punch has broken his nose.

Bella cleans the Professor's face with a sponge and warm water. She asks for no explanation, for she has no doubts that the Professor will give one in his own time. Instead, she smooths down his hair. She kisses him on the forehead. Then, humming, she undresses. Face-up on the bed she suddenly realizes that the events of the evening have excited her. And the Professor, also carried along by the momentum of the night, finds an erect member in his pants, a single drop glittering at the tip; overwhelmed, seized with joy, he kneels and pushes his penis between Bella's warm and palpy walls.

With a yelp of amazed pleasure Bella clasps the Professor of Philosophy, and wildly out of control thrashes her hips crying, 'Fuck me, fuck me, daddy-o!'

His last restraint vanishing with that cry the Professor gives himself over utterly to his grotesque jerks, and with great shudders comes inside Bella at last. He rolls over gasping, his cock glistening, his eyes shining and his cheeks wet from crying.

When Bella returns home, long after everyone is in bed, she creeps straight into Quentin's darkened study and, carefully lighting a safety match, sets fire to all his bridges.

However, at his own house, the Professor of Philosophy is in an entirely different mood; part remorseful, over his behaviour at the party; part terrified by his spectacular return to potency. Bella had misinterpreted his tears as tears of joy, and he hadn't the heart to disabuse her; how could he tell her that he was weeping for shame? For he had suddenly seen, quite clearly, what had caused his impotence. But at least this awareness now gives him the opportunity to regain his freedom, to re-establish the primacy of rationality over desire, to obey his all-powerful sense of duty. So he sits at his desk and writes two letters. The first is a letter of apology to the American. The second is what is called an 'anonymous letter'. It is addressed to Quentin. It informs him that, for the past year, his wife has been unfaithful. Having completed the task the Professor stands up, a free man.

He feels good.

POPPY Z. BRITE

The Sixth Sentinel

I first knew Hard Luck Rosalie Smith when she was a thin frayed rope of a child, twenty years old and already well acquainted with the solitude at the bottom of a whiskey bottle. Her hair was brittle from too many dye jobs, bright red last week, black as the grave today, purple and green for Mardi Gras. Her face was fine-boned and faintly feral, the eyes carefully lined in black, the rouged lips stretched tight over the sharp little teeth. If I had been able to touch Rosalie, her skin would have felt silky and faintly dry, her hair would have been like electricity brushing my face in the dark.

But I could not touch Rosalie, not so that she would notice. I could pass my fingers through the meat of her arm, pale as veal and packed like flaky fish flesh between her thin bones. I could wrap my hand around the smooth porcelain ball of her wrist. But as far as she was concerned, my touch went through her like so much dead air. All she could feel of me was a chill like ice crystallizing along her spine.

'Your liver has the texture of hot, wet velvet,' I would tell her, reaching through her ribs to caress the tortured organ.

120

She'd shrug. 'Another year in this town and it'll be pickled.'

Rosalie came to the city of New Orleans because it was as far south as her money would take her – or so she said. She was escaping from a lover she would shudderingly refer to only as Joe Coffeespoon. The memory of his touch made her feel cold, far colder than my ectoplasmic fingers ever could, and she longed for the wet kiss of tropical nights.

She moved into an apartment in one of the oldest buildings in the French Quarter, above a 'shoppe' that sold potions and philters. At first I wondered whether she would be pleased to find a ghost already residing in her cramped quarters, but as I watched her decorate the walls with shrouds of black lace and photographs of androgynous sunken-cheeked musicians who looked more dead than alive, I began to realize I could show myself safely, without threat of eviction. It is always a nuisance when someone calls in the exorcist. The priest himself is no threat, but the demons that invariably follow him are large as cats and annoying as mosquitoes. It is these, not the intonations and holy water, that drive innocent spirits away.

But Rosalie only gave me a cool appraising look, introduced herself, then asked me for my name and my tale. The name she recognized, having seen it everywhere from the pages of history books to the shingles hanging outside dubious 'absinthe' houses in the French Quarter. The tale – well, there were enough tales to entertain her for a thousand nights or more. (I, the Scheherazade of Barataria Bay!) How long had I wanted to tell those tales? I had been without a friend or a lover for more years than I could recall. (The company of other local ghosts did not interest me – they seemed a morbid lot, many of them headless or drenched in gore, manifesting only occasionally to point skeletal fingers at loose fireplace flagstones and then vanish without a word. I had met no personalities of substance, and certainly none with a history as exotic as mine.)

So I was glad for the company of Rosalie. As more old buildings are demolished I must constantly shift about the city, trying to find places where I resided in life, places where a shred of my soul remains to anchor me. There are still overgrown bayou islands and remote Mississippi coves I visit often, but to give up the drunken carnival of New Orleans, to forsake human companionship (witting or otherwise) would be to fully accept my death. Nearly two hundred years, and I still cannot do that.

'Jean,' she would say to me as evening fell like a slowly drifting purple scarf over the French Quarter, as the golden flames of the streetlights flickered on, 'do you like these panties with the silver bustier, Jean?' (She pronounced my name correctly, in the French manner, like John but with the soft J.) Five nights of the week Rosalie had a job stripping at a nightclub on Bourbon Street. She selected her undress from a vast armoire crammed full of the microscopic wisps of clothing she referred to as 'costumes', some of which were only slightly more substantial than my own flesh. When she first told me of the job she thought I would be shocked, but I laughed. 'I saw worse things in my day,' I assured her, thinking of lovely, shameless octoroon girls I had known, of famous 'private shows' involving poisonous serpents sent from Haiti and the oiled stone phalluses of alleged voodoo idols.

I went to see Rosalie dance two or three times. The strip club was in an old row building, the former site of a bordello I remembered well. In my day the place had been decorated entirely in scarlet silk and purple velvet; the effect was of enormous fleshy lips closing in upon you as you entered, drawing you into their dark depths. I quit visiting Rosalie at work when she said it unnerved her to suddenly catch sight of me in the hundreds of mirrors that now lined the club, a hundred spangle-fleshed Rosalies and a hundred translucent Jeans and a thousand pathetic weasel-eyed men all reflected to a point of swarming infinity far within the walls. I could see how the mirrors might make Rosalie nervous, but I believe she did not like me looking at the other dancers either, though she was the prettiest of a big-hipped, insipid-faced lot.

By day Rosalie wore black: lace and fishnet, leather and silk, the gaudy mourning clothes of the deather-children. I had to ask her to explain them to me, these deathers. They were children seldom older than eighteen who painted their faces stark white, rimmed their eyes with kohl, smudged their mouths black or blood-red. They made love in cemeteries, then plundered the rotting tombs for crucifixes to wear as jewelry. The music they listened to was alternately lush as a wreath of funeral roses and dark as four a.m., composed in suicidal gloom by the androgynes that decorated Rosalie's walls. I might have been able to tell these

123

children a few things about death. Try drifting through a hundred years without a proper body, I might have said, without feet to touch the ground, without a tongue to taste wine or kiss. Then perhaps you will celebrate your life while you have it. But Rosalie would not listen to me when I got on this topic, and she never introduced me to any of her deather friends.

If she had any. I had seen other such children roaming the French Quarter after dark, but never in Rosalie's company. Often as not she would sit in her room and drink whiskey on her nights off, tipping inches of liquid amber fire over crackling ice cubes and polishing it off again, again, again. She never had a lover that I knew of, aside from the dreaded Coffeespoon, who it seemed had been quite wealthy by Rosalie's standards. Her customers at the club offered her ludicrous sums if she would only grant them one night of pleasure more exotic than their toadlike minds could imagine. A few might really have been able to pay such fortunes, but Rosalie ignored their tumescent pleading. She seemed not so much opposed to the idea of sex for money as simply uninterested in sex at all.

When she told me of the propositions she received, I thought of the many things I had buried in the earth during my days upon it. Treasure: hard money and jewels, the riches of the robbery that was my bread and butter, the spoils of the murder that was my wine. There were still caches that no one had found and no one ever would. Any one of them would have been worth ten times the amounts these men offered.

Many times I tried to tell Rosalie where these caches were, but unlike some of her kind, she thought buried things should stay buried. She claimed that the thought of the treasure hidden under mud, stone, or brick, with people walking near it and sometimes right over it each day, amused her more than the thought of digging it up and spending it.

I never believed her. She would not let me see her eyes when she said these things. Her voice trembled when she spoke of the deathers who pursued grave-robbing as a sport. ('They pried up a granite slab that weighed fifty pounds,' she told me once, incredulously. 'How could they bear to lift it off, in the dark, not knowing what might come out at them?') There was a skeleton in a glass-topped coffin downstairs, in the voodoo shoppe, and Rosalie hardly liked to enter the shoppe because of it – I had seen her glancing out of the corner of her eye, as if the sad little bones simultaneously intrigued and appalled her.

It was some obsessive fear of hers, I realized. Rosalie shied away from all talk of dead things, of things buried, of digging in the ground. When I told her my tales she made me skip over the parts where treasures or bodies were buried; she would not let me describe the fetor of the nighttime swamp, the faint flickering lights of Saint Elmo's fire, the deep sucking sound the mud made when a shovel was thrust into it. She would allow me no descriptions of burials at sea or shallow bayou graves. She covered her ears when I told her of a rascal whose corpse I hung from the knotted black bough of a hundred-year-old oak. It was a remarkable thing, too – when I rode past the remote spot a

125

year later, his perfect skeleton still hung there, woven together by strands of gray Spanish moss. It wound around his long bones and cascaded from the empty sockets of his eyes, it forced his jaws open and dangled from his chin like a long gray beard – but Rosalie did not want to hear about it.

When I confronted her with her own dread, she refused to own up to it. 'Whoever said graveyards were romantic?' she demanded. 'Whoever said I had to go digging up bones just because I lust after Venal St Claire?' (Venal St Claire was a musician, one of the stick-thin, mourning-shrouded beauties that adorned the walls of Rosalie's room. I saw no evidence that she lusted after him or anyone else.) 'I just wear black so that all my clothes will match,' she told me solemnly, as if she expected me to believe it. 'So I won't have to think about what to put on when I get up in the morning.'

'But you *don't* get up in the morning.'

'In the evening, then. *You* know what I mean.' She tipped her head back and tongued the last drop of whiskey out of her glass. It was the most erotic thing I had ever seen her do. I ran my finger in among the smooth folds of her intestines. A momentary look of discomfort crossed her face, as if she had suffered a gas pain – attributable to the rotgut whiskey, no doubt. But she would not pursue the subject further.

So I watched her drink until she passed out, her brittle hair fanned across her pillow, the corner of her mouth drooling a tiny thread of spit onto her black silk coverlet.

Then I went into her head. This was not a thing I liked to do often – on occasion I had noticed her looking askance at me the morning after, as if she remembered seeing me in her dreams and wondered how I had got there. If I could persuade Rosalie to dig up one cache of loot – just one – our troubles would end. She would never have to work again, and I could have her with me all the time. But first I had to find her fear. Until I knew what it was, and could figure out how to charm my way around it, my treasures were going to stay buried in black bayou mud.

So within moments I was sunk deep in the spongy tissue of Rosalie's brain, sifting through her childhood memories as if they were gold coins I had just lifted off a Spanish galleon. I thought I could smell the whiskey that clouded her dreams, a stinging mist.

I found it more quickly than I expected to. I had reminded Rosalie of her fear, and now – because she would not let her conscious mind remember – her unconscious mind was dreaming of it. For an instant I teetered on the edge of wakefulness; I was dimly aware of the room around me, the heavy furniture and flocked black walls. Then it all swam away as I fell headlong into Rosalie's childhood dream.

A South Louisiana village, built at the confluence of a hundred streams and riverlets. Streets of dirt and crushed oyster-shells, houses built on pilings to keep the water from lapping up onto the neat, brightly painted porches. Shrimp nets draped over railings, stiffening with salt, at some houses; crab traps stacked up to the roof at others. Cajun country.

(Hard Luck Rosalie a Cajun girl, she who claimed she had never set foot in Louisiana before! *Mon petit chou!* 'Smith' indeed!)

On one porch a young girl dressed in a T-shirt and a home-sewn skirt of fresh calico perches on a case of empty beer bottles. The tender points of her breasts can be seen through the thin fabric of the T-shirt. A medallion gleams at the hollow of her throat, a tiny saint frozen in silver. She is perhaps twelve. It can only be her mama beside her, a large regal-faced woman with a crown of teased and fluffed black hair. The mama is peeling crawfish. She saves the heads in a coffee can and throws the other pickings to some speckled chickens scratching in the part of the dirt yard that is not flooded. The water is as high as Mama has ever seen it.

The young girl has a can of Coca-Cola, but she hasn't drunk much of it. She is worried about something: it can be seen in the slump of her shoulders, in the sprawl of her thin legs beneath the calico skirt. Several times her eyes shimmer with tears she is just able to control. When she looks up, it becomes clear that she is older than she appeared at first, thirteen or fourteen. An air of *naïveté*, an awkwardness of limb and gesture, makes her seem younger. She fidgets and at last says, 'Mama?'

'What is it, Rosie?' The mother's voice seems a beat too slow; it catches in her throat and drags itself reluctantly out past her lips.

'Mama – is Theophile still under the ground?'

(There is a gap in the dream here, or rather in my

awareness of it. I do not know who Theophile is – a childhood friend perhaps. More likely a brother; in a Cajun family there is no such thing as an only child. The question disturbs me, and I feel Rosalie slipping from me momentarily. Then the dream continues, inexorable, and I am pulled back in.)

Mama struggles to remain calm. Her shoulders bow and her heavy breasts sag against her belly. The stoic expression on her face crumbles a little. 'No, Rosie,' she says at last. 'Theophile's grave is empty. He's gone up to Heaven, him.'

'Then he wouldn't be there if I looked?'

(All at once I am able to recognize my Rosalie in the face of this blossoming girl. The intelligent dark eyes, the quick mind behind them undulled by whiskey and time.)

Mama is silent, searching for an answer that will both satisfy and comfort. But a bayou storm has been blowing up, and it arrives suddenly, as they will: thunder rolls across the sky, the air is suddenly alive with invisible sparks. Then the rain comes down in a solid torrent. The speckled chickens scramble under the porch, complaining. Within seconds the yard in front of the house is a sea of mud. It has rained like this every day for a month. It is the wettest spring anyone has ever seen in this part of the bayou.

'You ain't goin' anywhere in this flood,' Mama says. The relief is evident in her voice. She shoos the girl inside and hurries around the house to take washing off the line, though the faded cotton dresses and patched denim trousers are already soaked through.

Inside the warm little house, Rosalie sits at the kitchen window watching rain hammer down on the bayou, and she wonders.

The storm lasts all night. Lying in her bed, Rosalie hears the rain on the roof; she hears branches creaking and lashing in the wind. But she is used to thunderstorms, and she pays no attention to this one. She is thinking of a shed in the side yard, where her father's old crab traps and tools are kept. She knows there is a shovel in there. She knows where the key is.

The storm ends an hour before dawn, and she is ready.

It is her own death she is worried about, of course, not that of Theophile (whoever he may be). She is at the age where her curiosity about the weakness of the flesh outweighs her fear of it. She thinks of him under the ground and she has to know whether he is really there. Has he ascended to Heaven or is he still in his grave, rotting? Whatever she finds, it cannot be worse than the thing she has imagined.

(So I think at the time.)

Rosalie is not feeling entirely sane as she eases out of the silent house, filches her father's shovel, and creeps through the dark village to the graveyard. She likes to go barefoot, and the soles of her feet are hard enough to walk over the broken edges of the glittering wet oystershells, but she knows you have to wear shoes after a heavy rain or worms might eat their way into your feet. So she slogs through the mud in her soaked sneakers, refusing to think about what she is going to do.

It is still too dark to see, but Rosalie knows her way by heart through these village streets. Soon her hand finds the rusty iron gate of the graveyard, and it ratchets open at her touch. She winces at the harsh sound in the predawn silence, but there is no one around to hear.

At least, no one who *can* hear.

The crude silhouettes of headstones stab into the inky sky. Few families in the village can afford a carved marker; they lash two sticks together in the shape of a rough cross, or they hew their own stone out of granite if they can get a piece. Rosalie feels her way through a forest of jagged, irregular memorials to the dead. She knows some of them are only hand-lettered oak boards wedged into the ground. The shadows at the base of each marker are wet, shimmering. Foul mud sucks at her feet. She tells herself the smell is only stagnant water. In places the ground feels slick and lumpy; she cannot see what she is stepping on.

But when she comes near the stone she seeks, she can see it. For it is the finest stone in the graveyard, carved of moon-pale marble that seems to pull all light into its milky depths. His family had it made in New Orleans, spending what was probably their life's savings. The chiseled letters are as concise as razor cuts. Rosalie cannot see them, but she knows their every crevice and shadow. Only his name, stark and cold; no dates, no inscriptions, as if the family's grief was so great that they could not bear to say anything about him. Just inscribe it with his name and leave him there.

The plot of earth at the base of the stone is not visible, but she knows it all too well, a barren, muddy rectangle.

There has been no time for grass or weeds to grow upon it; he has only been buried a fortnight, and the few sprouts that tried to come up have been beaten back down by the rain. But can he really be under there, shut up in a box, his lithe body bloating and bursting, his wonderful face and hands beginning to decay?

Rosalie steps forward, hand extended to touch the letters of his name THEOPHILE THIBODEAUX. As she thinks – or dreams – the name, her fingers poised to trace its marble contours, an image fills her head, a jumble of sensations intense and erotic. A boy older than Rosalie, perhaps seventeen: a sharp pale face, too thin to be called handsome, but surely compelling; a curtain of long sleek black hair half-hiding eyes of fierce, burning azure. Theophile!

(All at once it is as if Rosalie's consciousness has merged completely with mine. My heart twists with a young girl's love and lust for this spitfire Cajun boy. I am dimly aware of Rosalie's drunken twenty-year-old body asleep on her bed, her feminine viscera twitching at the memory of him. O, how he touched her – O, how he tasted her!

She had known it was wrong in the eyes of God. Her mama had raised her to be a good girl. But the evenings she had spent with Theophile after dances and church socials, sitting on an empty dock with his arm around her shoulders, leaning into the warm hollow of his chest – that could not be wrong. After a week of knowing her he had begun to show her the things he wrote on his ink-blackened relic of an Olympia typewriter, poems and stories, songs of the swamp. And that could not be wrong.

132

And the night they had sneaked out of their houses to meet, the night in the empty boathouse near Theophile's home – that could not be wrong either. They had begun only kissing, but the kisses grew too hot, too wild – Rosalie felt her insides boiling. Theophile answered her heat with his own. She felt him lifting the hem of her skirt and – carefully, almost reverently – sliding off her cotton panties. Then he was stroking the dark down between her legs, teasing her with the very tips of his fingers, rubbing faster and deeper until she felt like a blossom about to burst with sweet nectar. Then he parted her legs wider and bent to kiss her there as tenderly as he had kissed her mouth. His tongue was soft yet rough, like a soapy washcloth, and Rosalie had thought her young body would die with the pleasure of it. Then, slowly, Theophile was easing himself into her, and yes, she wanted him there, and yes, she was clutching at his back, pulling him farther in, refusing to heed the sharp pain of first entry. He rested inside her, barely moving; he lowered his head to kiss her sore developing nipples, and Rosalie felt the power of all womanhood shudder through her. This could not be wrong.)

With the memories fixed firmly in her mind she takes another step toward his headstone. The ground crumbles away beneath her feet, and she falls headlong into her lover's grave.

The shovel whacks her across the spine. The rotten smell billows around her, heavy and ripe: spoiling meat, rancid fat, a sweetish-sickly odor. The fall stuns her. She struggles in the gritty muck, spits it out of her mouth.

Then the first pale light of dawn breaks across the sky, and Rosalie stares into the ruined face of Theophile.

(Now her memories flooded over me like the tide. Some time after they had started meeting in the boathouse she began to feel sick all the time; the heat made her listless. Her monthly blood, which had been coming for only a year, stopped. Mama took her into the next town to see a doctor, and he confirmed what Rosalie had already dreaded: she was going to have Theophile's baby.

Her papa was not a hard man, nor cruel. But he had been raised in the bosom of the Church, and he had learned to measure his own worth by the honor of his family. Theophile never knew his Rosalie was pregnant. Rosalie's father waited for him in the boathouse one night. He stepped in holding a new sheaf of poems, and Papa's deer shot caught him across the chest and belly, a hundred tiny black eyes weeping red tears.

Papa was locked up in the county jail now and Mama said that soon he would go someplace even worse, someplace where they could never see him again. Mama said it wasn't Rosalie's fault, but Rosalie could see in her eyes that it was.)

It has been the wettest spring anyone can remember, a month of steady rains. The water table in Louisiana bayou country is already so high that a hole will begin to draw water at a depth of two feet or less. All this spring the table has risen steadily, soaking the ground, drowning grass and flowers, making a morass of the sweet swamp earth. Cattails have sprung up near the edge of the graveyard. But the storm last night pushed the groundwater to saturation point and beyond. The wealthy folk of New Orleans bury their dead in vaults above ground to protect them from this very danger. But no one here can afford a marble vault, or even a brick one.

And the village graveyard has flooded at last.

Some of the things that have floated to the surface are little more than bone. Others are swollen to three or four times their size, gassy mounds of decomposed flesh rising like islands from the mud; some of these have silk flower petals stuck to them like obscene decorations. Flies rise lazily, then descend again in glittering, circling clouds. Here are mired the warped boards of coffins split open by the water's relentless pull. There floats the plaster figurine of a saint, his face and the color of his robes washed away by rain. Yawning eyeless faces thrust out of stagnant pools, seeming to gasp for breath. Rotting hands unfold like blighted tiger lilies. Every drop of water, every inch of earth in the graveyard is foul with the effluvium of the dead.

But Rosalie can only see the face thrust into hers, the body crushed beneath her own. Theophile's eyes have fallen back into their sockets and his mouth is open; his tongue is gone. She sees thin white worms teeming in the passage of his throat. His nostrils are widening black holes beginning to encroach upon the greenish flesh of his cheeks. His sleek hair is almost gone; the few strands left are thin and scummy, nibbled by waterbugs. (Sitting on the dock, Rosalie and Theophile used to spit into the water and watch the shiny black beetles swarm around the white gobs; Theophile had told her they would eat hair and toenails too.) In places she can see the glistening dome of his skull. *The skull behind the dear face, the skull that cradled the thoughts and dreams . . .*

She thinks of the shovel she brought and wonders what she meant to do with it. Did she *want* to see Theophile like this? Or had she really expected to find his grave empty, his fine young body gone fresh and whole to God?

No. She had only wanted to know where he was. Because she had nothing left of him – his family would give her no poems, no lock of hair. And now she had even lost his seed.

(The dogs ran Papa to earth in the swamp where he had hidden and the men dragged him off to jail. As they led him toward the police car, Theophile's mother ran up to him and spat in his face. Papa was handcuffed and could not wipe himself; he only stood there with the sour spit of sorrow running down his cheeks, and his eyes looked confused, as if he was unsure just what he had done.

Mama made Rosalie sleep in bed with her that night. But when Rosalie woke up the next morning Mama was gone; there was only a note saying she would be back before sundown. Sure enough, she straggled in with the afternoon's last light. She had spent the whole day in the swamp. Her face was scratched and sweaty, the cuffs of her jeans caked with mud.

Mama had brought a basketful of herbs. She didn't fix dinner, but instead spent the evening boiling the plants down to a thin syrup. They exuded a bitter, stinging scent as they cooked. The potion sat cooling until the next night. Then Mama made Rosalie drink it all down.

136

It was the worst pain she had ever felt. She thought her intestines and her womb and the bones of her pelvis were being wrung in a giant merciless fist. When the bleeding started she thought her very insides were dissolving. There were thick clots and ragged shreds of tissue in the blood.

'It won't damage you,' Mama told her, 'and it will be over by morning.'

True to Mama's word, just before dawn Rosalie felt something solid being squeezed out of her. She knew she was losing the last of Theophile. She tried to clamp the walls of her vagina around it, to keep him inside her as long as she could. But the thing was slick and formless, and it slid easily onto the towel Mama had spread between her legs. Mama gathered the towel up quickly and would not let Rosalie see what was inside.

Rosalie heard the toilet flush once, then twice. Her womb and the muscles of her abdomen felt as if they had gone through Mama's kitchen grater. But the pain was nothing compared to the emptiness she felt in her heart.)

The sky is growing lighter, showing her more of the graveyard around her: the corpses borne on the rising water, the maggot-ridden mud. Theophile's face yawns into hers. Rosalie struggles against him and feels his sodden flesh give beneath her weight. She is beyond recognizing her love now. She is frantic; she fights him. Her hand strikes his belly and punches in up to the wrist.

Then suddenly Theophile's body opens like a flower made of carrion, and she sinks into him. Her elbows are trapped in the brittle cage of his ribs. Her face is pressed into the bitter soup of his organs. Rosalie whips her head to one side. Her face is a mark of putrescence. It is in her hair, her nostrils; it films her eyes. She is drowning in the body that once gave her sustenance. She opens her mouth to scream and feels things squirming in between her teeth.

'My *chérie* Rosalie,' she hears the voice of her lover whispering.

And then the rain pours down again.

Unpleasant.

I tore myself screaming from Rosalie – screaming silently, unwilling to wake her. In that instant I was afraid of her for what she had gone through; I dreaded to see her eyes snap open like a doll's, meeting me full in the face.

But Rosalie was only sleeping a troubled slumber. She muttered fitful disjointed words; there was a cold sheen of sweat on her brow; she exuded a flowery, powerful smell of sex. I hovered at the edge of the bed and studied her ringed hands clenched into small fists, her darting, jumping eyelids still stained with yesterday's makeup. I could only imagine the ensuing years and torments that had brought that little girl to this night, to this room. That had made her want to wear the false trappings of death, after having wallowed in the truth of it.

But I *knew* how difficult it would be to talk these memories out of her. There could be no consolation and no compensation for a past so cruel. No treasure, no matter how valuable, could matter in the face of such lurid terror.

So I assure you that the thing I did next was done out of

pure mercy – *not* a desire for personal gain, or control over Rosalie. I had never done such a thing to her before. She was my friend; I wished to deliver her from the poison of her memories. It was as simple as that.

I gathered up my courage and I went back into Rosalie's head. Back in through her eyes and the whorled tunnels of her ears, back into the spongy electric forest of her brain.

I cannot be more scientific than this: I found the connections that made the memory. I searched out the nerves and subtle acids that composed the dream, the morsels of Rosalie's brain that still held a residue of Theophile, the cells that were blighted by his death.

And I erased it all.

I pitied Theophile. Truly I did. There is no existence more lonely than death, especially a death where no one is left to mourn you.

But Rosalie belonged to me now.

I had her rent a boat.

It was easy for her to learn how to drive it: boating is in the Cajun blood. We made an exploratory jaunt or two down through Barataria – where two tiny hamlets, much like Rosalie's home village, both bore my name – and I regaled a fascinated Rosalie with tales of burials at sea, of shallow bayou graves, of a rascal whose empty eye sockets dripped with Spanish moss.

When I judged her ready, I guided her to a spot I remembered well, a clearing where five enormous oaks grew from one immense, twisted trunk. The five sentinels, we called them in my day. The wind soughed in the upper branches. The swamp around us was hushed expectant.

After an hour of digging, Rosalie's shiny new shovel unearthed the lid and upper portion of a great iron chest. Her brittle hair was stringy with sweat. Her black lace dress was caked with mud and clay. Her face had gone paler than usual with exertion; in the half-light of the swamp it was almost luminescent. She had never looked so beautiful to me as she did at that moment.

She stared at me. Her tired eyes glittered as if with fever.

'Open it,' I urged.

Rosalie swung the shovel at the heart-shaped hasp of the chest and knocked it loose on the first try. Once more and it fell away in a shower of soggy rust. She glanced back at me once more – looking for what, I wonder; seeing what? – and then heaved open the heavy lid.

And the sixth sentinel sat up to greet her.

I always took an extra man along when I went into the swamp to bury treasure. One I didn't trust, or didn't need. He and my reliable henchmen would dig the hole and drag the chest to the edge of it, ready to heave in. Then I would gaze deep into the eyes of each man and ask, in a voice both quiet and compelling, 'Who wishes to guard my treasure?' My men knew the routine, and were silent. The extra man – currying favor as the useless and unreliable will do – always volunteered.

Then my top lieutenant would take three steps forward and put a ball in the lowly one's brain. His corpse was laid tenderly in the chest, his blood seeping into the mounds of gold or silver or glittering jewels, and I would tuck in one of my mojo bags, the ones I had specially made in New Orleans. Then the chest was sunk in the mire of the swamp, and my man, now rendered trustworthy, was left to guard my treasure until I should need it.

I was the only one who could open those chests. The combined magic of the mojo bag and the anger of the betrayed man's spirit saw to that.

My sixth sentinel wrapped skeletal arms around Rosalie's neck and drew her down. His jaws yawned wide and I saw teeth, still hungry after two hundred years, clamp down on her throat. A mist of blood hung in the air; from the chest there was a ripping sound, then a noise of quick, choking agony. I hoped he would not make it too painful for her. After all, she was the woman I had chosen to spend eternity with.

I had told Rosalie that she would never again have to wriggle out of flimsy costumes under the eyes of slobbering men, and I had not lied. I had told her that she would never have to worry about money any more, and I had not lied. What I had neglected to tell her was that I did not wish to share my treasures – I only wanted her dead, my Hard Luck Rosalie, free from this world that pained her so, free to wander with me through the unspoiled swamps and bayous, through the ancient buildings of a city mired in time.

Soon Rosalie's spirit left her body and flew to me. It had nowhere else to go. I felt her struggling furiously against my love, but she would give in soon. I had no shortage of time to convince her.

I slipped my arm around Rosalie's neck and planted a kiss on her ectoplasmic lips. Then I clasped her wisp of a hand in mine, and we disappeared together.

CHARLES BUKOWSKI

The Copulating Mermaid of
Venice, California

The bar had closed and they still had to make the walk to
the rooming house, and there it was – the hearse had driven
up across the street where the Stomach Hospital was.

'I think this is THE night,' said Tony. 'I can feel it in my
blood, I really can!'

'The night for what?' asked Bill.

'Look,' said Tony, 'we know their operation well by now.
Let's get one! What the fuck? You got the guts?'

'Whatsa matta? You think I'm a coward because that runty
sailor whipped my ass?'

'I didn't say that, Bill.'

'*You're* the coward! I can whip you, easy . . .'

'Yeah. I know. I'm not talking about *that*. I say, let's grab
a stiff just for laughs.'

'Shit! Let's grab TEN stiffs!'

'Wait. You're drunk now. Let's wait. We know the operation. We know how they operate. We been watching every
night.'

'And you're *not* drunk, eh? You wouldn't have the GUTS otherwise!'

'Quiet now! Watch! Here they come. They've got a stiff. Some poor guy. Look at that sheet pulled over his head. It's sad.'

'I *am* looking. And it *is* sad . . .'

'OK, we know the operation: if it's just one stiff, they toss him in, light their cigarettes and drive off. But if it's two stiffs, they don't bother locking the hearse door twice. They're real cool boys. It's just old stuff with them. If it's two stiffs, they just leave the guy on the roller there behind the hearse, go in and get the other stiff, then toss them in together. How many nights have we watched it?'

'I dunno,' said Bill, 'sixty, at least.'

'Okay, now there's the one stiff. If they go back in for another – that stiff belongs to us. *You game for grabs if they go in for another stiff?*'

'I'm game! I got double your guts!'

'Okay, then, watch. We'll know in a minute . . . Oops, there they go! *They're going in for another stiff!*' said Tony. 'You game?'

'Game,' said Bill.

They sprinted across the street and grabbed the corpse by the head and feet. Tony had the head, that sad head wrapped so tight in the sheet, while Bill grabbed the feet.

Then they ran across the street, the pure white sheet of the corpse floating in the momentum – sometimes you could see an ankle, an elbow, a thigh of flesh, and then they ran it up the rooming house front steps, got to the door

nd Bill said, 'Jesus Christ, who's got the key? Look, I'm
cared!'

'We don't have much time! Those bastards are gonna be
ut soon with the other stiff! Throw him in the hammock!
Quick! We gotta find a goddamned key!'

They tossed the stiff into the hammock. It rocked back
nd forth in the hammock under the moonlight.

'Can't we take the body *back*?' asked Bill. 'Good God oh
Mother o Mighty, can't we take the body back?'

'No time! Too late! They'd see us. HEY! WAIT!' yelled
Tony. 'I found the key!'

'THANK JESUS!'

They unlocked the door, then grabbed the thing on the
hammock and ran up the stairway with it. Tony's room was
closest. Second floor. There was quite a bit of bumping with
he corpse along the stairway wall and railing.

Then they had it outside Tony's door and stretched it out
while Tony looked for his door key. They got the door open,
plopped the stiff on the bed and then went to the refrigerator
nd got hold of Tony's cheap gallon of muscatel, had half a
waterglass full each, then refilled, came back to the bed-
oom, sat down and looked at the stiff.

'Do you suppose anybody saw us?' asked Bill.

'If they had, I think the cops would be up here by now.'

'Do you think they'll search the neighborhood?'

'How can they? How can they go knocking on doors at
his time of the morning, asking, "Do you have a dead
ody?"'

'Shit, I guess you're right.'

'Sure, I'm right,' said Tony, 'still, I can't help wondering how those two guys felt when they came back and saw the body gone? It must have been kind of funny.'

'Yeah,' said Bill, 'it musta been.'

'Well, funny or not, we've got the stiff. There he *is*, right on the bed.'

They looked at the thing under the sheet, had another drink.

'I wonder how long he's been dead?'

'Not very long, I don't think.'

'I wonder when they begin to stiffen up? I wonder when they begin to stink?'

'That rigor mortis takes a bit of time, I think,' said Tony. 'But he'll probably begin to stink pretty soon. It's just like garbage left in the sink. I don't think they drain the blood until they reach the mortuary.'

So, two drunks, they went on drinking the muscatel; they even forgot at times about the body, and they spoke of those vague and important other things in their rather inarticulate way. Then it was back to the body again.

The body was still there.

'What we gonna do with it?' asked Bill.

'Stand it up in the closet after it stiffens up. It seemed pretty loose when we were carrying it. Probably died about a half an hour ago or so.'

'So, okay, we stand it up in the closet. Then what do we do when it starts to stink?'

'I never thought about that part,' said Tony.

146

'Think about it,' said Bill, pouring a good one.

Tony tried to think about it. 'You know, we might go to jail for this. *If* we get caught.'

'Sure. So?'

'Well, I think we made a mistake, but it's too late.'

'Too late,' repeated Bill.

'So,' said Tony, pouring a tall one, 'if we are stuck with this stiff we might as well have a look at him.'

'Look at him?'

'Yeah, look at him.'

'You got the guts?' asked Bill.

'I dunno.'

'You scared?'

'Sure. No training in this sort of thing,' said Tony.

'All right. *You* pull the sheet back,' said Bill, 'only fill my glass first. Fill my glass, then pull the sheet back.'

'Okay,' said Tony.

He filled Bill's glass. Then walked over.

'All right,' said Tony, 'here GOES!'

Tony pulled the sheet straight back over the body. He kept his eyes closed.

'Good GOD!' said Bill, 'it's a woman! A *young* woman!'

Tony opened his eyes. 'Yeah. *Was* young. Christ, look at that long blonde hair, goes way down past her asshole. But she's DEAD! Terribly and finally dead, for ever. What a shame! I don't understand it.'

'How old you figure she was?'

'She doesn't *look* dead to me,' said Bill.

147

'She is.'

'But look at those *breasts*! Those *thighs*! That *pussy*! That pussy: it still looks alive!'

'Yeah,' said Tony, 'the pussy, they say: it's the first thing to come and the last thing to go.'

Tony walked over to the pussy, touched it. Then he lifted a breast, kissed the damned dead thing. 'It's so sad, everything is so sad – that we live all our lives like idiots and then finally die.'

'You shouldn't touch the body,' said Bill.

'She's beautiful,' said Tony, 'even dead, she's beautiful.'

'Yeah, but if she were alive she wouldn't even look at a bum like you twice. You know that, don't you?'

'Sure! And that's just the point! Now she can't say, "NO!"'

'What the hell are you talking about?'

'I mean,' said Tony, 'that my cock is hard. VERY HARD!'

Tony walked over and poured a glassful from the jug. Drank it down.

Then he walked over to the bed, began kissing the breasts, running his hands through her long hair, and then finally *kissing* that dead mouth in a kiss from the living to the dead. And then he mounted.

It was GOOD. Tony rammed and jammed. Never such a fuck as this in all his days! He came. Then rolled off, toweled himself with the sheet.

Bill had watched the whole thing, lifting the gallon muscatel jug in the dim lamplight.

'Christ, Bill, it was beautiful, beautiful!'

'You're crazy! You just fucked a dead woman!'

'And *you've* been fucking dead women all your life – dead women with dead souls and dead pussies – only you didn't know it! I'm sorry, Bill, she was a beautiful fuck. I have no shame.'

'Was she *that* good?' asked Bill.

'You'll never believe it.'

Tony walked to the bathroom to take a piss.

When he got back, Bill had mounted the body. Bill was going good. Moaning and groaning a bit. Then he reached over, kissed that dead mouth, and came.

Bill rolled off, hit the edge of the sheet, wiped off.

'You're right. Best fuck I *ever* had!'

Then they both sat in their chairs and looked at her.

'Wonder what her name was?' asked Tony. 'I'm in love.'

Bill laughed. 'Now I *know* you're drunk! Only a damn fool falls in love with a living woman; now you gotta get hooked on a dead one.'

'Okay, I'm hooked,' said Tony.

'All right, you're hooked,' said Bill, 'whatta we do now?'

'Get her the hell outa here!' answered Tony.

'How?'

'Same way we got her in – down the stairway.'

'Then?'

'Then into your car. We drive her down to Venice Beach, throw her into the ocean.'

'That's cold.'

'She won't feel it any more than she felt your cock.'

'And how about your cock?' asked Bill.

'She didn't feel that either,' answered Tony.

There she was, double-fucked, dead-laid on the sheets.

'Let's make it, baby!' screamed Tony.

Tony grabbed the feet and waited. Bill grabbed the head. As they rushed out of Tony's room the doorway was still open. Tony kicked it shut with his left foot as they moved toward the top of the stairway, the sheet no longer wound about the body but, more or less, flopped over it. Like a wet dishrag over a kitchen faucet. And again, there was much bumping of her head and her thighs and her big ass against the stairway walls and stairway railings.

They threw her into the back seat of Bill's car.

'Wait, wait, baby!' screamed Tony.

'What for?'

'The muscatel jug, asshole!'

'Oh, sure.'

Bill sat waiting with the dead cunt in the back seat.

Tony was a man of his word. He came running out with the jug of muski.

They got on the freeway, passing the jug back and forth, drinking good mouthfuls. It was a warm and beautiful night and the moon was full, of course. But it wasn't exactly night. By then it was 4:15 a.m. A good time anyhow.

They parked. Then had another drink of the good muscatel, got the body out and carried it that long sandy, sandy walk toward the sea. Then they got down to that part of the sand where the sea reached now and then, that part of the sand that was wet, soaked, full of little sand crabs and air holes. They put the body down and drank from the jug.

Now and then an excessive wave rolled a bit over all of them: Bill, Tony, the dead cunt.

Bill had to get up to piss and having been taught nineteenth-century morals he walked a bit up the shore to piss. As his friend did so, Tony pulled back the sheet and looked at the dead face in the seaweed twist and swirl, in the salty morning air. Tony looked at the face as Bill was pissing offshore. A lovely kind face, nose a little too sharp, but a very good mouth, and then with her body stiffening already, he leaned forward and kissed her very gently upon the mouth and said, 'I love you, dead bitch.'

Then he covered her with the sheet.

Bill finished pissing, came back. 'I need another drink.'

'Go ahead. I'll take one too.'

Tony said, 'I'm going to swim her out.'

'Can you swim good?'

'Not too well.'

'I'm a good swimmer. I'll swim her out.'

'NO! NO!' screamed Tony.

'Goddamn it, stop yelling!'

'I'm going to swim her out!'

'All right! All right!'

Tony took another drink, pulled the sheet aside, picked her up and carried her step by step toward the breakers. He was drunker than he figured. Several times the big waves knocked them both down, knocked her out of his arms, and he had to get to his feet, run, swim, struggle to find the body. Then he'd see her – that long, long hair. She was just

151

like a *mermaid*. Maybe she *was* a mermaid. Finally Tony floated her out beyond the breakers. It was quiet. Halfway between moon and sunrise. He floated with her some moments. It was very quiet. A time within time and a time beyond time.

Finally, he gave the body a little shove. She floated off, half underwater, the strands of long hair whirling about the body. She was still beautiful, dead or whatever she was.

She began to float away from him, caught in some tide. The sea had her.

Then suddenly he turned from her, tried to swim back toward the shore. It seemed very far away. He made it in with the last stroke of his strength, rolling in with the force of the last breaker. He picked himself up, fell, got up, walked forward, sat down beside Bill.

'So, she's gone,' said Bill.

'Yeah. Shark meat.'

'Do you think we'll ever be caught?'

'No. Give me a drink.'

'Go easy. We're getting close to the bottom.'

'Yeah.'

They got back to the car. Bill drove. They argued over the final drinks on the way home, then Tony thought about the mermaid. He put his head down and began to cry.

'You were always chickenshit,' said Bill, 'always chickenshit.'

They made it back to the rooming house.

Bill went to his room, Tony to his. The sun was coming up. The world was awakening. Some were awakening with hangovers. Somm were awakening with thoughts of church. Most were still asleep. A Sunday morning. And the mermaid, the mermaid with that dead sweet tail, she was well out to sea. While somewhere a pelican dove, came up with a glittering, guitar-shaped fish.

LISA TUTTLE

Manskin, Womanskin

He said, 'I think we'd be more comfortable in the bedroom, don't you?' and I said, 'Where's the loo?'

It was our first time alone together in his house and we both knew what we were there for. We'd met at a friend's party and had gone out together seven times in three weeks. Although we were still on our best behaviour, and I was aware that I still knew very little about him, the urge to get closer was strong, very strong. A lot is made of the loss of virginity as a great moment of decision, as a trauma, even, but the loss of mine had been easy and inevitable, and my first boyfriend and I had been together for nearly eight years. Making up my mind to go to bed with my second boyfriend had been much more difficult, and now I felt that I had taken too long and been over-cautious. I'd been so determined not to make a mistake, to be certain that this relationship would last – and in the end we'd broken up after less than two years. This time, although I still wanted it to be the last first time, this man my final one-and-only, I'd decided to take a chance and be a little braver about the unknown.

After three weeks of increasing warmth and interest the time was right. I was nervous, but willing. I'd meant to conquer my nervousness by staying close to him, so close that clothed kisses on the sofa would progress without any major break to the naked intimacies in his bed. But when you've gotta go, you've gotta go. So off I went and didn't realize until the door was closed with me inside the little room that the light-switch was on the wall outside. But I didn't need light for what I had to do, and if I had, the moonlight sifting dreamily through frosted glass would have been enough.

I wondered, as I sat on the pot, if Fred was as nervous as I was. It seemed unlikely. He was thirty-nine, ten years older than me, and he'd never been married. Although he hadn't itemized his girlfriends for me, I gathered there had been quite a few. He didn't seem to have much luck with sustaining relationships, a fact about which he seemed rueful and a bit bewildered. It was obvious to me that he just hadn't met the right woman. Was I the right woman? I thought of the sense of intimacy and understanding between us already, despite the fact that we'd known each other only three weeks. Was it a false understanding? Sexual attraction was like moonlight, casting a glamour on things that would look terribly ordinary in daylight, like that garment, whatever it was, hanging from a hook on the back of the bathroom door. The moonlight made it look like a cast-off human skin, if humans could cast off their skins.

I remembered a movie I wished I'd never seen, about a psycho who murdered women for their skins, and I jumped up. I felt a little sick. Yet there was nothing grisly or horrible about the thing. When I touched it, it was so cool and fine between my fingertips that it might have been spun from the moonlight itself.

It came down from the hook into my hands as if I wanted it, and the sensation of all that impossibly light mass tumbling into my arms made me dizzy with desire. I just had to put it on.

It was the weirdest sort of garment I'd ever encountered, a full body suit with hands and feet and head. It seemed all of a piece, yet as soon as I looked for an opening it was open in my hands, inviting me out of my clumsy, constricting clothes and inside it. There was no zip or other form of fastening, yet when I pressed the edges of the skin together they bonded fast. It seemed that a light veil had fallen over my face, I could feel something lighter than the finest silk against my skin, yet there was no obstruction. I could breathe as freely as ever, open and shut my eyes, even open my mouth and put out my tongue. I thought my vision was slightly affected, as if veiled, yet that may have been the moonlight.

I ran my hands over my naked/not naked body, finding it both familiar and strange. I had changed, the skin had changed me, but I was still myself. For the first time in my life I knew, absolutely, that I was beautiful, and, for the first time since childhood, felt completely at home in my body. No longer nervous, I went out to meet my lover.

He was waiting for me in the bedroom, in the moonlight which streamed through net curtains, as naked as I was. His unexpected handsomeness took my breath away. His body was more impressive than his clothes revealed, and the shadows chiselled what I'd first thought were the fairly ordinary – though very nice – features of his round face into more pleasing, classical proportions. I should have felt utterly intimidated by the sight of this stranger, but instead I was engulfed by a wave of lust that carried all my qualms and hesitancies out to sea, and washed me onto the bed, into his arms.

The first time I tried to make bread it was awful. I felt clumsy and irritable, did everything wrong, and in the end I threw the batch out. After that, it was fine. In fact, baking bread is one of my favourite things to do. But my first experience with it sums up my attitude towards first times in bed with someone new: it'll be awful, but worth it in the long run. Since there's no way of avoiding the first time you might as well just be as relaxed as you can about it, get through it, perform the mental equivalent of throwing it out uneaten, and take your reward from the pleasures to come.

Things I'd heard from my friends made me believe it was true for everyone – certainly for all women – but *that* first time, in the skin, was totally different. Our bodies seemed to recognize each other, our bodies *adored* each other, and it was impossible to put a hand or a foot or anything else wrong. All, all was mutual delight.

It was the skin, of course, but while I was in it, I thought it was me. A me wonderfully, gloriously changed, but still me.

I fell asleep in the skin. In the morning, I'd forgotten I

had it on, but in the bathroom, just as I was about to step into the shower, the skin suddenly fell away from me, running down my body and dropping smooth as water to puddle at my feet.

I picked it up and examined it in the dull and murky daylight. It was a silvery no-colour, like a snake's shed skin, but without brittleness. Fine, supple and strong, it had no weight, almost no mass. I crushed it into the palm of my hand, closed my fingers on it until it was invisible and felt like nothing at all. I could carry it in my purse or pocket, keep it with me always, I thought – then I hung it back on the door where I'd found it.

In the kitchen, amid the smells of coffee and charred toast, Fred looked ordinary again, ordinary and a little shy, and I knew that must be how I looked, too. He didn't seem to mind, though. He seemed to like looking at me, and he didn't avoid my eye, rather he caught it, and smiled.

An accidental bump led to a fervent clutch and a kiss and very soon, clutching and groping at each other, we made our way back down the hall to the bedroom. He seemed different in daylight, the whole thing was different, clumsier and sweatier, no less urgent yet somehow scarier, a new first time. And then he paused and drew back a little. 'Shall we . . . uh, do you want to . . . ?'

'Of course.' I rolled away from him just enough to reach the box of condoms on the table, but when I looked back I could see that wasn't what he meant. 'No?'

'Oh, yes, that too, but I meant – like last night. In the skins.'

It shocked me to hear him say it. How could I have thought it was my secret when it was his house I'd found it in? Yet since it had fallen off the memory of the womanskin had moved into the part of my mind where dreams and sexual fantasies lived, and to have Fred refer to it gave me the creepiest feeling, as if he'd somehow got inside my head.

He misinterpreted the look on my face. 'Of course we don't have to, if you didn't like it. I thought it was rather special, that's all . . .'

'Yes, yes, I did too.' Belatedly I twigged. '*You* were wearing one, too!'

'Yes, of course.'

'Fred, what are they?' I rolled on to my side, propping myself up on an elbow, and he mirrored me.

'I don't know. A manskin and a womanskin, just what they seem to be. No, honestly, I don't know any more than you do.'

'You must. Where did they come from?'

'I don't know. I found them in the garden.'

'In your garden?' I looked at the bedroom window, still curtained in net, at the greenish blur beyond. I hadn't seen his garden yet, but I was familiar enough with the pocket-handkerchief gardens of this neighbourhood of London to imagine the narrow, fenced-in rectangle of grass bounded on at least two sides by flower beds or shrubberies, all most unmagical. 'You found them in your garden? How? When? Tell me, Fred!'

'Well, did you think I'd bought them in a shop?' He grinned at me. 'The garden's nothing special; I'll show you later. There's a little shed down at the bottom, and a compost heap; the skins were lying on the grass in between. It was about a month ago – well, it must have been exactly a month ago because the moon was full, like it was last night. It was about a week before we met – you see, I haven't had them very long. I was feeling a little lonely and a little restless and I wasn't quite ready to go to bed, although it was late enough. It wasn't raining and I could see the moon shining away when I went to draw the curtains, so I thought I'd go out into the garden for a breath of air. That was when I saw something shining like moonlight on the grass. It looked like – you know quicksilver? That's what I thought of, quicksilver flowing in the shape of a person. Like a shadow on the grass, but light instead of dark, almost like a concentrated essence of light, shining up from the dark grass. I went over to it and bent down to touch it, and it was as I was lifting it up that it fell apart into two, and I realized I was holding – well, you know.'

'So you just kept them?'

'What would you have done?'

'Did you try them on?'

'Just the manskin,' he said swiftly, so swiftly that the qualification made me wonder. 'Once I had it on I knew that it was no good by itself, that they were meant to be a couple, were for a couple.'

'So a few days later you asked me out.'

'I would have asked you out anyway. It might have taken me a little longer, that's all. The skin gave me an extra – it gave me courage.'

'And then yesterday you left the womanskin hanging on the back of the bathroom door hoping – what? That I'd just see it and happen to try it on?'

He nodded.

'What if I hadn't?'

'But you did.' He smiled his sweet, shy smile. 'Shall we put them on again?'

I wasn't feeling the slightest bit sexy, the mood had gone to something else entirely, and I wanted to go on exploring it, exploring him by talking, but I was so moved by his strange story, and by him, that I did what he said, got up and went to the bathroom and slipped into the womanskin. I knew as soon as I returned that he was wearing his – there was nothing to see, but I sensed it, like an aura. As soon as the two skins came into contact they began making love. Of course it was *we* who did all those things, our two bodies fitting together as if we'd been lovers for years, and of course we experienced the arousal, the growing excitement, the climax, and yet all the while there was some small part of me which remained remote, aware that Fred and I were two strangers, separated by the skins, and that all the passion they generated had nothing really to do with us.

At first, in the beginning days and weeks of our deepening relationship, I didn't like to say anything about it. Sex in the skins was so reliably wonderful that it seemed sheer perversity to ask to try it without them. And besides, I thought naked sex was bound to happen naturally before long – we'd just get carried away and do it without thinking of the skins.

But it didn't. If we were caught in the throes of passion

on the couch in the middle of watching the late-night movie, we had to pause for contraception, and given a pause, the skins would insert themselves. I could have protested, of course, made a joking or a serious request to leave them out of it. But I guess I wanted it to come from Fred. I was afraid of finding out that the skins meant more to him than I did.

Every night Fred would slip into his skin at bedtime, the way that I might have inserted my diaphragm, just in case. But there was no 'just in case' about it, because once he'd put the manskin on, I seemed to feel a yearning from the womanskin which would have been cruel to ignore. I couldn't just be myself when Fred had on the manskin; I had to be her.

They were no good on their own, the skins. It was as Fred had told me, they were a couple, made for a couple. One morning I had the notion of wearing the womanskin out into the world, of going to work in it and seeing how other people would react. But I couldn't do it. The skin which clasped me so close whenever I was alone with Fred simply refused to stay on; it would not be worn under clothes or without sexual intent.

I don't mean to imply that the skins dominated our lives. The skins were only for sex, and when we weren't wearing them, or about to, even the memory of them seemed to slip away, at least from me. There's always more to life than sex in even the most passionate relationship. Fred and I began to spend all our spare time together. Although I still, cautiously, continued to pay rent on my single room, and left my out-of-season clothes hanging in the wardrobe there,

162

I was effectively living with him. I met his friends and he met mine, we cooked for each other and went shopping together, joked and argued and shared a life. It should have been perfect – the sex could not have been better – yet I felt there was something missing. I wanted a greater closeness. Fred didn't know what I meant. How could we be closer? We did everything together and the sex, every night, was great. I thought maybe we should talk more about ourselves. Fred didn't, but he did his best to oblige, answering my questions about his past, or what he felt about something, even when I could tell he found them annoying or unimportant or intrusive. I couldn't explain what was wrong, what was missing, but something was. After awhile I became obsessed with the notion that the skins were coming between us, and that the intimacy I craved would be ours only if we made love without them.

Of course I should have said something about how I was feeling, but our love was still too new: I didn't want him to think I was dissatisfied, or to make him unhappy. So, in time-honoured female fashion, I resorted to trickery.

We were on our way to the cinema, a route which took us right past the house where I rented a room, when I suddenly expressed a need for a particular sweater I'd left there. Obligingly he went along with me, and as soon as we were together behind the closed door of my room I faked an overwhelming passion to get us on to my single bed. But even before all our clothes were off he'd revealed that, alongside the emergency condom I already knew he carried in his wallet, he also carried both the skins.

'They fold down to nothing at all, you must have noticed,' he said. 'I don't always carry them with me, but this morning I just thought I'd see if they'd fit . . . lucky chance, huh?'

I burst into tears and confessed. He was astonished. Why hadn't I said?

Now, too late, I tried to make light of my desire. I hadn't asked because I hadn't wanted to make it seem important. It wasn't important. Our relationship, most particularly the sexual side of it, was wonderful. Only, now and then I wondered if we might not be even closer if we made love without the skins. Hadn't he ever wondered about that, about how it would feel?

He said he had not. He said he couldn't imagine being any closer to anyone than he already was to me. He said that sex with me, in the skins, was the best he'd ever known and, that being so, why should he want anything different? But now that he knew what I wanted . . .

Now that he knew what I wanted, we had to do it there and then, the skins folded back into his wallet. Was it their presence, like uninvited ghosts, which made what followed so unsatisfactory? Or was it my guilt at having tried to deceive him? How could I complain we weren't close enough when I kept my own feelings hidden? It was a pretty wretched coupling, all told. I'd seldom felt less like having sex, and it was easy to imagine the pressures on Fred struggling to satisfy me unaided. No wonder that we ended up farther apart, more alone than ever. No wonder it was such a relief to put the skins on again later that night and feel ourselves drawn back together. In my imagination the skins had been coming between us, blocking a more perfect understanding, but now I could see it was the skins which saved us from our differences. Without the skins we were only ordinary. With them we were special.

We soon took great sex for granted, as our right. We were spoiled by the skins which made sex instant and easy and completely detached from the rest of life. It still made me uneasy because it was so unnatural. We were in the unlikely situation of being in a sexual relationship in which the sexual part was completely unaffected by the relationship.

The sex was magic, but the sex belonged to the skins. It didn't matter if we'd just been arguing about whose turn it was to clean the bathroom, or whether someone who voted Conservative could be, in any sense of the word, a *good* person – it didn't matter if he was tired or I had a hangover – whatever our moods, whatever our differences, if we put on the skins we were instantly ready for love. The skins took us into another world, their world, where only one thing mattered. Tiredness, anger, irritation, menstrual cramps either vanished or stopped mattering for a little while. Yet it was the same if I was feeling particularly loving towards Fred for some reason, or if I was already aroused by some fantasy I'd been having – none of it mattered, nothing made any difference, positive or negative, in the realm of the skins. Fred and I were involved in a sexual relationship, but it was not our own.

Our relationship did not influence the sex, but the sex definitely influenced our relationship. It's hard to share several hours of physical bliss with someone and not feel, at the very least, *warm* towards them the next day. Kitchen and bathroom foibles, odd and even disgusting personal habits are easily forgiven in the afterglow, differences forgotten because unimportant. I don't know what sort of lovers we would have been without the skins; neither of us was eager to find out, unwilling to spoil what we did have. And yet there were times when I was with Fred when I felt lonelier than I'd ever felt on my own. I put it down to hormones.

I still don't know why I put on the manskin one night. Opportunity, I suppose, and curiosity. I had never examined it, I don't think I'd ever even touched it except when Fred was wearing it. We'd just been getting ready for bed when the telephone rang and he went out of the room to answer it, leaving his skin lying on the bed.

Wondering how different it was to mine, I picked it up, and, because I was naked already, put it on.

I didn't expect it to fit. My skin fit me, as his fit him, as if they'd been specially tailored to our proportions, and Fred was nearly six inches taller than I was, with broader shoulders and longer arms. Yet the manskin settled on to my nakedness like my own skin. Looking down at myself, I thought there'd been some mix-up: his skin couldn't possibly fit me so tightly and comfortably. This must be a woman's skin.

But I knew it wasn't mine. Fred had been wearing this skin; it was unmistakably his. Something of his essence still clung to it the way that a smell, perfume or body odour will cling to much-worn, unwashed clothes. This wasn't a smell,

166

though; it was emotion, it was personality, it was cast of mind, a sort of echo of Fred himself, which I recognized as surely as I recognized his voice on an answering machine, his arms around me in a dark room.

It was almost like being Fred, knowing what he knew, feeling what he felt. It was intimacy beyond anything I'd ever experienced, a way of knowing what I'd only struggled to imagine, before, and the knowledge overwhelmed me with love.

Fred came back into the room and I tossed him my skin. 'Put it on,' I said. 'Quickly!'

I don't think he understood what I had done until he had put it on. I saw the astonishment on his face, the melting into love, in the minute or so before we came together to make love.

It was the best ever. In the past I'd sometimes felt more like a passenger than a participant, aware that it could be someone else, anyone else, inside without making any difference to what was happening between manskin and womanskin. Great sex, yet somehow anonymous.

This could not have been less anonymous. I was engulfed by Fred himself, by the sensual, sensory memories of the man. I was in *his* skin, and yet I was myself, making love to him, the man I felt with every part of me, in *my* skin. Words can't explain or do it justice. I'm not even sure I can really remember it now, not the way it really was, but one thing is certain: it was the high point of our love affair.

The problem with heights is that once you've reached the highest there is nowhere to go but down. The next few nights afterwards we made love the old way: Fred in the manskin, I in the womanskin, until I began to grow restless and want something more.

When I suggested we swap skins, Fred was adamantly opposed. I didn't quite believe his opposition – it had been so wonderful, how could he not want it again? – and I teased and pressed and pestered for a reason.

'It's not right, that's why. It's not natural.'

'Oh, and the skins are?'

'Of course they are!' He glared at me. 'I can understand curiosity, once, but you should be satisfied now. Aren't you satisfied with being a woman?'

'But it's not about being a woman! I'm still a woman, with the skin or without it – whichever skin I wear. It doesn't make any difference.'

'If it doesn't make any difference, why do you want to wear the manskin?'

'It's not about being a man or a woman, it's about being you. Well, *feeling* you, knowing you better than – knowing you from the inside. That's what it's like, that's why I liked it. Not because it was a MANskin – really, I couldn't tell any difference between them – but because it was yours. Didn't you like being in my skin?'

'It's not your skin, it's just something I let you wear. And no, I didn't like it particularly. I don't like feeling like a woman. I'm a man.'

I was suddenly frightened, aware that I was on dangerous ground. All at once the skins were his and I was – who was I, what was I, to him?

'Of course you're a man. It's because you *are* a man, and I'm not, and it's because I love you, that I want to know you in every way there is. I want to get closer to you, I don't want to take anything away from you—'

'Then you shouldn't try. Loving me isn't wanting to *be* me; it isn't wanting to turn me into a woman. If you really loved me you'd want to be even MORE of a woman, to make me feel more of a man. That's what the skins are all about.'

'I'm sorry.' It was hard for me to accept the truth, that what had been for me a high point of intimacy and understanding had been no such thing for him. Instead of feeling closer to me in my skin he had simply felt, unhappily, like a woman. Any woman, I guess, with me as any man. I gave up trying to explain it to him. If he didn't want to be inside my skin I wasn't going to try to force him.

After that we made love less often. His aversion to wearing the womanskin created an ambivalence in me, an insecurity. Was the woman he had encountered traces of in the skin so unlovable? Who did he imagine that I was? We made love a few times without the skins in pursuit of our old closeness but it was never satisfactory. We tried very hard for a time and then we gave up trying.

We were drifting apart. The term implies a gradualness, and it was certainly not abrupt, yet it happened very quickly once it began. Both of us became busy with things that kept us out of the house and out of each other's way. I went back to my room more often, and even spent the night there, especially if I was going out with friends after work or if he said he would be out late.

169

Yet it wasn't easy, giving up on Fred. I'd always liked being part of a couple, and I'd never entered a relationship without intending it to last for ever. And I missed him. Memories of the early days of our romance haunted me, memories of intimacy, wordless feelings I would never have again.

Neither of us said anything about what was happening, reluctant to bring it to a formal, final close. We spent two or three nights a week together, and although I had been gradually, unobtrusively shifting my things back to my own room, I still had my own key to his house.

One evening which we had planned to spend together I happened to get there first. I took my bottle of wine into the kitchen, and then went down the hall to the bathroom.

The skins, both of them, were hanging from the hooks on the back of the door. It gave me quite a start to see them, for Fred had long been in the habit of folding his carefully away after use. When it wasn't in his wallet he kept it in a small, round, leather stud-box on the bedroom dresser. I had tended to leave the womanskin hung on the back of the door where I'd first found it, but after feeling his disapproval of 'picking up after me' a few times, I'd found a Chinese red silk purse and used that faithfully. I was sure that I'd folded it away after the last time; certainly the skins had not been hanging in the bathroom when I left on Sunday night.

Then I noticed that they were moving. It was only the faintest of gentle waving motions, as if they stirred in a breeze, but there was no breeze in the closed room, and if there had been, it would have impelled the skins to move

170

both in the same direction not, as I could plainly see, in gentle flutterings towards each other.

What I saw, and I knew it, was pure yearning. They longed for each other all the time, but only by human intervention could they come together. We could live without them, but they needed us.

I lifted them down from their hooks, took them into the bedroom, and lay them flat on the bed, one on top of the other. I watched for a little while but there was no visible movement – maybe, for them, no movement was necessary now they were so close. Then, feeling embarrassed by my own curiosity, I left the room, turning out the light when I went.

Fred and I had dinner in – a take-away from the local Indian – and then watched a production of *Don Giovanni* on television. Opera is not really my sort of thing, and he had offered to tape it and watch it by himself later, but I was getting the prickly sensation that Fred had decided it was time at last for our serious talk, and I was grateful for anything that would postpone it. Our relationship was nearly over, but I was determined it should last long enough for us to make love once more.

When we went into the bedroom together he looked startled at the sight of the skins on the bed.

'Oh, maybe not,' he said. 'Maybe it wouldn't be such a good idea tonight – I've been meaning to talk to you—'

'Later. Don't say anything now. We'll put on the skins – we could be any man, any woman – we can talk tomorrow.'

Hastily I stripped off my clothes, knowing that once I was

in the skin he wouldn't argue with me, he would feel the yearning, too, and the compulsion to satisfy it.

Then I was in the skin and – it wasn't mine any more. All at once I was suffocatingly close to, intimate with, a complete stranger. It was like waking up in the middle of a rape, and the worst part about it was the hot, heavy desire all around – I felt it as if it was mine, and it was directed at Fred – but I knew it belonged to somebody else. I wanted to scream but I couldn't. Somehow I managed to peel the thing off me, and then I stood naked, trembling, staring outraged at my lover.

'You've had someone else here – you've been making love with someone else!'

'I was going to tell you – I tried—'

'You were going to tell me! And that makes it all right?'

'Oh – please. Don't go all – as if I'd broken your heart. You know perfectly well that things were already all but finished between us.' His calm, weary, rational tone made me aware that I was playing a role lifted from soap opera, but I couldn't seem to stop.

'All but, yes. All but. But not completely finished. It would have been nice if you could at least have waited, instead of ending it like this, humiliating me, and – and why did you have to bring her here? Why did you have to use the skins?'

He stopped looking defensive.

'You know why,' he said quietly. 'You know perfectly well why. The same reason you dragged me in here and tore off all your clothes ten minutes ago. Nothing to do with love for me. Nothing much to do with you, either.'

172

Anger and hurt rushed out of me like air from a pricked balloon, leaving me limp. I began to put my clothes back on. 'I wasn't the first, was I?'

He sighed and shook his head. 'But it felt like the first time with you, it really did. That's all I meant. I didn't want you thinking it was routine, or old hat, or – because it really was special with you, like the very first time.'

'Did you really find them in your garden?'

'Different garden. Down in Suffolk. Years ago – the night I lost my virginity. Some fifty-odd women ago.'

I was all dressed now. I looked at my watch, saw that the underground would still be running, I could go home. 'Well – good luck. I hope you're happy. Maybe she'll be the one.'

He smiled a little, mocking my conventional expectations. 'That's not what it's about. I don't need *one*.'

YASUNARI KAWABATA

One Arm

'I can let you have one of my arms for the night,' said the girl. She took off her right arm at the shoulder and, with her left hand, laid it on my knee.

'Thank you.' I looked at my knee. The warmth of the arm came through.

'I'll put the ring on. To remind you that it's mine.' She smiled and raised her left arm to my chest. 'Please.' With but one arm, it was difficult for her to take the ring off.

'An engagement ring?'

'No. A keepsake. From my mother.'

It was silver, set with small diamonds.

'Perhaps it does look like an engagement ring, but I don't mind. I wear it, and then when I take it off it's as if I were leaving my mother.'

Raising the arm on my knee, I removed the ring and slipped it on the ring finger.

'Is this the one?'

'Yes.' She nodded. 'It will seem artificial unless the elbow and fingers bend. You won't like that. Let me make them bend for you.'

She took her right arm from my knee and pressed her lips gently to it. Then she pressed them to the finger joints.

'Now they'll move.'

'Thank you.' I took the arm back. 'Do you suppose it will speak? Will it speak to me?'

'It only does what an arm does. If it talks I'll be afraid to have it back. But try anyway. It should at least listen to what you say, if you're good to it.'

'I'll be good to it.'

'I'll see you again,' she said, touching the right arm with her left hand, as if to infuse it with a spirit of its own. 'You're his, but just for the night.'

As she looked at me she seemed to be fighting back tears.

'I don't suppose you'll try to change it for your own arm,' she said. 'But it will be all right. Go ahead, do.'

'Thank you.'

I put her arm in my raincoat and went out into the foggy streets. I feared I might be thought odd if I took a taxi or a streetcar. There would be a scene if the arm, now separated from the girl's body, were to cry out, or to weep.

I held it against my chest, toward the side, my right hand on the roundness at the shoulder joint. It was concealed by the raincoat, and I had to touch the coat from time to time with my left hand to be sure that the arm was still there. Probably I was making sure not of the arm's presence but of my own happiness.

She had taken off the arm at the point I liked. It was

plump and round – was it at the top of the arm or the beginning of the shoulder? The roundness was that of a beautiful Occidental girl, rare in a Japanese. It was in the girl herself, a clean, elegant roundness, like a sphere glowing with a faint, fresh light. When the girl was no longer clean that gentle roundness would fade, grow flabby. Something that lasted for a brief moment in the life of a beautiful girl, the roundness of the arm made me feel the roundness of her body. Her breasts would not be large. Shy, only large enough to cup in the hands, they would have a clinging softness and strength. And in the roundness of the arm I could feel her legs as she walked along. She would carry them lightly, like a small bird, or a butterfly moving from flower to flower. There would be the same subtle melody in the tip of her tongue when she kissed.

It was the season for changing to sleeveless dresses. The girl's shoulder, newly bared, had the color of skin not used to the raw touch of the air. It had the glow of a bud moistened in the shelter of spring and not yet ravaged by summer. I had that morning bought a magnolia bud and put it in a glass vase; and the roundness of the girl's arm was like the great, white bud. Her dress was cut back more radically than most sleeveless dresses. The joint at the shoulder was exposed, and the shoulder itself. The dress, of dark green silk, almost black, had a soft sheen. The girl was in the rounded slope of the shoulders, which drew a gentle wave with the swelling of the back. Seen obliquely from behind, the flesh from the round shoulders to the long, slender neck came to an abrupt halt at the base of the upswept hair, and the black hair seemed to cast a glowing shadow over the roundness of the shoulders.

She had sensed that I thought her beautiful, and so she lent me her right arm for the roundness there at the shoulder.

Carefully hidden under my raincoat, the girl's arm was colder than my hand. I was giddy from the racing of my heart, and I knew that my hand would be hot. I wanted the warmth to stay as it was, the warmth of the girl herself. And the slight coolness in my hand passed on to me the pleasure of the arm. It was like her breasts, not yet touched by a man.

The fog yet thicker, the night threatened rain, and wet my uncovered hair. I could hear a radio speaking from the back room of a closed pharmacy. It announced that three planes unable to land in the fog had been circling the airport for a half-hour. It went on to draw the attention of listeners to the fact that on damp nights clocks were likely to go wrong, and that on such nights the springs had a tendency to break if wound too tight. I looked for the lights of the circling planes, but could not see them. There was no sky. The pressing dampness invaded my ears, to give a wet sound like the wriggling of myriads of distant earthworms. I stood before the pharmacy awaiting further admonitions. I learned that on such nights the fierce beasts in the zoo, the lions and tigers and leopards and the rest, roared their resentment at the dampness, and that we were now to hear it. There was a roaring like the roaring of the earth. I then learned that pregnant women and despondent persons should go to bed early on such nights, and that women who applied perfume directly to their skins would find it difficult to remove afterwards.

At the roaring of the beasts, I moved off, and the warning about perfume followed me. That angry roaring unsettled me, and I moved on lest my uneasiness be transmitted to the girl's arm. The girl was neither pregnant nor despondent, but it seemed to me that tonight, with only one arm, she should take the advice of the radio and go quietly to bed. I hoped that she would sleep peacefully.

As I started across the street I pressed my left hand against my raincoat. A horn sounded. Something brushed my side, and I twisted away. Perhaps the arm had been frightened by the horn. The fingers were clenched.

'Don't worry,' I said. 'It was a long way off. It couldn't see. That's why it honked.'

Because I was holding something important to me, I had looked in both directions. The sound of the horn had been so far away that I had thought it must be meant for someone else. I looked in the direction from which it came, but could see no one. I could see only the headlights. They widened into a blur of faint purple. A strange color for headlights. I stood on the curb when I had crossed and watched it pass. A young woman in vermilion was driving. It seemed to me that she turned toward me and bowed. I wanted to run off, fearing that the girl had come for her arm. Then I remembered that she would hardly be able to drive with only one. But had not the woman in the car seen what I was carrying? Had she not sensed it with a woman's intuition? I would have to take care not to encounter another of the sex before I reached my apartment. The rear lights were also a faint purple. I still did not see the car. In the ashen fog a lavender blur floated up and moved away.

'She is driving for no reason, for no reason at all except to be driving. And while she drives she will simply disappear,' I muttered to myself. 'And what was that sitting in the back seat?'

Nothing, apparently. Was it because I went around carrying girls' arms that I felt so unnerved by emptiness? The car she drove carried the clammy night fog. And something about her had turned it faintly purple in the headlights. If not from her own body, whence had come that purplish light? Could the arm I concealed have so clothed in emptiness a woman driving alone on such a night? Had she nodded at the girl's arm from her car? Perhaps on such a night there were angels and ghosts abroad protecting women. Perhaps she had ridden not in a car but in a purple light. Her drive had not been empty. She had spied out my secret.

I made my way back to my apartment without further encounters. I stood listening outside the door. The light of a firefly skimmed over my head and disappeared. It was too large and too strong for a firefly. I recoiled backwards. Several more lights like fireflies skimmed past. They disappeared even before the heavy fog could suck them in. Had a will-o'-the-wisp, a death-fire of some sort, run on ahead of me, to await my return? But then I saw that it was a swarm of small moths. Catching the light at the door, the wings of the moths glowed like fireflies. Too large to be fireflies, and yet, for moths, so small as to invite the mistake.

Avoiding the automatic elevator, I made my way stealthily up the narrow stairs to the third floor. Not being left-handed, I had difficulty unlocking the door. The harder I tried the more my hand trembled – as if in terror after a crime. Something would be waiting for me inside the room, a room where I lived in solitude; and was not the solitude a presence? With the girl's arm I was no longer alone. And so perhaps my own solitude waited there to intimidate me.

'Go on ahead,' I said, taking out the girl's arm when at length I had opened the door. 'Welcome to my room. I'll turn on the light.'

'Are you afraid of something?' the arm seemed to say. 'Is something here?'

'You think there might be?'

'I smell something.'

'Smell? It must be me that you smell. Don't you see traces of my shadow, up there in the darkness? Look carefully. Maybe my shadow was waiting for me to come back.'

'It's a sweet smell.'

'Ah – the magnolia,' I answered brightly. I was glad it was not the moldy smell of my loneliness. A magnolia bud befitted my winsome guest. I was getting used to the dark. Even in pitch blackness I knew where everything was.

'Let me turn on the light.' Coming from the arm, a strange remark. 'I haven't been in your room before.'

'Thank you. I'll be very pleased. No one but me has ever turned on the lights here before.'

I held the arm to the switch by the door. All five lights went on at once: at the ceiling, on the table, by the bed, in the kitchen, in the bathroom. I had not thought they could be so bright.

The magnolia was in enormous bloom. That morning it had been in bud. It could have only just bloomed, and yet there were stamens on the table. Curious, I looked more closely at the stamens than at the white flower. As I picked up one or two and gazed at them, the girl's arm, laid on the table, began to move, the fingers like spanworms, and gathered the stamens in its hand. I went to throw them in the waste-basket.

'What a strong smell. It sinks right into my skin. Help me.'

'You must be tired. It wasn't an easy trip. Suppose you rest awhile.'

I laid the arm on the bed and sat down beside it. I stroked it gently.

'How pretty. I like it.' The arm would be speaking of the bed cover. Flowers were printed in three colors on an azure ground, somewhat lively for a man who lived alone. 'So this is where we spend the night. I'll be very quiet.'

'Oh?'

'I'll be beside you and not beside you.'

The hand took mine gently. The nails, carefully polished, were a faint pink. The tips extended well beyond the fingers.

181

Against my own short, thick nails, hers possessed a strange beauty, as if they belonged to no human creature. With such fingertips, a woman perhaps transcended mere humanity. Or did she pursue womanhood itself? A shell luminous from the pattern inside it, a petal bathed in dew – I thought of the obvious likenesses. Yet I could think of no shell or petal whose color and shape resembled them. They were the nails on the girl's fingers, comparable to nothing else. More translucent than a delicate shell, than a thin petal, they seemed to hold a dew of tragedy. Every day and every night her energies were poured into the polishing of this tragic beauty. It penetrated my solitude. Perhaps my yearning, my solitude, transformed them into dew.

I rested her little finger on the index finger of my free hand, gazing at the long, narrow nail as I rubbed it with my thumb. My finger touched the tip of hers, sheltered by the nail. The finger bent, and the elbow too.

'Does it tickle?' I asked. 'It must.'

I had spoken carelessly. I knew that the tips of a woman's fingers were sensitive when the nails were long. And so I had told the girl's arm that I had known other women.

From one who was not a great deal older than the girl who had lent me the arm but far more mature in her experience of men, I had heard that fingertips thus hidden by nails were often acutely sensitive. One became used to touching things not with the fingertips but with the nails, and the fingertips therefore tickled when something came against them.

I had shown astonishment at this discovery, and she had

gone on: 'You're, say, cooking – or eating – and something touches your fingers, and you find yourself hunching your shoulders, it seems so dirty.'

Was it the food that seemed unclean, or the tip of the nail? Whatever touched her fingers made her writhe with its uncleanness. Her own cleanness would leave behind a drop of tragic dew, there under the long shadow of the nail. One could not assume that for each of the ten fingers there would be a separate drop of dew.

It was natural that I should want all the more to touch those fingertips, but I held myself back. My solitude held me back. She was a woman on whose body few tender spots could be expected to remain.

And on the body of the girl who had lent me the arm they would be beyond counting. Perhaps, toying with the fingertips of such a girl, I would feel not guilt but affection. But she had not lent me the arm for such mischief. I must not make a comedy of her gesture.

'The window.' I noticed not that the window itself was open but that the curtain was undrawn.

'Will anything look in?' asked the girl's arm.

'Some man or woman. Nothing else.'

'Nothing human would see me. If anything it would be a self. Yours.'

'Self? What is that? Where is it?'

'Far away,' said the arm, as if singing in consolation. 'People walk around looking for selves, far away.'

'And do they come upon them?'

'Far away,' said the arm once more.

183

It seemed to me that the arm and the girl herself were an infinity apart. Would the arm be able to return to the girl, so far away? Would I be able to take it back, so far away? The arm lay peacefully trusting me; and would the girl be sleeping in the same peaceful confidence? Would there not be harshness, a nightmare? Had she not seemed to be fighting back tears when she parted with it? The arm was now in my room, which the girl herself had not visited.

The dampness clouded the window, like a toad's belly stretched over it. The fog seemed to withhold rain in mid-air, and the night outside the window lost distance, even while it was wrapped in limitless distance. There were no roofs to be seen, no horns to be heard.

'I'll close the window,' I said, reaching for the curtain. It too was damp. My face loomed up in the window, younger than my thirty-three years. I did not hesitate to pull the curtain, however. My face disappeared.

Suddenly a remembered window. On the ninth floor of a hotel, two little girls in wide red skirts were playing in the window. Very similar children in similar clothes, perhaps twins, Occidentals. They pounded at the glass, pushing it with their shoulders and shoving at each other. Their mother knitted, her back to the window. If the large pane were to have broken or come loose, they would have fallen from the ninth floor. It was only I who thought them in danger. Their mother was quite unconcerned. The glass was in fact so solid that there was no danger.

'It's beautiful,' said the arm on the bed as I turned from

the window. Perhaps she was speaking of the curtain, in the same flowered pattern as the bed cover.

'Oh? But it's faded from the sun and almost ready to go.' I sat down on the bed and took the arm on my knee. 'This is what is beautiful. More beautiful than anything.'

Taking the palm of the hand in my own right palm, and the shoulder in my left hand, I flexed the elbow, and then again.

'Behave yourself,' said the arm, as if smiling softly. 'Having fun?'

'Not in the least.'

A smile did come over the arm, crossing it like light. It was exactly the fresh smile on the girl's cheek.

I knew the smile. Elbows on the table, she would fold her hands loosely and rest her chin or cheek on them. The pose should have been inelegant in a young girl but there was about it a lightly engaging quality that made expressions like 'elbows on the table' seem inappropriate. The roundness of the shoulders, the fingers, the chin, the cheeks, the ears, the long, slender neck, the hair, all came together in a single harmonious movement. Using knife and fork deftly, first and little fingers bent, she would raise them ever so slightly from time to time. Food would pass the small lips and she would swallow – I had before me less a person at dinner than an inviting music of hands and face and throat. The light of her smile flowed across the skin of her arm.

The arm seemed to smile because, as I flexed it, very gentle waves passed over the firm, delicate muscles, to send waves of light and shadow over the smooth skin. Earlier, when I had touched the fingertips under the long nails, the light passing over the arm as the elbow bent had caught my eye. It was that, and not any impulse toward mischief, that had made me bend and unbend her arm. I stopped, and gazed at it as it lay stretched out on my knee. Fresh lights and shadows were still passing over it.

'You ask if I'm having fun. You realize that I have permission to change you for my own arm?'

'I do.'

'Somehow I'm afraid to.'

'Oh?'

'May I?'

'Please.'

I heard the permission granted, and wondered whether I could accept it. 'Say it again. Say "please".'

'Please, please.'

I remembered. It was like the voice of a woman who had decided to give herself to me, one not as beautiful as the girl who had lent me the arm. Perhaps there was something a little strange about her.

'Please,' she had said, gazing at me. I had put my fingers to her eyelids and closed them. Her voice was trembling. '"Jesus wept. Then said the Jews, Behold how he loved her!"'

'Her' was a mistake for 'him'. It was the story of the dead Lazarus. Perhaps, herself a woman, she had remembered it wrong, perhaps she had made the substitution intentionally.

The words, so inappropriate to the scene, had shaken me.

I gazed at her, wondering if tears would start from the closed eyes.

She opened them and raised her shoulders. I pushed her down with my arm.

'You're hurting me!' She put her hand to the back of her head.

There was a small spot of blood on the white pillow. Parting her hair, I put my lips to the drop of blood swelling on her head.

'It doesn't matter.' She took out all her hairpins. 'I bleed easily. At the slightest touch.'

A hairpin had pierced her skin. A shudder seemed about to pass through her shoulders, but she controlled herself.

Although I think I understand how a woman feels when she gives herself to a man, there is still something unexplained about the act. What is it to her? Why should she wish to do it, why should she take the initiative? I could never really accept the surrender, even knowing that the body of every woman was made for it. Even now, old as I am, it seems strange. And the ways in which various women go about it: unalike if you wish, or similar perhaps, or even identical. Is that not strange? Perhaps the strangeness I find in it all is the curiosity of a younger man, perhaps the despair of one advanced in years. Or perhaps some spiritual debility I suffer from.

Her anguish was not common to all women in the act of surrender. And it was with her only the one time. The silver thread was cut, the golden bowl destroyed.

'Please,' the arm had said, and so reminded me of the

other girl; but were the two voices in fact similar? Had they not sounded alike because the words were the same? Had the arm acquired independence in this measure of the body from which it was separated? And were the words not the act of giving itself up, of being ready for anything, without restraint or responsibility or remorse? It seemed to me that if I were to accept the invitation and change the arm for my own I would be bringing untold pain to the girl.

I gazed at the arm on my knee. There was a shadow at the inside of the elbow. It seemed that I might be able to suck it in. I pressed it to my lips, to gather in the shadow.

'It tickles. Do behave yourself.' The arm was around my neck, avoiding my lips.

'Just when I was having a good drink.'

'And what were you drinking?'

I did not answer.

'What were you drinking?'

'The smell of light? Of skin.'

The fog seemed thicker; even the magnolia leaves seemed wet. What other warnings would issue from the radio? I started toward my table radio and stopped. To listen to it with the arm around my neck seemed altogether too much. But I suspected I would hear something like this: because of the wet branches and their own wet feet and wings, small birds have fallen to the ground and cannot fly. Automobiles passing through parks should take care not to run over them. And if a warm wind comes up, the fog will perhaps change color. Strange-colored fogs are noxious. Listeners should therefore lock their doors if the fog should turn pink or purple.

'Change color?' I muttered. 'Turn pink or purple?'

I pulled at the curtain and looked out. The fog seemed to press down with an empty weight. Was it because of the wind that a thin darkness seemed to be moving about, different from the usual black of night? The thickness of the fog seemed infinite, and yet beyond it something fearsome writhed and coiled.

I remembered that earlier, as I was coming home with the borrowed arm, the head and tail beams of the car driven by the woman in vermilion had come up indistinctly in the fog. A great, blurred sphere of faint purple now seemed to come toward me. I hastily pulled away from the curtain.

'Let's go to bed. Us too.'

It seemed as if no one else in the world would be up. To be up was terror.

Taking the arm from my neck and putting it on the table, I changed into a fresh night-kimono, a cotton print. The arm watched me change. I was shy at being watched. Never before had a woman watched me undress in my room.

The arm in my own, I got into bed. I lay facing it, and brought it lightly to my chest. It lay quiet.

Intermittently I could hear a faint sound as of rain, a very light sound, as if the fog had not turned to rain but were itself forming drops. The fingers clasped in my hand beneath the blanket grew warmer; and it gave me the quietest of sensations, the fact that they had not warmed to my own temperature.

189

'Are you asleep?'

'No,' replied the arm.

'You were so quiet, I thought you might be asleep.'

'What do you want me to do?'

Opening my kimono, I brought the arm to my chest. The difference in warmth sank in. In the somehow sultry, somehow chilly night, the smoothness of the skin was pleasant.

The lights were still on. I had forgotten to turn them out as I went to bed.

'The lights.' I got up, and the arm fell from my chest.

I hastened to pick it up. 'Will you turn out the lights?' I started toward the door. 'Do you sleep in the dark? Or with lights on?'

The arm did not answer. It would surely know. Why had it not answered? I did not know the girl's nocturnal practices. I compared the two pictures, of her asleep in the dark and with the lights on. I decided that tonight, without her arm, she would have them on. Somehow I too wanted them on. I wanted to gaze at the arm. I wanted to stay awake and watch the arm after it had gone to sleep. But the fingers stretched to turn off the switch by the door.

I went back and lay down in the darkness, the arm by my chest. I lay there silently, waiting for it to go to sleep. Whether dissatisfied or afraid of the dark, the hand lay open at my side, and presently the five fingers were climbing my chest. The elbow bent of its own accord, and the arm embraced me.

There was a delicate pulse at the girl's wrist. It lay over

my heart, so that the two pulses sounded against each other. Hers was at first somewhat slower than mine, then they were together. And then I could feel only mine. I did not know which was faster, which slower.

Pcrhaps this identity of pulse and heartbeat was for a brief period when I might try to exchange the arm for my own. Or had it gone to sleep? I had once heard a woman say that women were less happy in the throes of ecstasy than sleeping peacefully beside their men; but never before had a womam slept beside me as peacefully as this arm.

I was conscious of my beating heart because of the pulsation above it. Between one beat and the next, something sped far away and sped back again. As I listened to the beating, the distance seemed to increase. And however far the something went, however infinitely far, it met nothing at its destination. The next beat summoned it back. I should have been afraid, and was not. Yet I groped for the switch beside my pillow.

Before turning it on, I quietly rolled back the blanket. The arm slept on, unaware of what was happening. A gentle band of faintest white encircled my naked chest, seeming to rise from the flesh itself, like the glow before the dawning of a tiny, warm sun.

I turned on the light. I put my hands to the fingers and shoulder and pulled the arm straight. I turned it quietly in my hands, gazing at the play of light and shadow, from the roundness at the shoulder over the narrowing and swelling of the forearm, the narrowing again at the gentle roundness of the elbow, the faint depression inside the elbow, the narrowing roundness to the wrist, the palm and back of the hand, and on to the fingers.

'I'll have it.' I was not conscious of muttering the words. In a trance, I removed my right arm and substituted the girl's.

There was a slight gasp – whether from the arm or from me I could not tell – and a spasm at my shoulder. So I knew of the change.

The girl's arm – mine now – was trembling and reaching for the air. Bending it, I brought it close to my mouth.

'Does it hurt? Do you hurt?'

'No. Not at all. Not at all.' The words were fitful.

A shudder went through me like lightning. I had the fingers in my mouth.

Somehow I spoke my happiness, but the girl's fingers were at my tongue, and whatever it was I spoke did not form into words.

'Please. It's all right,' the arm replied. The trembling stopped. 'I was told you could. And yet—'

I noticed something. I could feel the girl's fingers in my mouth, but the fingers of her hand, now those of my own right hand, could not feel my lips or teeth. In panic I shook my right arm and could not feel the shaking. There was a break, a stop, between arm and shoulder.

'The blood doesn't go,' I blurted out. 'Does it or doesn't it?'

For the first time I was swept by fear. I rose up in bed. My own arm had fallen beside me. Separated from me, it was an unsightly object. But more important – would not the pulse have stopped? The girl's arm was warm and pulsing; my own looked as if it were growing stiff and cold. With the girl's, I grasped my own right arm. I grasped it, but there was no sensation.

'Is there a pulse?' I asked the arm. 'Is it cold?'

'A little. Just a little colder than I am. I've gotten very warm.' There was something especially womanly in the cadence. Now that the arm was fastened to my shoulder and made my own, it seemed womanly as it had not before.

'The pulse hasn't stopped?'

'You should be more trusting.'

'Of what?'

'You changed your arm for mine, didn't you?'

'Is the blood flowing?'

'"Woman, whom seekest thou?" You know the passage?'

'"Woman, why weepest thou? Whom seekest thou?"'

'Very often when I'm dreaming and wake up in the night I whisper it to myself.'

This time of course the 'I' would be the owner of the winsome arm at my shoulder. The words from the Bible were as if spoken by an eternal voice, in an eternal place.

'Will she have trouble sleeping?' I too spoke of the girl herself. 'Will she be having a nightmare? It's a fog for herds of nightmares to wander in. But the dampness will make even demons cough.'

'To keep you from hearing them.' The girl's arm, my own still in its hand, covered my right ear.

It was now my own right arm, but the motion seemed to have come not of my volition but of its own, from its heart. Yet the separation was by no means so complete.

'The pulse. The sound of the pulse.'

I heard the pulse of my own right arm. The girl's arm had come to my ear with my own arm in its hand, and my own wrist was at my ear. My arm was warm – as the girl's arm had said, just perceptibly cooler than her fingers and my ear.

'I'll keep away the devils.' Mischievously, gently, the long, delicate nail of her little finger stirred in my ear. I shook my head. My left hand – mine from the start – took my right wrist – actually the girl's. As I threw my head back, I caught sight of the girl's little finger.

Four fingers of her hand were grasping the arm I had taken from my right shoulder. The little finger alone – shall we say that it alone was allowed to play free? – was bent toward the back of the hand. The tip of the nail touched my right arm lightly. The finger was bent in a position possible only to a girl's supple hand, out of the question for a stiff-jointed man like me. From its base it rose at right angles. At the first joint it bent in another right angle, and at the next in yet another. It thus traced a square, the fourth side formed by the ring finger.

It formed a rectangular window at the level of my eye. Or rather a peep-hole, or an eyeglass, much too small for a window; but somehow I thought of a window. The sort of window a violet might look out through. The window of the little finger, the finger-rimmed eyeglass, so white that it gave off a faint glow – I brought it nearer my eye. I closed the other eye.

'A peep show?' asked the arm. 'And what do you see?'

'My dusky old room. Its five lights.' Before I had finished the sentence I was almost shouting. 'No, no! I see it!'

'And what do you see?'

'It's gone.'

'And what did you see?'

'A color. A blur of purple. And inside it little circles, little beads of red and gold, whirling around and around.'

'You're tired.' The girl's arm put down my right arm, and her fingers gently stroked my eyelids.

'Were the beads of gold and red spinning around in a huge cogwheel? Did I see something in the cogwheel, something that came and went?'

I did not know whether I had actually seen something there or only seemed to – a fleeting illusion, not to stay in the memory. I could not remember what it might have been.

'Was it an illusion you wanted to show me?'

'No. I came to erase it.'

'Of days gone by. Of longing and sadness.'

On my eyelids the movement of her fingers stopped.

I asked an unexpected question. 'When you let down your hair does it cover your shoulders?'

'It does. I wash it in hot water, but afterward – a special quirk of mine, maybe – I pour cold water over it. I like the feel of cold hair against my shoulders and arms, and against my breasts too.'

It would of course be the girl again. Her breasts had never

been touched by a man, and no doubt she would have had difficulty describing the feel of the cold, wet hair against them. Had the arm, separated from the body, been separated too from the shyness and the reserve?

Quietly I took in my left hand the gentle roundness at the shoulder, now my own. It seemed to me that I had in my hand the roundness, not yet large, of her breasts. The roundness of the shoulder became the soft roundness of breasts.

Her hand lay gently on my eyelids. The fingers and the hand clung softly and sank through, and the underside of the eyelids seemed to warm at the touch. The warmth sank into my eyes.

'The blood is going now,' I said quietly. 'It is going.'

It was not a cry of surprise as when I had noticed that my arm was changed for hers. There was no shuddering and no spasm, in the girl's arm or my shoulder. When had my blood begun to flow through the arm, her blood through me? When had the break at the shoulder disappeared? The clean blood of the girl was now, this very moment, flowing through me; but would there not be unpleasantness when the arm was returned to the girl, this dirty male blood flowing through it? What if it would not attach itself to her shoulder?

'No such betrayal,' I muttered.

'It will be all right,' whispered the arm.

There was no dramatic awareness that between the arm and my shoulder the blood came and went. My left hand, enfolding my right shoulder, and the shoulder itself, now mine, had a natural understanding of the fact. They had come to know it. The knowledge pulled them down into slumber.

I slept.

I floated on a great wave. It was the encompassing fog turned a faint purple, and there were pale green ripples at the spot where I floated on the great wave, and there alone. The dank solitude of my room was gone. My left hand seemed to rest lightly on the girl's right arm. It seemed that her fingers held magnolia stamens. I could not see them, but I could smell them. We had thrown them away – and when and how had she gathered them up again? The white petals, but a day old, had not yet fallen; why then the stamens? The automobile of the woman in vermilion slid by, drawing a great circle with me at the center. It seemed to watch over our sleep, the arm's and mine.

Our sleep was probably light, but I had never before known sleep so warm, so sweet. A restless sleeper, I had never before been blessed with the sleep of a child.

The long, narrow, delicate nail scratched gently at the palm of my hand, and the slight touch made my sleep deeper. I disappeared.

I awoke screaming. I almost fell out of bed, and staggered three or four steps.

I had awakened to the touch of something repulsive. It was my right arm.

Steadying myself, I looked down at the arm on the bed. I caught my breath, my heart raced, my whole body trembled. I saw the arm in one instant, and the next I had torn the

197

girl's from my shoulder and put back my own. The act was like murder upon a sudden, diabolic impulse.

I knelt by the bed, my chest against it, and rubbed at my insane heart with my restored hand. As the beating slowed down a sadness welled up from deeper than the deepest inside me.

'Where is her arm?' I raised my head.

It lay at the foot of the bed, flung palm up into the heap of the blanket. The outstretched fingers did not move. The arm was faintly white in the dim light.

Crying out in alarm I swept it up and held it tight to my chest. I embraced it as one would a small child from whom life was going. I brought the fingers to my lips. If the dew of woman would but come from between the long nails and the fingertips!

TANITH LEE

The Beautiful Biting Machine

When the two suns go down and it starts to get dark, the Nightfair wakes up, a beast with a thousand bright eyes.

Five miles long, four miles wide, the valley is full of lights, noises, musics, between the tall and echoing hills.

This world's a pleasure planet. It has many and various attractions. The Nightfair is only one. Here there are spinning wheels of yellow sparks against the dusk, and glimmering neon ghost towers ringing with screams, and carousels that maybe come alive. Not everyone cares for these, or the candy awnings, the peppermint arenas, the cries of fortune-tellers in glass cages, the crashing of pre-arranged safe vehicular accidents, the soaring space-flights that never leave the ground. Those that don't care for them don't come. But for those that do, there are the cuisine and superstition and popular art, the sex and syntax and the sin of twenty worlds, to be sampled for a night, or a week of nights. (Who could tolerate more?)

So visit the Valley of Lights. Hurry, hurry, don't be slow or sly or shy.

Welcome to the Nightfair.

'This gentlevyrainian's gotta slight complaint.'

'Tell him to see a doctor.'

'Don't cheek me, Beldek.'

'No, Mr Qire. What seems to be the trouble, sir?'

Beldek and Qire looked through the one-way window at the gentleman from Vyraini. Like all Vyrainians, he was humanoid, greenish, fretful. Vyraini did not esteem the human race, but was patronizingly intrigued by it and its culture. Anything human, where possible, should be experienced, explored. Now this Vyrainian had come to Qire's pavilion at the Nightfair, and was not quite satisfied, had a slight complaint.

'Go and talk to it – him,' said Qire.

'*Me*, sir?'

'You. You speak their lingo. You speak half the damn gurglings of half the damn galaxy, don't you, Beldek? You lazy son-of-a-ghex.'

'If you say so, Mr Qire.'

Beldek opened the long window and stepped through. The other side of the window it looked like a door, glamorous with enamel paint and stained glass. Beldek bowed to the gentlevyrainian with his hands to his face, which was the correct form of greeting from an outworlder. The Vyrainian stood impassive, ears folded.

'*Fo ogch m'mr bnn?*' Beldek inquired courteously.

The Vyrainian seemed gratified, lifted its ears and broke into staccato Vyrainese.

The glottal conversation continued for two and a half minutes. After which, feeling Qire's beady little eyes on him through the one-way door-window, Beldek leisurely set the computer for a twenty per cent refund.

The Vyrainian took its cash, and offered Beldek the salute used when bidding farewell to an inferior but valuable alien. Not all Earthmen knew exactly what the salute implied (a rough translation was: I will let you lick my feet another time, O wise one). Beldek, who did, smiled pleasantly.

The whaal-ivory screens of the outer doors closed on the Vyrainian's exit.

Beldek turned as Qire came storming from the inner office. Qire was a bulging, broad-faced type, the little eyes somewhat slanting, the mane of golden hair an implant. His clothes, though gaudy, were the best – real silk shirt, whaal-leather sandals. A ruby in his neckchain.

'Why d'yah do that?'

'What, Mr Qire, sir?'

'Refund the bastard his money.'

'Twenty per cent. The amount he agreed would compensate for the slight complaint.'

'What was wrong with her?'

Beldek said, ultra-apologetically, fawningly, 'A little something I told you about, that clicks—'

'Why the Garbundian Hell didn't you, for Christ's sake, get it fixed?'

'I have tried, Mr Qire,' said Beldek humbly. 'I truly have.'

201

Qire glowered.

'I should put you out on your butt. Why don't I?'

'I'm useful?' Beldek, attempting humbly to be helpful, now.

'Like urx-faron you are. All right. Give me the receipts. I'm going over to Next Valley. I'll be here again five-day week. Chakki'll be by in three days.'

Beldek keyed the computer for the cash receipts, tore them off when they came, and presented them to Qire. Qire riffled through them, glancing for mistakes. 'Okay, Beldek. I want to hear from Chakki that *she's* back in good order, you savvy?'

'Oh yes, Mr Qire, *sir*.'

Qire swore. At the whaal-ivory doors he turned for one last snarl.

'I've got other concerns on this planet, Beldek. If Malvanda packs up, it's no great loss to me. You're the one'll suffer. Back to hoofing the space-lanes with your card tricks and your dipscop seventh-rate jaar. You get me?'

'To the heart, sir,' said Beldek. 'And all the way up *yours*, Mr Qire.'

Qire cursed him and slammed out.

The doors, ever-serene, whispered shut in his wake.

Beldek leaned on the ornamental counter, keying the computer, which he had long ago rigged, to count the amount he had creamed off Qire's takings for the last five-day period. Qire, of course, guessed he did this. It was an inevitable perk of the job. All told, Qire seemed to value disliking

Beldek. Value the hypertensive rage that came to the boil whenever Beldek's cool clear eyes met his with such angelic sweetness above the long, smiling mouth that said: Yes, Mr Qire, *sir*. Most of the human portion of the Valley of Lights knew about Qire's hatred of his employee Beldek, the drifter from the space-lanes. Beldek who could speak half the languages of the galaxy, and could charm rain from a desert sky, if he wanted. Usually he didn't want. Beldek, whose un-implanted long thick lank brass-coloured hair hung on his shoulders and over his high wide forehead. Lean as a sculpture and tall, from birth on some unspecified lower-gravity world. Pale and pale-eyed. Something about him: more than the rumoured past, card-shark, kept creature of male, female, humanoid ... tales of a man murdered out among the stars ... More than the fact of working for Qire, in attendance on one of the weirdest novelties of the Nightfair. Be careful of Beldek.

The pavilion stood on a rise. A quarter of a mile below, a bowl of dizzy fires, the Arena of Arson, flashed and flared. Back a way, one of the great wheels whirled gold against the black sky. But the crimson pavilion was clouded round with Sirrian cedars. Far-off lamps winked on their branches; the apex of the pavilion, a diadem of rose-red glass lit subtly from within, just pierced, with a wicked symbolism of many carnal things, from the upper boughs. Once among the trees, the rest of the Fair seemed siphoned off. You came to the kiosk with the ivory doors. You went in, read something, signed something, paid something, and were let through another door, this one of black Sinoese lacquer. And then the Fair was very far away indeed. For then you were in the Mansion of Malvanda. And she was there with you . . .

A faint bell chimed on the console. Beldek killed the read-out and looked urbanely at the door-screens. Another customer.

The doors opened.

A new-worlder stepped through. He was alone. Most of them came alone, the same as most were men, or rather, most were male. A mixture of human and some genetically adhesive other-race, the new-worlder was fresh-skinned, grinning, handsome, and without whites to his eyes.

'Say,' he said.

'Good-evening, gentlenewman. You wish to visit Malvanda's Mansion?'

'Su-ure,' said the new-worlder.

'Take a seat, please.'

Grinning, the new-worlder rippled on to a couch. Double-jointed, too. That should offer Malvanda a challenge.

Beldek came around the counter and extended a small steel wafer.

'You understand, this entertainment being of the kind it is, you must first—'

'Sign a disclaimer? Yes, su-ure.' The new-worlder was already excited, a little drunk or otherwise stimulated. That had usually happened too, before they got themselves to these doors.

The newman accepted the wafer, which hummed, and spoke to him, telling him of possible dangers involved in what he was about to experience. As it droned on, the newman grinned and nodded, nodded and grinned, and sometimes his all-blue eyes went to Beldek, and he grinned wider, as if they were in a conspiracy. When the machine finished, the new-worlder was already up at the counter, his six fingers out for the disclaimer and stylus. He signed with a flourish. He paid the fee in one large bill, and shiftily counted his change from habit, not really concentrating.

'What now?'

'Now you meet the lady.'

'Say,' said the newman.

Beldek fed the disclaimer into the computer. The back of the kiosk murmured and rose, revealing the black lacquer door. The new-worlder tensed. There was sudden sweat on his face and he licked his lips. Then the door opened, inward.

Standing well-back by the counter, Beldek got a glimpse of sombre plush, sulky, wine-smoked light, the vague shimmer of draperies in a smooth wind scented with camellias and sorrow-flowers, the floral things of drugged funerals. He had seen the poisonously alluring aperture, that throbbing cornelian camellia vulva of doorway, many thousands of times. The new-worlder had not. Mindlessly, helplessly, he went forward, as if mesmerized, and poured over the threshold. A heavy curtain fell. The door swung shut. The ultimate orifice had closed upon him.

Beldek moved around behind the counter and touched

the voyeur-button. He watched for less than a minute, his face matt as fresh linen, ironed young and expressionless. Then he cut off the circuit.

Such a device, mostly unknown to clients, was necessary by law, which did not call it a voyeur-button. Persons who underwent such events as Malvanda had to be monitored and easy of access should an emergency occur. Twice, before Beldek joined the show, a client had died in there. Because the disclaimers were in order, and medical aid was rushed to the spot, Qire was covered and no action resulted. The newman, however, had registered healthy on the wafer. Beldek had told at a glance he was strong. There was no need to watch.

Qire sometimes came around just to do that. There was a more private extension of the voyeur-button in the cubicle off the inner office. Qire had not invented Malvanda's Mansion, only sponsored the design and then bought the product. But he liked it. He *liked* to watch. Sometimes, Qire brought a friend with him.

Beldek went into the inner office and dropped crystals in his ears which would play him an hour of wild thin music, a concerto for celestina and starsteel.

He did not need to watch Malvanda.

He knew what happened

When the hour was up, Beldek tidied the office, and reset the computer. The panels dimmed one by one as the lamps softened in the kiosk and the carnal peak on the roof went

206

out. The new-worlder was the last customer of the night. In thirty minutes, dawn would start to seep across the eastern hills.

As Beldek was revamping the computer program for tomorrow night, the black lacquer door shifted open behind him. He heard the newman emerge, stumbling a little on his double joints.

The hiccuping footsteps got all the way to the whaal-ivory doors before the voice said, 'Say.' The voice had changed. It was husky, demoralized. 'Say.'

Reluctantly, abrasively polite, Beldek turned. He levelled a wordless query at the sagging male by the kiosk doors. The newman's eyes were muddy, looking sightless. He seemed to go on trying to communicate.

'Yes, sir?'

'Nothing,' said the new-worlder. 'Just – nothing.' The doors opened and like a husk he almost blew into the diluting darkness, and away through the dregs and embers of the Fair.

Whatever else, the click in the mechanism obviously hadn't spoiled it for him at all.

By day, the Nightfair goes to ground. Some of the big architectures and marts sink down literally into the bedrock. Others close up like clams. Coming over the hills too early, you get a view of acres of bare earth, burned-looking, as if after some disaster. Here and there the robot cleaning-machines wander, in a snowstorm of rinds, wrappers, drugstick butts, lost tinsels. Places that stand, naked to the two eyes of heaven, the pair of dog-suns, have a look of peeled potatoes, indecent and vulnerable.

Awnings of durable wait like rags, dipped flags, for the glow and glitter of neon night.

The peoples of the Nightfair are wolves, foxes, coomors, they sleep by day in their burrows, or their nests up in the scaffolded phantom towers, among the peaceful wrecks of sky-buses, their wry lemon dreams filling the air with acids.

In the last of the afternoon there begins to be some movement, furtive, rats on a golden hill of rubbish littered with tin-can calliopes.

'Beldek, is that you, you ghexy guy?'

Qire's runner, Chakki, having used his key to the whaal-ivory doors, peered about the office.

'Who else did you hope to find?'

Beldek was tinkering with a small box of wires and three or four laser-battery tools. He did not turn round. Chakki now and then dropped by, never when expected, checking up for Mr Qire, or just nosing. Scrawny and pretty, Chakki was a being of instinct rather than thought or compunction, an alley cat that runs in, steals a chicken dinner, pees in a corner, and, soulless physical ghost, is gone.

'What ya doing, lovely Beldek?'

'Trying to repair a click.'

'My . . . Malvanda clicketh. Yeah, I heard aboul it. Better now?'

'We shall see.'

'You going in to give it her?'

Beldek walked past him towards the back wall of the kiosk which was going up to reveal the door of Sinoese lacquer.

'You lucky buck. Bet she bends ya.'

'So long, Chakki.'

The lacquer door started to open. Chakki stared tiptoe over Beldek's shoulder into camellia, cornelian, lilies-go-roses, funereal virgo unintacta.

'Let's have a piece, Bel?'

'If you can afford it. Come back tonight with the other clientele.'

'Go swiff yourself, Bell*rung*.'

The curtain fell. The door had closed.

Beyond the door, no matter the time of day or season, it was always midnight in Indian Summer.

Around the great oval room there were long windows that seemed to give on to a hot perfumed night mobile only with the choruses of crickets. There were lush gardens out there, under the multiplicity of stars, the best constellations of ten planets, and beyond the garden, hills, the backs of black lions lying down. Now and then a moth or two fluttered like bright flakes of tissue past the open glass. They never came in. It might distract the customer.

The roof apparently was also of glass, ribbed into vanes, like the ceiling of a conservatory. You saw the stars through it, and soon a huge white moon would come over, too big to be true.

There were carpets on the walls. Draperies hung down, plum velvets, transparencies with embroidery and sequins, dividing the room like segments of a dream. Everything bathed in the aromatic smoke of a church of incense candles. The other scent was flowers. They bloomed out of the bodies of marble animals grouped around little oases of water thick with sinuous snake-fish. Redblack flowers, albino flowers, flowers stained between red and white and black, grey flowers, fever and blush flowers, bushes of pale, sighing faints.

The marble stair went up to shadows, and reflected in the polished floor. If you looked in the floor at the reflection presently something moved, upside down, a figure in fluid. Then you looked up again at the stair. And saw Malvanda, out of the shadows, coming down.

Malvanda was tall and twenty-two years old, slim but not slender, her shoulders wide for elegance, her hips wide as if to balance panniers, her waist to be spanned by a man's hands, her breasts high and firm and full to fill them, spill them. Malvanda's skin was as white as the sorrow-flowers, with just that vague almost-colourless flush, at the temples, ear-lobes, hollow of the throat, insteps, wrists ... that the sorrow-flowers had at the edges of their petals. She was platinum blonde. Flaxen hair without a trace of gold or yellow, hair that is white, like moonlight blanching metal. Her eyebrows were just two shades darker, but her lashes were like tarnished brass and her eyes were like untarnished brass. Wolf-colour eyes, large; glowing now, fixed on him.

A small movement of her head shifted the coils of

platinum hair away over her shoulder. The column of her throat went down and down into the crimson dress. The V of the neckline ended just under her breasts. She smiled a little, just a very little. Her lips were a softer crimson than the gown. Rose mouth. She began to come towards him, and her hand stole from her side, moving out to him ahead of her, as if it couldn't wait to make contact.

Beldek walked up to her, and, as the smooth hand floated to his arm, he guided her fingers away. He ran his own hand in under the heavy silk hair to the base of her skull and touched.

Switched off, Malvanda stood quite still, her lips slightly parted, her eyes dreaming, brazen, swimming with late afternoon veldt.

Beldek ran his thumb around her throat and jabbed into the hollow. He pressed the second disc under her right ear, and the third under her left index fingernail, de-activating the safety. There had to be a suitably obtuse series of pressures, to avoid random de-activation by a client, when caressing her. Beldek knelt at Malvanda's feet. He raised the hem of her gown and drew one flawless foot on to his knee. He gripped under the instep, and drew out the power-booster from the panel.

Then he got up and went around, undoing the cling-zip on the back of her gown. The keyboard opened where her lower spine should be. He compared it to the box of wires he had brought in, then, selecting one of the fine plumbing needles, he began to work on her.

After four and a half minutes he found the fault that

might be responsible for the unfortunate *click* which had offended the aesthetic values of the Vyrainian. Two levers, the size of whiskers, had unaligned and were rubbing together. Looking through the magnifier, he eased them away and put in a drop of stabilizer. That area of the board could be overheating, so causing the levers' unwanted expansion together. He would need to check it again in a couple of days.

Having closed the panel and sealed her dress, he replaced the power-booster in her foot. The gauge in her board had showed nearly full, so it was time to empty the sac before reactivating.

Very gently, Beldek parted her beautiful carmine lips, and reached in, past the beautiful teeth, to the narrow tube of throat.

The sac was not too easy to come at, of course. When Qire took him on, the first two things he had wanted to see were Beldek's hands. Articulate and long-fingered, they had passed the test.

Beldek was halfway through disposing of the sac's contents when he heard a noise behind him.

The moon was coming up over the glass ceiling, augmenting the candle-and-lamplight. Not that he really needed it to see Chakki, transfixed there, against the curtain with his mouth open and his eyes bulging.

Before coming in, Beldek always cut off the voyeur-button, both on the console and in the office cubicle. At such times as this, the computer would only release the black lacquer door to Beldek. Somehow, Chakki had found a way either to fool the computer or to force the door.

'What the Garbundian Hop-Hell are you doing, Beldek?' said Chakki, all agog.

'Emptying the sac,' said Beldek. 'As you saw.'

'Yeah but—' Chakki burst into a wild laugh. 'Holla, man. You're kinkier than I ever thought.'

Chakki, unable to spy in the usual way, had obviously badly wanted to see Beldek in operation with Malvanda. Chakki had always, blatantly, imagined Beldek liked to get free what the patrons paid for. If he'd managed an entry one minute earlier, or one minute later, it need not have mattered.

'Kinkier than you thought? Of course I am, Chakki.' Beldek resettled the sac in Malvanda's mouth, and let it go down the throat, always an easier manoeuvre this, than retraction. He keyed on the relays. Malvanda did not move just yet. She took a moment to warm up after de-activation. 'I suppose I'll have to bribe you, now, Chakki. Won't I?'

Chakki giggled. He looked nervous. In a second he would start to back away.

'How about,' said Beldek, 'a free ride with Malvanda?' Then he sprinted, faster than any alley cat, straight through the candlelamp moonlight. He caught Chakki like a lover. 'How about that?' he asked, and Chakki shivered against him, scared now, but not quite able to make up his mind to run.

Beldek led him firmly, kindly stroking him a little, to the centre of the floor where Malvanda had been left standing.

As they got near, her eyelids flickered.

'She's something,' said Chakki. 'Maybe I could come round tonight.'

'Busy tonight. Do it now. You always wanted to. Have fun.'

Chakki's shiver grew up into a shudder, he glanced towards the curtained door. Then Malvanda woke up.

Beldek moved aside. Malvanda's hand went to Chakki's face, sensuous and sure.

She was taller than Qire's runner. Beldek's height. Her mouth parted naturally now, the wonderful strange smile, inviting, certain. Just showing the tips of the teeth.

This time, Beldek *would* watch.

Chakki wriggled, still afraid. But the drugs in the candles were affecting him by now, and the water-lily touches, on the neck, the chest, slipping, lingering. He put out one hand, careful, into her neckline, and found a breast. Half-frightened, aroused, wanting approval, he looked at Beldek. 'She feels *real*.'

'She's meant to, Chakki.'

'Hey, I never really saw what you—'

'That's okay, Chakki. Enjoy.'

Malvanda's strawberry tongue ran over Chakki's lips. Her left arm held him like a loved child, her right hand moved like a small trusting animal seeking shelter, and discovered it, there in Chakki's groin, and played and tickled, and burrowed, and coiled.

They were on the couch now. Chakki with his clothes off,

with handfuls of Malvanda's gown clenched in his fists, his nose between her breasts, was writhing and squeaking. Malvanda bent her head to do the thing they paid for, and the thing Chakki had not paid for. The true thrill, the perverse unique titillation that Malvanda offered. Her platinum hair fell over them, obscuring. But Beldek knew what went on under the wave of hair. Chakki was coming, noisily and completely, the way most of them did.

Beldek walked quickly across to the couch. He tapped Malvanda on the right shoulder, just once.

He had had the maintenance of her a long while. He had been able to innovate a little. A very little. Enough. Provision for a Chakki day.

Chakki was subsiding. Then struggling.

'Beldek,' he said, 'she's still – ah – Christ – Beldek!'

His arms flailed and his legs, as naked and puny, Chakki tried to push Malvanda away. But Malvanda was strong as only a machine could be. She held him down, pinned beneath her, her marmoreal body oblivious of the kicks and scratches that did not even mar its surface, as she went on doing what Beldek had just told her to go on doing.

Ignoring the screams, that gradually became more frenzied and more hopeless, Beldek walked out of Malvanda's Mansion.

The marks where the door had been forced were not bad but quite plain. A paint job would see to it. Chakki would have planned to do that before Qire got back. Now Qire would have to see them.

Beldek shut the door and Chakki's last wailing thinning shrieks were gone.

Just before suns' set, Beldek called Qire on the interphone. He broke the news mildly. Qire's runner had got through the Mansion door when Beldek was in the bathroom. Entering the Mansion to check Malvanda, Beldek found Chakki. He had died of haemorrhage, and shock, the way the two others had. There was, obviously, no disclaimer. What did Qire want him to do?'

He could hear the boss-man sweating all along the cable from Next Valley.

'You called anyone else, Beldek?'

'No.'

'The pol?'

'Not yet.'

He listened to Qire bubbling over, over there. The two prior deaths in Qire's pavilion made things awkward, despite all the cover on the world. This third death, minus cover, could look like shoddy goods. And Chakki was a private matter. Beldek had known what Qire would do.

'All right. Don't call 'em. You listening, Beldek?'

'Oh yes, Mr Qire. Most attentively.'

'Don't scad me, Beldek. I'm gonna give you a number. You call *that*. Someone'll come see to things. Okay?'

'Anything you say, Mr Qire.'

'And keep your mouth shut.'

'Yes, *sir*.'

Qire gave him the number and he used it. The voice at

the other end was mechanized. He said to it the brace of phrases Qire had briefed him with, and then there were noises, and the line went blind.

The suns were stubbed out and the wild flame wheels began to turn on the sky of Indian ink, and the coloured arsons shot across the arena bowl below, and the carousels practised their siren-songs and got them perfect.

Someone came and tried to breach the darkened pavilion.

Beldek went out and stood on the lawn.

Two Pheshines stared from their steamy eyes, lashing their tails in the grass.

'*Dena mi ess, condlu ess, sollu ess. Dibbit?*'

Beldek had told them, in Phesh, the show was closed. The gentlephesh did *dibbit*, and went off spitting to each other.

The nondescript carry-van drew up an hour later. Men walked into the kiosk and presently into the Mansion. They walked out with a big plastic bag and took it away.

Beldek had already cleaned up, before they came.

Not much later, Beldek lit the pavilion and opened for business, but no one else stopped by that night.

Beldek sat up in the tall echoing hills, watching the dawn borning and the Nightfair slink to ground.

Malvanda, had she been real, would not have been able to do this. Sunlight was anathema to Malvanda's kind. Sunlight and mirrors and garlic-flowers, and thorns, and crucifixes and holy wafers, and running water. It just went to show.

Beldek leaned back on the still-cool slate, looking down the four by five miles of the valley.

Gorgeous Malvanda, Terran turn-on, Phesh *tasha-mi*,
Venusian wet dream; Angel of Orgasm, kiss of death.
Malvanda, the Beautiful Biting Machine. Malvanda the robot
vampire.

He didn't know her whole history. How some sick-minded
talent had thought her up and put her together. Her place of
origin was a mystery. But what she did. He knew that. A
connoisseur's sexual desideratum. The actual bite was controlled to a hair's breadth by her keyboard. The teeth went
in, naturally. She sucked out blood. That's what they paid
for, was it not? Money's worth. Blood money. Only a little,
of course. More would be dangerous. And the teeth left
built-in coagulant behind them, zippering up the flesh all
nice. Unimpaired, the client staggers forth, only a bit
whoozy. A bite whoozy.

Some of them even came back, days, months, years later,
for another turn.

It was harmless, unless you were sick, had some
weakness . . .

Or unless Beldek tapped Malvanda's right shoulder that
particular way he had when she was with Chakki. Then
another key snapped down its command through her wires
and circuits. And Malvanda kept on biting, biting and
sucking, like a bloody vacuum cleaner. Till all the blood was
in Malvanda's throat sac and spilling over and on the floor
and everywhere. But Beldek had cleaned that away, and
bathed her, and changed her gown, before Qire's goonfriends
arrived with their big plastic bag.

It had been fairly uncomplex to tidy his mistake, this

time. But he must beware of mistakes from now on. Tomorrow, today, Beldek would work something out to make the Mansion door impregnable.

Even so, Beldek didn't really mind too much. It had been a bonus, all that blood. Better than just the contents of the sac, which Chakki had, unfortunately for Chakki, seen Beldek drinking earlier.

Beldek sunned himself on the hills for several hours. He never browned in sunshine, but he liked it, it was good for him. His hair, the tone of Malvanda's eyes, gleamed and began playfully to curl.

When he strolled back through the valley, the Fair was in its somnolent jackal-and-bone midday phase. Qire's buggy was at the entry to the pavilion. Qire was inside, in the Mansion, pawing Malvanda over, and the furnishings, making sure everything had been left as the customers would wish to find it.

Beldek followed him in.

'I should throw you out on your butt,' said Qire.

'Throw me,' said Beldek. 'I'll have some interesting stories to tell.'

Qire glared.

'Don't think you can make anything outa what happened. It was your, for Christ's sake, negligence.'

They both knew Qire would never fire him. Beldek was too handy at the job. And knew too much. And would be too difficult to dispose of.

Presently they went into the office and Qire handed Beldek a sheaf of large notes. 'Any noise,' said Qire, 'something

219

might happen you might not be happy about. And fix that damn door. *She* seems okay. She damaged at all?'

'No. Still what your pamphlets say. The Night-Blooming Bella Donna of Eternal Gothic Fantasy.'

When Qire had gone, Beldek listened to symphonies on music crystals in the office.

It had always rather fascinated him, the way in which vampires, a myth no one any longer believed, had become inextricably and dependently connected with sex. Actually, vampirism had nothing to do with sex. Beldek could have told them that. Just as it had nothing to do with sunlight or mirrors or crosses. It was simply and solely (though not sourly), about basic nourishment.

Later, he set the program for the night. He had a premonition there would be a lot of custom. Somehow, without anyone knowing about it in any logical way, some enticing whiff of velvet morbidity would be blowing around the pavilion luring them in like flies. The sac would have to be emptied many times tonight, in Beldek's own special way, which was not the way in which the instruction manual advocated.

Just before it got dark and he lit up the lights to match the exploding ignition of the Fair, Beldek looked in on Malvanda. She had been returned to her shadowy alcove above the marble stair, and was waiting there for the first client to come in and gaspingly watch her descend. Beldek climbed the steps and brushed her platinum hair, and refilled the perfumery glands behind her ears.

He cared nothing for the sentient races which were his

prey. But for the beautiful biting machine, he felt a certain malign affection. Why not? After a century or so of insecure, monotonous, and frequently inadequate hit-and-miss hunting, which left little space for other pursuits, the Nightfair had provided Beldek the softest option on twenty worlds. Now Malvanda saw to everything. She paid his bills. She kept him fed.

STEVEN BERKOFF

Gross Intrusion

'Gross Intrusion' is the term given by auto-engineers when a car penetrates another causing death or injury to the occupant of the weaker car, whose body structure may have caved in too easily due to lack of what is called 'Structural Integrity'.

The guy poured some olive oil out of a bottle on to the palm of his hand, set the bottle down with his free hand and rubbed the olive oil first into both palms then onto his prick ... then he casually, and not before checking the nail of his index finger plunged the same finger into H's ass ... took his finger out again as if satisfied with its location and pushed his prick in which entered slowly and gradually as the shocked sphincter was having to adjust its role from delivering to receiving. Slowly yielded the flesh and its co-ordinated network of fine muscles ... they relaxed between moments of revulsion when all the sphincter wanted to do was to purge itself of the monster that was threatening it (what kind of turd is this?) and harness its forces to an almighty gesture of expulsion when the hole would resemble the iris of a camera at its smallest aperture, but each time the sphincter relaxed itself for a further intake of power that might crush the invader the cunning prick would advance further into his fleshy ranks. It was painful now as it made its inexorable journey against the natural grain of his tunnel . . . it pushed, quelling any resistance, and each advance into his groin was followed by an almost involuntary withdrawal affording the active guy ecstasy since longitudinal rubbing and latitudinal squeezing is what petrassage is all about . . . the push in needs to be followed almost immediately by a slow coursing out, as if having prepared the way by its initial attack the prick too withdraws to rally its forces to return and joyfully confirm its victory, and so as not to lose ground the next movement in was even stronger in its thrusting power. For H, pain as it went in, and the incredible sensation as the prick withdrew, of shitting, plus the fear that he actually was and half expected a strong smell of shit to come floating up to his nostrils. H was not familiar with these sensations which are part of the ecstasy of the passive recipient; that sense of possessing a cunt in one's ass, a strong centre of feeling whose payoff on being buggered is a sensation of shitting (the two, somehow, ineluctably combined). H was not yet refined in this more arcane pleasure of lovemaking, and to this end his curiosity became a seductive devil that tempted him to the present experiment. But this curiosity was born less out of the passion of the explorer than out of an evil growth that fed itself in the dank fields of waste and boredom and the desire to flagellate his skin and spirit into some sense of being alive . . . and needed. This sense to be needed had perverted itself as it twisted away from its original course through lack of fulfilment, and careered blindly to another world . . . any world where he could be of use. Or used. In normal times he would distribute his golden load one way only, disturbing and caressing a whole battery of nerves that clicked on, as the sphincter, like a chief electric nodule sensitized the area; and the charting of a torpedo-like turd to the lower depths was subtly and satisfyingly felt, right to its last tapering tail which reluctantly leaves, vacating the area that stretched and contracted for its expulsion, and as soon as it hit water the great lower intestine or ass-hole was already mourning its loss. Its loss of nag in the bum by the tenant that satisfies too. The ass was a normally dormant theatre compared to the sheer activity of the crazy twitchings in the tubes of flesh hanging and lolling in the front. But certain and gradual reversals were taking place . . . the desire dormant for so long was beginning to stir as if awaking from a long sleep. H would vaguely try to cast it back to oblivion but it had incubated for too long and wanted out. Who or what planted the seed one cannot here go into . . . suffice to say that it existed. H remembered those heaving and hot summer shits in the fields feeling the motions of almost burningly large turds coursing out of his system in the shape of men's pricks, so huge at times, even the size of pricks. Did that one come out of my tight little rosebud? H would simper to himself, occasionally delighting his skull's porn-box by gently inserting his little finger up his ass and feeling with wonder at how tightly even his little finger would be gripped, and thrillingly and frighteningly would conjecture how on earth the hard, large cocks of men would or could penetrate him. So, he would sit in the fields distantly gazing at the horizon with misty and soft-focused eyes, dim for pleasure . . . the pleasure of feeling so much in his hole. This new or gradually awaking discovery of an unexplored planet of delights within his being led him to fantasize about being taken unaware as he sat there with naked loins, by an irate farm labourer and his mate who would be so incensed at the sight of H's naked joints that they would rudely throw him to the ground and slide their pricks up his still moist ass. In these moments H felt indeed like a quivering virgin. Now was reality . . . now was the pain . . . the guy was holding on to his prey like a terrier holds a rat, pushing deeper and deeper . . . so deep it must be wounding me, H thought . . . but he mustn't complain or shout out . . . that would seem so silly. The man supported H under his belly pulling him up to encourage him onto his knees and almost making H impale himself on the stranger's weapon . . . odd words came out from the man between quick hard breaths . . . *'Hurt? You OK. . . . Enjoying yourself cocksucker? . . . Wan' it deeper? . . . I'll fuck your head off!'* . . . as passion grew inflamed, the stranger's text became more ribald and even ridiculous . . . *'I'll kill you when I come you mother-fucker! . . . I'll eat you up you bastard!'* . . . mixed with a reasonable variety of *'Ooohs'* and *'Heyssss'* and *'Haaaaaas'* . . . *'Honey, Oh honey you make me feel so good!!!'* . . . H said nothing but allowed it all, or rather submitted to it . . . feelings now spent if they were ever there to spend . . . sex sucked out of his being the way a raging fire sucks the oxygen out of a room . . . as if sex had never existed except in his mind . . . or in the fields with his little finger probing the little mouse of sensuality that had errantly taken lodging there . . . or in the swollen bulges of men, in their nude swarthy flesh stiffening in the illicit camouflaging steam of Turkish baths; the haven of all the third sex. Now it was pain . . . and yes, even now the acrid smell of shit came winging up as he crouched, beasted by a stranger now who fell for his erecting penis, fantasy-fed in the urinals of a favoured gay toilet and followed H, whose bait had hooked a monster that would not be easily assuaged by the little mouse. He followed, no words exchanged, just Harry's thumping heart led the way (the throb of fear not joy) to his room. And H sacrificed himself to the idea that at some point ecstasy would return and trade itself with this ridiculous fear . . . and that as the stranger undid his flies and fire started to ignite his loins, it would continue and not abate . . . but the size of him! . . . it was a threat . . . it was violent and would hurt . . . H felt an unworthy combatant . . . felt small and puny. The man was black and yes it was true . . . it was no myth, since this one was indeed set like a donkey . . . they do have vast quantities of cock . . . and the small flame that lit a candle for H shrank away as the guy, without asking, took some oil off the shelf in the bathroom and poured it onto his hands like a gladiator oiling himself for the battle to the death . . . or as if a complex operation was about to take place. He was priming his cock with a large palmful of oil, too much, but of course with that weapon how necessary! The black knew that his shaft needed bountiful lubrication and whereas a normal, hard and shrewd queen would have told him with no qualms where to get off in an act of self-preservation – what good is a stretched out queen? – Harry could not. Harry was still shy in his exploration into the realm of his sexual indentity. The black had said nothing but sensed his alarm and his fear . . . was even used to guys freaking out over his tool and even turning on him, and he usually in those cases ended up with a blow-job or a friendly wank. He didn't mind which really, as long as he released a binful of spunk with a whitey . . . as long as he could be free in his body, and he sensed in Harry a victim but read masochism in Harry's weakness where he could have read simply fear . . . the black was experienced and gave value to what he read in men's faces when their voices were too shy to betray their deepest longings . . . in this case he was unaware that he was torturing H. How often do you come across a gay in his thirties who is still a virgin? As sex had removed itself from H it left a dry room where nothing could grow (the black senses the cold dry room deep within H and has no desire to enter that particular abode). H's sexual barometer remained flaccid . . . and as the black squeezed and pummelled H's hanging appendage of skin, the emptiness of which drove the master even further into his quest for pain, he seemed determined to split poor H's intestines as an axe splits oak. How dare whitey not be 'hard on' with my beautiful black prick up his ass and halfway up his stomach, his renewed vigour seemed to imply . . . but H's hips ceased to move and just presented themselves to the black like some meagre sacrificial offering from a poor pagan to a demon deity, as if to say that's all we have . . . it's not much, but it's living. '*Move, fuck you!! . . . move onto my prick!!*' He seemed to shriek at H's dumb, prostrate white buttocks going gradually red with impatient kneading . . . Harry wobbled uneasily on his knees and wanted to collapse onto his stomach, but the black, incensed now with the strength that lust loans to muscles (no matter how tired) to complete the act, held H up like a bag of flesh and bones with his right arm and pulled him onto the hilt where seemingly it could go no further . . . the black lifted his head and bared his teeth like a donkey about to bray, arched his back . . . said . . . 'OH FUCK FUCK FUCK OOOH SHIT YOU FUCKER (what pain) OOH FUUUCK YOU MOTHER YOU MOTHER FUCKING COCKSUCKER . . . I'LL EAT YOU OOH MMMYY . . . LICK MY SPUNK . . . EAT MY SHIT OOOH OOOH NOOO WOW WOW WOWEE OH FUCK OH!! HONEY! NICE NICE HONEY? CHRIST-OFUCK!' The black shuddered then fell down like a shot bull . . . panting over H's back . . . the weight of him collapsing finally H's precarious position . . . dead feelings crept into the proceedings . . . the world seemed to go very still and shadows would flit in and out of H's eyes as if bats or even vultures were in the room . . . waiting . . . numbness . . . did not even feel the shrinking of the black's penis as its spent swill having whooshed into H was now returning to the folds of peace . . . a death smell lingered, cold and dank around the prostrate limbs of the victim which seemed to impersonate the spread-eagled and twisted corpses of Auschwitz . . . sleep: H wanted sleep or to wrench himself free to throw himself out of the window . . . but most of all, what the sane part of his mind wanted, wanted more than anything else in the entire earth, was to cradle in his arms a soft gentle woman, a soft gentle and unfearful thing that had no pain . . . no threat . . . no hard muscle or rough bristle . . . no vile hot stabbing greed investing him with agony . . . no scummy dirt or breath-stink-shit-sour. Soft . . . soft . . . soft . . . the word comforted; talcum-powdered and tinkling voices . . . soft faces . . . soft cheeks . . . soft bosoms and ribbons . . . innocent vulnerable thighs and always soft, soft, soft downy brown . . . his ass felt cold and wet and even torn, as the organic compost of shit, sperm and blood dripped its unsightly mixture onto the sheets . . . He was sick and weak and was sure some time had passed; feeling a heavy weight on him, the sleeping black. So H had drifted off . . . had drifted off into a dream world peopled with the soft bodies, the sweet smelling bodies of women and woke to the shocking realization of what the dead weight pinning him down was . . . and with it came the burning, like corrosive acid, from his anus and the awful memory of the *thing* that felt as if still there, still undulating and thrusting and the black screaming invectives, the chorus for his excited secretions. Harry barely turned his head but could just see out of the corner of his eye a large red patch near his hips . . . his or mine? But more than likely mine. He was circumcized and less likely to tear than a man who hadn't been. H felt sick and tearful and wanted the black growth like a burden from hell off of his back and out . . . out for

229

ever ... but H could only mutter ... 'Please ... Please ...
would you get off me please ... please ... off me please ...
do you hear?' *'Hello sweetheart ... who's had a nappy then
... Hey! I must have had a shut eye ... Ha! Ha! Ha! nice one
though, eh! Nice!'* As if the thought had encouraged him and
the ghastly sleep refreshed him, H to his horror felt the
man's slimy, sticky penis reswelling itself for the act. No,
the black couldn't resume at this stage, must see how injured
one of them was. 'No ... get off ... please, I'm ill.' But if
fates worse than death had existed in H's imagination this
must answer for the supreme ... once again he penetrated
... H attempted to twist away, though still on his belly, not
on his knees ... *'Hold still cunt or I give it you!'* ... he took
Harry's throat in his hands and gave a vicious but quick
squeeze, as if to say how simple it would be for my powerful
hands to snap this scrawny neck and how I hate your
scrawny neck and what it's attached to but you must be
obedient until I have had my fill ... H passed out for a
second but had no doubt and read well messages of violence!
They need no analysis and are not famous for innuendo.
With his hands still holding onto his throat the black moved,
gyrating like a dancer into the wound of the world ...
Harry's poor torn sphincter ... he moved like he had all the
time he needed and could indulge and savour as a gourmet
whose first fierce hunger having been appeased, is able to
relax and enjoy rather than satisfy ... 'please, please don't'
... a pathetic whine gurgled from his bloody mouth ...
wherefore doth blood come into his mouth!!! Did he bite
his tongue or did his heart burst!! The black heaved with a

230

more spikey vigour ... *'On your knees ... Oh come on turd ... I'm nearly there ... Shit I nearly ... Nearly ... Come on ... I can't like this ... On your knees you fucker ... Come on mother ... Thaaats better ... Heeeeah ... Oh wow ... Hey thats wuuunderful ... Oh ... Oh ... Ohh!!!!! Ow Woow!'* The negro still held Harry by the throat and H was impaled to the hilt ... he was thrusting hard now and arched his back once more and as his moment of triumph came, bared his teeth, as if to holler it to the whole world ... did not of course see the blood seeping out of Harry's mouth nor feel the slackness when death calmly extinguishes the lights of a body ... OOW ... OW ... OW ... OW ... OW ... OW ... OW ... OW ... OH YEAH!!!!! YEAH!!!! OOOOO-OOOOH!

LUCY ELLMANN

Love: The World's Oldest Profession

. . . loveable, desirable, likeable, congenial, after one's heart, winsome, amiable, sweet, angelic, divine, adorable, beautiful, intriguing, seductive, appealing, prepossessing, cuddly . . .

Christ! Give me a break, muttered Maisy in exasperation. She reached for her note-pad and crossed off 'Reading the Thesaurus' from her list of Things To Do In London For Free. She was preparing a shortish book on the subject, getting ever shorter. All her pleasures seemed to be transitory or increasingly expensive, and her free-thinking was becoming distinctly uninspired. She suggested, for instance, that you could go to the Barbican and various other theatres and watch the play on the latecomers' TV set. You could sit around hospital waiting-rooms and see injured people. You could go on long walks with eyes to the ground in search of pound coins, buttons and the occasional aubergine. You could count the number of playgrounds that have turned into carparks during Thatcher's rule. To alleviate loneliness, you could phone Free-Phone numbers or pretend to be a house-buyer or lie around reading the thesaurus, but that was now ruled out.

Frank woke early, as usual of late. The sun was just peeping under the blind, giving a weird glow to the vase of dried flowers that adorned his windowsill. He tiptoed round to Annabelle's side of the bed, trying not to disturb her as he collected his clothes. A light sleeper, Annabelle was now lightly sleeping off back pain, mild conjunctivitis and menstrual trouble, either pre or post or concurrent – he wasn't sure what stage they were at with it. Annabelle had amassed a number of physical ailments that made her life of leisure, security and solitary confinement a cause for concern and frequent, if inexpert, back rubs administered by Frank.

Strange, this early morning race for the train and traipse across London for rough sex with Maisy, followed by the torment of her nosing around in his balls while he tried to rid himself of raunchy smells with the soap and shampoo they'd romantically bought together in obscene but perfect imitation of the brands he used at home. And other suchlike sensual experiences.

But Maisy was irresistible. A woman without back trouble, who admired his gentles as she called them. He couldn't remember when Annabelle had last found him acceptable in any way. His body was too hairy, his penis too big, his hand wobbled when pouring wine, TV documentaries put him to sleep and he had an inaccurate understanding of the right night to put out the rubbish.

His mother had liked him. He'd been the one exception to her belief that men were not to be trusted (his father had once had a brief affair and had spent all his time growing turnips ever since). She'd fed Frank sardine sarnies as a sign of their confederacy, while he leant back against the kitchen cupboards in his customary pose – one ungainly knee thrust forward and the foot somewhere underneath propping him up – relating the events, sorry though they might be, of his schooldays.

From the bedroom Annabelle listened to Frank moving about the house, collecting his briefcase and the lunch money she'd carefully allocated from the Food Expenses Jar the night before. She didn't move for fear the bed might creak and she would be called upon to make early morning chit-chat. Obscuring herself under the covers, she clung to vestiges of oblivion, the unadult world of blankets and half-light in which mussed hair and bad breath and the sad intimacy of the warmed bed could not yet trouble her. She needed to collect herself at a dignified pace, feeling dishevelled by her dreams. In one, tube train doors had opened to emit a surge of giant Heinz spaghetti. After which, she had ridden up a number of escalators in search, apparently, of chamois leather camiknickers.

When she heard the quiet implosion of the front door shutting behind Frank, Annabelle lugged her body to the bathroom where she began to engage in the power and glory of existence by dealing with excreta and a pain in her lower spine. She rose as quickly as possible from the loo and went downstairs to drink herbal tea and to hoover. The house was in perfect shape.

Annabelle then wandered around desultorily dusting. She was compiling a compendium of compassion for suffering throughout the world. It was her Christian faith, she felt, that led her to take a particular interest in such matters. There was no limit to her indignation, outrage and despair on behalf of the meek, the poor and the ugly. The radio gently fed her capacious sensibility.

A call-in programme had just begun on the question of women priests, yes or no. A woman phoned to say that God had created Man and Woman in His Own Image. She repeated this a number of times, but the studio guest was unimpressed. The role of priest, he said, was based on that of the twelve apostles, and they had all been male. Genesis was passé.

It didn't take him long to convince Annabelle. The female body was too heathen, too prone to mess, to be a messenger of God. Into her mind came images of white-robed choristers spattered with menstrual blood, Carefree panty-pads let loose amongst the Communion wafers, and the church lit by Tampax candles.

Annabelle proceeded to the loo again to check that she herself wasn't leaking any unseemly substances at the moment, and found that she wasn't. She then lay down on the pristine-clean, still-wrapped-in-polythene sofa-bed they'd bought for the front room, where she could watch TV in relative calm while awaiting 10.30, the time when she always called Frank at the office.

Why were sheets and blankets and pillows and pillowcases and mattresses suspended somewhere above the floor so common worldwide as a means of sleeping? mused Maisy (forgetting all about Japanese bedtime arrangements). Rather whimsically, she added 'Musing' to her list of urban freedoms. Eventually she would assemble them all according to the mood one might wish to accommodate or generate: what to do on a good/bad/indifferent day.

Maisy's own day was improving. Frank had a meeting in the afternoon so she was planning to skive off to a film with Tim, who still pined for her. The trouble, she found, with married men is all the gaps they leave in your life. She was counter-attacking by creating, and filling, free time where there wasn't supposed to be any.

When the phone rang, Maisy put it through with her customary efficiency, using an American drawl. 'Fra-ank, Hollywood calling. Your chance to break into the movies!'

It was of course Annabelle. Frank thought Maisy was admirably patient about Annabelle's daily interruptions of their smooth-running office life. This time Annabelle wanted him to buy soured cream and pork chops at Sainsbury's on his way home. She'd seen a recipe whereby you fry the pork chops, flambé them in brandy and then plop a spoonful of soured cream on each one and simmer a few more minutes.

Frank wished Annabelle didn't read so many women's magazines – all about how, if you slop this on your face or hair or pork chops, exercise those abdominal muscles, keep abreast of cultural events in which you have no intention of participating, and get your perverser impulses under control by reading some romantic fiction, your Partner has got to Love you more.

Then there was Maisy, so pleasingly indifferent to pleasing anyone but herself. She didn't even shave her legs. She'd achieved a quality of autonomy that made him want to spend the whole day in her arms.

Of course, she was a bit cynical. Within days of arriving at his office she had filled Frank in on many of the astounding inadequacies of the dozens of men to whom she had at some point given the benefit of the doubt. Frank had felt no inclination at all to join this discredited crowd. Not only fearful of competition, he didn't even fancy Maisy at first. She was too tall, too stocky, too loud-mouthed and uncouth. He'd never before heard a woman talk so unguard-edly, so unendingly and so off-puttingly about sex.

So it had been something of a revelation when she waylaid him at the annual booze-up and fucked him and sucked him as if he were a frog who'd just turned into a prince and was long overdue for a good time. He'd never been quite sure his existence was one of his unhappy parents' happiest acci-dents. But now he walked tall in the knowledge that whatever antipathy Annabelle had felt for him since they'd met as virgin undergraduates, he was in fact, according to Maisy, a godsend to womankind.

Frank forgot all about the pork chops.

At the pub at lunchtime, he paid for their drinks with the Maisy Fund, a clandestine accumulation of lunch money from Annabelle that he'd managed to piece together over the months – it wasn't fair to expect Maisy to pay all the time. She had enough to put up with already. Maisy was presently going on and on about free things to do in London, a subject of conversation surely geared to elicit sympathy for her poverty. But if she was so poor, how was she able to afford those new boots? Frank had to admit he was a little afraid of Maisy's new stiletto-heeled cowboy boots. It wasn't their pointedness that depressed him, but their cocksure air. For some reason they made him uncomfortably aware of her other lovers, the ones she saw in the evenings. In restaurants. In pubs. In clubs. IN SOHO. His only consolation was: those guys had to endure the boots too.

Annabelle made herself a toasted cheese sandwich with their sandwich maker, and served it up on an old blue paper plate. She didn't feel she deserved a brand-new one, much less a plate made from some more durable substance. Through little acts of self-denial followed by self-pity, Annabelle got through her days.

After lunch, her eye caught a magazine which said that there were approximately 5,000 million people in the world. The thought that over half of these must be *women* made Annabelle feel faint. She took to her bed for most of the afternoon.

*

Maisy lay on her front with legs apart on Tim's posh carpet, enjoying its thick white springiness beneath her. She was reading old Sunday papers and feeling seriously annoyed with Frank, who'd confessed at lunchtime that he was still reluctantly carrying on his monthly endeavours to impregnate his infantile and self-indulgent wife.

'She probably doesn't even buy coloured toilet paper,' Maisy mumbled to herself. 'Trying to save the whale all day or something.' Maisy had lately taken against ecology.

On and on Frank had gone about how much Annabelle needed him, how she wasn't strong like Maisy. Maisy was familiar with this notion that mistresses are automatically strong and never needy. What Frank didn't seem to realize was that what most women NEED is two men per day, and two new ones the next.

Maisy felt a sudden wave of despondency at the prospect of going home to her monastically empty bed, preserved these days for her initiate, Frank. I'll never find a man who can give me enough. They like depriving us, she summarized, and reached for the magazine section.

Tim came into the room and said she looked like she was making snow fairies. He explained the child's game of lying in the snow and waving one's arms and legs about in order to make indentations like the wings and gown of a fairy. In fact, he lay on top of her to show her how.

A Sunday. Frank is doing the ironing as Annabelle, who usually does it, has morning sickness and pain in her knees. Frank is feeling overwhelmed. The loneliness of weekends, stuck in the outskirts of London performing rituals of various kinds which he once fully endorsed. The shopping and gardening and home-making, the bickering and punitive sulking, the massages and embarrassments and silences and indignity of lovelessness that seem to stretch into eternity as he waits anxiously for his release on Monday morning: Married Life.

As for the baby-making, Frank has for some time been treasuring the realization that he no longer fancies Annabelle. So small and pretty and unattainable, her sexual unwillingness had formerly given structure to his life. He can still remember the poignancy of those rare encounters when his desires and her surrender briefly united in a shared shame. Her endurance of the pain of it for his sake: the only moments of certainty that she cared. He'd grown accustomed to the cycle of forgiveness, which took for ever, and reward, which could be momentary. Annabelle had eroticized her own sullenness for him.

But since Maisy enlightened him as to his own considerable charms, Annabelle's spell has been broken. It was only at Annabelle's insistence (she wanted a child) that their sex life has continued at all. And has now borne fruit.

Feeling increasingly alienated toward the house and its contents, toward Annabelle and her contents, Frank burns a shirt.

Annabelle, gloomy, made her way to a hospital where she was booked to see a skin specialist. There was a mole on her head that Frank had commented on once in a tone of

240

distaste. She wanted to please him. She was willing to risk a local anaesthetic and minor surgery to please him. There was a row of six medical students in the consulting room, being steered towards omnipotence by a doctor who never looked up from his desk. Annabelle's heart sank. She had hoped for an anonymous meeting, with a minimum of interrogation and deliberation – not all these youngsters tentatively rubbing her nodule, her excrescence, her embossed carbuncle, her deformity, and wondering how a pregnant woman could be so vain. The doctor kept referring to it ominously as a lump, and the students couldn't decide whether it was part of her dermis or her epidermis. They were still puzzling over it when she was dismissed from the room. Epidermis or otherwise, she would never know.

Annabelle's nodule was removed in a comparatively private ceremony. She bought a woolly hat afterwards on her way to Frank's office, to cover the unsightly spot where the unsightly lump had been (a tuft of royal blue stitches encrusted with blood had taken its place).

It wasn't pleasant for Frank when Annabelle, still jittery from surgery, turned up at his office a little later. Annabelle didn't immediately seem to understand why Frank's secretary was leaning over his desk with her hand inside his belt and her mouth on his mouth. Maisy, unruffled, turned to Annabelle and said, 'Loosen up, babe. Breathe some air now and then – there's plenty to go round.'

'I just came to tell Frank I got the mole cut off my head he didn't like,' Annabelle replied.

'Frank,' said Maisy. 'Am I to take it that this hatted figure with an evident bun in the oven is your WIFE?'

It seemed to Frank in the days that followed that his delicacy and discretion toward both ladies had badly misfired. They began to complain, at their different times of the day, about his lack of Frankness. In desperation he renewed his pledges to both parties, assuring Annabelle that he would sack Maisy, have nothing more to do with her, not even by telephone, and that he would try to prove to Annabelle his loyalty and devotion in the physically and emotionally arduous days to come; and telling Maisy that he had to see Annabelle through the pregnancy and stay with her for three months afterwards in order to avert post-natal depression, but after that he would move in with Maisykins, pretty please, and get a divorce.

From now on the two women took Frank with a pinch of salt: Annabelle made him do the hoovering before he left for work and Maisy objected to the name 'Maisykins'.

The Marriage Guidance Counsellor, for whom Frank's parents were paying, shook Annabelle's hand with a grip capable of fracturing bones. Trying to prove he was confident about something or other, she supposed. Which was more than she felt, what with all the energy sucked out of her by the fluttering foetus and the philandering fandangoing fellatio-prone (for all she knew) Frank.

She was getting a lot of sympathy these days, but underneath it all she felt blamed for everything. Frank's waywardness, as well as his previous uxoriousness, Frank's father's waywardness thirty years before, their ten years of childlessness and their present fecundity, Frank's discontent, Annabelle's discontent, her suicidal tendencies and frigidity – it was all her fault.

What wasn't?, she wondered. Hurricanes in Eastern Japan perhaps? *Coups d'état* in the Maldive Islands? Great mishaps of the world were suddenly a comfort. While Frank droned on beside her with illustrations of his own blamelessness, Annabelle thought with satisfaction of the negligible chance that she had played any part in the deaths of 56,000 men in an hour during the First World War, or had in any way encouraged the bee disease spreading across Europe or the incidence of AIDS amongst New York heterosexual women. But then it occurred to her that Frank had probably contracted AIDS and given it to her, and she would no doubt be blamed for passing it on to their unborn child.

'You seem, Annabelle, to have a very irregular sleeping pattern,' suggested the counsellor, with an uncalled-for amount of eyebrow movement. Frank too looked at her piercingly, as if her difficulties with sleep, which he had just been describing to the counsellor, might indeed be the root of all their problems.

'I think I sleep as well as most women who've just found out their husband's screwing his secretary,' said Annabelle, and two tears dripped simultaneously down her cheeks.

The counsellor, having previously considered Annabelle radiant, now began to find her repellent. Obviously a selfpitier who hid from marital responsibilities behind moral righteousness and ill-health. This mother-to-be had to grow up.

It was a difficult birth. Despite every available drug being administered, it was clear that the frail and spiritual Annabelle was not well-designed to bear a baby engendered by Frank. It was nobody's fault – God had made her pelvis too small. She called for forceps, a Caesarian, any unnatural method of birth she could think of. The midwife kept checking Annabelle's genitals and making philosophical remarks about Mother Nature.

'FUCK mother-fucking Nature!' spat Annabelle at the height of her agony.

A little shocked, Frank wiped her forehead with a sweaty cloth and reflected spitefully that Annabelle seemed to find giving birth about as enjoyable as conception, before the bleating bloody baby was suddenly thrust into his stiff grasp.

It was a moving, tender moment.

When Frank left her for Maisy a few weeks after Isabel's birth, Annabelle wrote him pathetic, pleading letters which he wept over and hid at the office. Leaving the baby to cry in her cot, Annabelle wrote about all the wonderful times they'd had together at university and the Christian Summer Camp and their honeymoon in Malta where she'd refused to swim at the Blue Grotto but did get lasciviously drunk once. She told him how the roses and turnips were doing, and that if he came home now she would forgive him. She

244

reminded him of how well, how patiently and uncomplain-ingly, how *nobly* she had ironed his shirts. 'Does this woman iron them or what? You see, I worry about you,' she scrawled. She told him how lovely the wailing baby looked in pink. Annabelle had never been so communicative, so loving, in the whole of their life together.

His parents wrote to him too, saying that they would never speak to him again. But he now felt committed to Maisy. They'd finally mentioned Love to each other. He was the Man for her, she the Woman for him.

Maisy and Frank drove down to his house on the fringes of Essex one night when he knew Annabelle and the baby would be out. Frank thought this would be the most diplomatic time to rescue some of his belongings since Annabelle tended to weep all through his visits to Isabel – searching for his camera and climbing boots had therefore proved tricky.

Appalled by the semi-detached brick number from which her otherwise well-endowed lover had emanated, Maisy sat uncomfortably in the car. A goofy rose-bush grew from a grassless circle in the middle of the patioed front garden. Where the vegetables could be she had no idea. As Frank scoured the house, one room lit up after another, revealing a tiny bunch of dried flowers in every window.

Maisy wasn't convinced by this cohabitation lark. As the poor fellow didn't know how to live alone, she said she'd give it a try. But she didn't like all the housework. Frank squeamishly removed her dirty knickers from every corner and crevice, and did the washing-up at all hours. The question of Supper had taken on a newfound significance. And now he wanted to regulate all this with a rota system. She could see he was just aching to dust her collection of peacock feathers.

He was around a lot more, but spent most of the time talking about Annabelle and how much alimony he ought to give her (about 90 per cent of his income, as far as Maisy could work out). She liked him best, as before, in the early morning – although he still hadn't quite mastered the mature ejaculation.

Maisy took to going out at night on her own to the Kitsch & Chintz Club, where she danced with Tim for whom she still pined. On her return, the domesticated Frank would be fast asleep. Maisy masturbated noisily beside him, another free thing to do in London.

BRIAN STABLEFORD

A Career in Sexual Chemistry

There are some names which are more difficult to wear than others. Shufflebottoms, Bastards and Pricks start life with a handicap from which they may never recover, and one can easily understand why those born into families which have innocently borne since time immemorial such surnames as Hitler and Quisling often surrender such birthrights in favour of Smith or Villanova. People who refuse to change embarrassing names are frequently forced into an attitude of defensive stubbornness, brazenly and pridefully staring out the mockery of the world. For some people, an unfortunate surname can be a challenge as well as a curse, and life for them becomes a field of conflict in which heroism requires them to acquit themselves well.

One might be forgiven for thinking that Casanova is a less problematic name than many. It is by no means vulgar and has not the slightest genocidal connotation. It is a name that some men would be glad to have, conferring upon them as it would a mystique which they might wittily exploit. It is nevertheless a label which might be parent to a host of embarrassments and miseries, especially if worn by a gawky schoolboy in an English inner-city comprehensive school, which was where the Giovanni Casanova who had been born on 14 February 1982 first became fully aware of its burdensome nature.

Giovanni's father, Marcantonio Casanova, had always been fond of the name, and seemed well enough equipped by fate to wear it well. He was not a tall man, but he had a handsome face and dark, flashing eyes which were definitely no handicap in the heart-melting stakes. He had made no serious attempt to live up to the name, though, accepting it as a nice joke that he found contentment in placid monogamy. His grandparents had come to Britain in the 1930s, refugees from Mussolini's Italy, and had settled in Manchester at the height of the Depression. Marcantonio therefore came from a line of impoverished intellectuals who had been prevented by social circumstance from achieving their real potential.

Giovanni's mother had also had no opportunity to fulfil her intellectual potential. Her maiden name was Jenny Spencer, and she had been born into that kind of respectable working-class family which would make every effort to set its sons on the road of upward social mobility, but thought that the acme of achievement for a daughter was to be an apprentice hairdresser at sixteen, a wife at seventeen and a mother at eighteen. All of these expectations Jenny had fulfilled with casual ease.

The whims of genetic and environmental fortune combined to give these humble parents a uniquely gifted son, for Giovanni soon showed evidence of a marvellous intelligence beyond even the latent potentialities of his parents. Nature's generosity was, however, restricted entirely to qualities of mind; in terms of looks and physique Giovanni was a non-starter. He was undersized, out of proportion, and had an awful complexion. A bout of measles in infancy added insult to injury by leaving his eyesight terribly impaired; astigmatism and chronic myopia combined to force him to wear spectacles which robbed his dark eyes of any opportunity they ever had to flash heart-meltingly, and made him look rather cross-eyed. His voice was high-pitched, and never broke properly when he belatedly reached puberty. His hair insisted on growing into an appalling black tangle, and he began to go thin on top when he was barely seventeen. As dozens of thoughtless people were to remark to his face, and thousands more were to think silently to themselves, he certainly didn't *look* like a Casanova.

The class culture of England had proved remarkably resilient in the face of the erodent egalitarianism of the twentieth century, and bourgeois morality never did filter down to the poorer streets of Northern England, even when the old slums were demolished and new ones erected with indoor toilets and inbuilt social alienation. Where Giovanni spent his formative years very few girls preserved their virginity past the age of fourteen, and many a boy without a CSE to his name had done sufficient research to write a Ph.D. thesis on sexual technique by the time he was old enough to vote. This tide of covert sexual activity, however, passed Giovanni Casanova by. He was acutely conscious of the flood of eroticism which seethed all around him, and wished devoutly to be carried away by it, but to no avail.

Other ugly boys, who seemed to him as unprepossessing as himself, managed one by one to leap the first and most difficult hurdle, and subsequently gained marvellously in confidence and expertise, but Giovanni could not emulate them. His unattractiveness made things difficult, and his name added just sufficiently to his difficulties to make his task impossible, because it made even the girls who might have felt sorry for him laugh at him instead. Even the most feeble-minded of teenage girls could appreciate that there was something essentially rib-tickling about saying 'no' to a Casanova.

Giovanni had started out on his journey through adolescence bogged down by self-consciousness, and by the time he was seventeen he was filled with self-loathing and incipient paranoia. By then he was already doomed to a long career as a social misfit. He was so withdrawn, having suffered such agonies from his failures, that he had completely given up talking to members of the female sex, except when forced by absolute necessity.

His sanity was saved, though, because he found a haven of retreat: the world of scientific knowledge, whose certainties contrasted so sharply with the treacherous vicissitudes of the social world. Even his teachers thought of him as a slightly unsavoury freak, but they recognized that in intellectual terms he was a potential superstar. He compiled the most impressive scholarly record that his very moderate school had ever produced, and in October 2000 he went triumphantly to university to study biochemistry.

Biochemistry was the glamour science in those days, when every year that passed produced new biotechnological miracles from the laboratories of the genetic engineers. Giovanni was entranced by the infinite possibilities of the applied science, and set out to master the crafts of gene-mapping, protein design and plasmid construction. In everyday life he seemed extremely clumsy and slow of wit, but he was a very different character in the privacy of a laboratory, when he could manage the most delicate operation with absolute control, and where he had such a perfect intuition and understanding of what he was doing that he soon left his educators far behind.

In the new environment of the university, where intelligence was held in reasonably high esteem by female students, Giovanni tried tentatively to come out of his shell. He began talking to girls again, albeit with ponderous caution and unease. He helped other students with their work, and tried once or twice to move on from assistance to seduction. There was a black-haired Isabel who seemed to think him an interesting conversationalist, and a freckled Mary who even cooked a couple of meals for him because she thought he was neglecting himself, but they politely declined to enter into more intimate relationships with him. They could not think of him in such a light, and though they were prepared to consider Giovanni a friend of sorts, the boys they welcomed into their beds were of a very different type. Giovanni tried hard not to resent this, and to see their point of view. He certainly did not *blame* them, but his sympathy with their attitude only made him more disappointed with himself, and even more sharply aware of the mockery in his name.

Transforming bacteria by plasmid engineering was *passé* long before Giovanni's graduation, and he felt that the engineering of plants, though it certainly offered great opportunities for ingenuity and creativity, was not quite adventurous enough for him. He knew that his talents were sufficiently extraordinary to require something a little more daring, and so he channelled his efforts in the direction of animal engineering. His doctoral research was devoted to the development of artificial cytogene systems which could be transplanted into animal cells without requiring disruption of the nucleus or incorporation into the chromosomal system; these made it practicable to transform specific cells in the tissues of mature metazoans, avoiding all the practical and ethical problems which still surrounded work on zygotes and embryos.

Giovanni's early ambition was to apply this research to various projects in medical science. He produced in his imagination half a dozen strategies for conquering cancer, and a few exotic methods of combating the effects of ageing. Had he stayed in pure research, based in a university, this was undoubtedly what he would have done, but the early years of the new millennium were a period of economic boom, when big biotechnology companies were headhunting talent with a rare ruthlessness. Giovanni never applied for a job or made any inquiry about industrial opportunities, but found potential employers begging to interview him in the comfort of his own home or any other place he cared to name. They sent beautiful and impeccably manicured personnel officers to woo him with their tutored smiles and their talk of six-figure salaries. One or two were so desperate to net him that they seemed almost willing to bribe him with sexual favours, but they always stopped short of this ultimate tactic, much to his chagrin.

He was so fiercely dedicated to his work, and had such noble ideals, that he hesitated for a long time before selling out, but the temptations were too much for him in the end. He sold himself to the highest bidder – Cytotech, Inc. – and joined the brain drain to sunny California, being careful to leave most of his bank accounts in convenient European tax shelters so that he could be a millionaire before he was thirty. He had the impression that even the most ill-favoured of millionaires could easily play the part of a Casanova, and he could hardly wait to set himself up as a big spender.

Cytotech was heavily involved in medical research, but its dynamic company president, Marmaduke Melmoth, had different plans for this most extraordinary of hirelings. He invited Giovanni to his mansion in Beverly Hills, and gave him the most fabulous meal that the young man had ever seen. Then he told Giovanni where, in his terminology, 'the game was to be played'.

'The future', said Melmoth, sipping his pink champagne, 'is in aphrodisiacs. Cancer cures we can only sell to people with cancer. Life-expectation is great, but it isn't worth a damn unless people can *enjoy* extended life. To hell with better mousetraps – what this world wants is better beaver-traps. You make me a red-hot pheromone, and I'll make you a billionaire.'

Giovanni explained to Melmoth that there could be no such thing as a powerful human pheromone. Many insects, he pointed out, perceive their environment almost entirely in olfactory terms, so that it makes sense for female insects with limited periods of fertility to signal their readiness with a smelly secretion which, if produced in sufficient quantities, could draw every male insect from miles around. Humans, by contrast, make very little use of their sense of smell, and their females are unafflicted by short and vital phases of fertility which must at all costs be exploited for the con-tinued survival of the species.

'All this I know,' Melmoth assured him. 'And the fact that you thought to tell me about it reveals to me that you have an attitude problem. Let me give you some advice, son. It's easy to find people who'll tell me what isn't possible and can't be done. For that I can hire morons. I hire geniuses to say "If *that* won't work, what will?" Do you get my drift?'

Giovanni was genuinely impressed by this observation, though it could hardly be reckoned original. He realized that his remarks really had been symptomatic of an attitude problem, which had manifested itself all-too-powerfully in his personal life. He went to his laboratory determined to produce for Mr Melmoth something that would stand in for the impossible pheromone, and determined to produce for himself some sexual encounters that would put him on course for a career as an authentic Casanova. It was simply, he decided, a matter of strategy and determination.

In fact, Giovanni was now in a position where he had more than a little prestige and influence. Although he was notionally starting at the bottom at Cytotech, there was no doubting that he would go far – that he was a man to be respected no matter how unlovely his appearance might be.

Thus advantaged, he had little difficulty in losing his virginity at last, with a seventeen-year-old blonde lab assistant called Helen. This was a great relief, but he was all too well aware of the fact that it represented no considerable triumph. It was a fumbling affair, throughout which he was trembling with anxiety and embarrassment; he felt that his everyday clumsiness and awkwardness, though he could leave them behind in his laboratory work, were concentrated to grotesque extremes in his sexual technique. Pretty Helen, who was not herself overburdened with experience or sophistication, uttered not a word of complaint and made no reference to his surname, but Giovanni found himself quite convinced that in the privacy of her thoughts she was crying out 'Casanova! Casanova!' and laughing hysterically at the irony of it. He dared not ask her to his bed again, and tended to shun her in the workplace.

Deciding that he needed more practice, Giovanni arranged visits to whores whose telephone numbers he found scrawled on the walls of the payphones in the main lobby, and though he avoided by this means the embarrassment of knowing that his partners were aware of his name, he still found it appallingly difficult to improve his performance. If anything, he thought, he was getting worse instead of better, becoming steadily more ludicrous in his own eyes.

Clearly this was what Melmoth would have called an attitude problem, but Giovanni now knew that simply calling it by that name would no more solve it than calling him Casanova had made him into an avatar of his famous namesake. Self-disgust made him give up visiting prostitutes after his third such experience, and he could not bring himself to try to resuscitate his relationship with Helen. He had little difficulty convincing himself that celibacy was to be preferred to continual humiliation.

In his work, however, he was making great strides. Taking Melmoth's advice to heart, he asked himself what would constitute, in human terms, an alternative to pheromones. The dominant human sense is sight, so the nearest human analogue of an insect pheromone is an attractive appearance, but this has so long been taken for granted that it sustains a vast cosmetics industry dedicated to helping members of the desired sex to enhance their charms. Giovanni felt that there was relatively little scope in this area for his expertise, so he turned his attention instead to the sense of touch.

He eventually decided that what was needed was something that would make the touch of the would-be seducer irresistible to the target of his (or her) affections: a love-potion of the fingertips. If he could find a psychotropic protein which could be absorbed quickly through the skin, so that the touch of the donor could become associated with subsequent waves of pleasurable sensation, then it should be fairly easy to achieve an operant conditioning of the desired one.

Giovanni brought all his artistry in protein-design to bear on the production of a psychotropic which would call forth strong feelings of euphoria, tenderness, affection and lust. This was not easy – understanding of this kind of psycho-chemistry was then at a very primitive level – but he was the man for the job. Having found the ideal protein, he then encoded it in the DNA of an artificial cytogene which was tailored for incorporation in subepidermal cells, whose activation would be triggered by sexual arousal. The protein itself could then be delivered to the surface of the skin by the sweat-glands.

When the time came to explain this ingenious mechanism to Marmaduke Melmoth, the company president was not immediately enthused.

'Hell's bells, boy,' he said. 'Why not just put the stuff in bottles and let people smear it on their fingers?'

Giovanni explained that his new psychotropic protein, like the vast majority of such entities, was so awesomely delicate that it could not be kept in solution, and would rapidly denature outside the protective environment of a living cell. In any case, the whole point was that the object of desire could only obtain this particular fix from the touch of the would-be seducer. If it was to be used for condition-ing, then its sources must be very carefully limited. This was not a technology for mass distribution, but something for the favoured few, who must use it with the utmost discretion.

'Oh shit,' said Melmoth, in disgust. 'How are we going to make billions out of a product like that?'

Giovanni suggested that he sell it only to the very rich at an exorbitant price.

'If we're going to do it that way,' Melmoth told him, 'we're going to have to be absolutely sure that it works, and that there's not the ghost of an unfortunate side-effect. You work for customers like that, they have to get satisfaction.'

Giovanni agreed that this was a vital necessity. He set up a series of exhaustive and highly secret clinical trials, and did not tell Melmoth that he had already started exploring the effects and potentials of the tissue-transformation. In the great tradition of scientific self-sacrifice, he had volunteered to be his own guinea-pig.

To say that the method worked would be a feeble understatement. Giovanni found that he only had to look at an attractive girl, and conjure up in his imagination fantasies of sexual communion, to produce the special sweat that put magic at his fingertips. Once he was sufficiently worked up, the merest touch sufficed to set the psychochemical seduction in train, and it required only the simplest strategy to achieve the required conditioning. Girls learned very quickly, albeit subconsciously, to associate his touch with the most tender and exciting emotions. They quickly overcame their natural revulsion and began to think that although not *conventionally* attractive he was really rather fascinating.

Within three weeks of the experiment's launch four female lab assistants, two word-processing operatives, three receptionists, one industrial relations consultant and a traffic warden were deep in the throes of infatuation. Giovanni was on top of the world, and gloried in the victory of becoming a self-made Casanova. The dignity of celibacy was cast casually aside. Women were desperate now to get him into bed, and he obliged them with pleasure. He even managed to overcome some of the limitations of his awkwardness, and was soon troubled no more by premature ejaculation.

But the sense of satisfaction did not last. It took only three months more for him to become thoroughly disgusted with himself all over again. It was not so much guilt generated by the knowledge that he had cheated his partners into their passionate desire (though that did weigh somewhat upon his conscience); the real problem was that he became convinced that he was not giving them full value in return. He knew that however disappointing any particular session of love-making might be, each and every victim would continue to love him vehemently, but he thought that he could see how disappointed his paramours were, in him and in themselves. They loved him, but their love only made them unhappy. This was partly because they realized that they were all competing with one another for his attentions, but he was convinced that it was mainly because those attentions were so inherently unsatisfying.

Giovanni could now present to the world the image of a genuine Casanova. He was talked about, in wondering tones. He was envied. But in his own eyes, he remained in every sense a despicable fraud. It was not *he* that was beloved, but some organic goo that he had concocted in a test-tube; and the women who were its victims were condemned to the desperations of jealousy, the disappointments of third-rate sex, and the miseries of helplessness. Giovanni had not the stomach to be a wholesale heartbreaker; he was too familiar with misery and desperation to take pleasure from inflicting it on others – not, at any rate, on women that he liked and admired.

By the time the royalties began to roll in, when Melmoth's discreet marketing of the discovery to the world's richest men began to pay dividends, Giovanni was again deep in depression and cynicism. Others, he felt sure, would be able to exploit his invention to the full, as the means to illimitable pleasure, but not he. Casanova, the fool, had simply confirmed his own wretchedness. His cup of bitterness overflowed.

It was, as ever, Marmaduke Melmoth who brought it home to him that he was still suffering from an attitude problem.

'Look, Joe,' said Melmoth. 'We got a few little problems. Nothing you can't sort out, I'm sure, but it's kinda necessary to keep the customers happy and the cash coming in. The way we're playing this we have a restricted market, and a lot of the guys are getting on a bit. It's all very well to offer them a way of getting the slots in the sack, but what they really need is something to get the peg into the slot. You ever hear of this stuff called Spanish fly?'

Giovanni explained that *cantharides* was a beetle rather than a fly; that it was a powerful poison; and that it probably wasn't terribly satisfying to have a painfully rigid and itchy erection for hours on end.

'So make something better,' said Melmoth, with that mastery of the art of delegation which had made him rich.

Giovanni gave the matter some consideration, and decided that it was probably feasible to devise a biochemical mechanism which would make it possible for a man to win conscious control over his erections: to produce them at will, sustain them as long as might be required, and generate orgasms in any desired quantity. This would require a couple of new hormones which Mother Nature had not thought to provide, a secondary system of trigger hormones for feedback control, and a cytogene for transforming the cells of the pituitary gland. Even when the biochemistry was in place, people would have to learn to use the new system, and that would require a training programme, perhaps with computer-assisted biofeedback back-up.

But it could be done; there was no doubt about it.

So Giovanni set to work, patiently bringing his new dreamchild to perfection.

Naturally, he had to test the system to make sure it was worth going ahead with clinical trials. Once the genetic transplants had taken, he spent a couple of hours a night in solitary practice. It took him only a week to gain complete conscious control of his new abilities, but he had started with the advantage of understanding, so he mapped out a training programme for the punters that would take a fortnight.

Once again, he was filled with optimism with respect to his own personal problems. No longer would he have to worry about flaws in his technique; he could now be confident that any girl who was caused to fall in love with him would receive full measure of sexual satisfaction in return. Now, he was in a much better position to emulate his famous namesake.

But Giovanni was no longer a callow youth, and his optimism about the future was not based entirely on his biotechnological augmentation. He had undergone a more dramatic change of attitude, and had decided that the Casanova he needed to copy was not the ancient Giovanni but his father Marcantonio. He had decided that the answer lay in monogamy, and he wanted to get married. He was now in his mid-thirties, and it seemed to him that what he needed was a partner of his own age: a mature and level-headed woman who could bring order and stability into his life.

These arguments led him to fall in love with his accountant, a 33-year-old divorcée named Denise. He had ample opportunity to make the fingertip contacts necessary to make her besotted with him, because his fortune was steadily increasing and there were always new opportunities in tax avoidance for them to discuss over dinner. Giovanni orchestrated the whole affair very carefully and, he thought, smoothly, graciously allowing Denise the pleasure of seducing him on their third *real* date. He still felt clumsy and a little anxious, but she seemed quite delighted with his powers of endurance.

His parents were glad when he told them the news. His father cried with delight at the thought that the name of Casanova would now be transmitted to a further generation, and his mother (who looked upon getting married as the only worthwhile certificate of belonging to the human race) was euphorically sentimental for months.

Denise gave up work when she became pregnant, mere weeks after the honeymoon, abandoning to other financial wizards the job of distributing and protecting the spring tide of cash which began to pour into Giovanni's bank accounts when his new discovery was discreetly marketed by the ingenious Melmoth.

Giovanni loved Denise very much, and became more and more devoted to her as the months of her pregnancy elapsed. When she gave birth to a baby girl, named Jennifer after his mother, he felt that he had discovered heaven on earth.

Unfortunately, this peak in his experience was soon passed. Denise got post-natal depression, and began to find her energetic sex life something of a bore. She was still hooked, unknowingly, on the produce of Giovanni's finger-tips, but her emotional responses became perversely confused, and her feelings of love and affection generated floods of miserable tears.

Giovanni was overwrought, and knew not what to do. He was slowly consumed by a new wave of guilt. Whatever was the matter, he was responsible for it. He had made Denise love him, and had avoided feeling like a cheat only because he was convinced that she was reaping all the rewards that she could possibly have attained from a love that grew spontaneously in her heart. Now things were going wrong, he saw himself as her betrayer and her destroyer.

When Giovanni became anguished and miserable, Denise blamed herself. She became even more confused and even more desperate in her confusion. The unhappy couple fed one another's despair, and became wretched together. This intolerable situation led inexorably toward the one awful mistake that Giovanni was bound eventually to make.

He told her everything.

From every possible point of view, this was a disastrous move. When Denise heard how her husband had tied her finest and most intimate feelings to chemical puppet-strings her love for him underwent a purely psychosomatic transformation into bitter and resentful hatred. She left him forthwith, taking the infant Jenny with her, and sued for divorce. She also filed a suit demanding thirty million dollars' compensation for his biochemical interference with her affections. In so doing, of course, she made headline news of the enterprises which Marmaduke Melmoth had kept so carefully secret, and released a tempest of controversy.

The impact of this news can easily be imagined. The world of the 2010s was supposedly one in which the women of the overdeveloped countries had won complete equality with their menfolk. The feminists of the day looked back with satisfaction at centuries of fierce fighting against legal and attitudinal discrimination; their heroines had battled successfully against sexism in the workplace, sexism in education, sexism in the language and sexism in the psyche.

Though progress had brought them to the brink of their particular Millennium, they still had a heightened consciousness of the difficulties which had beset their quest, and a hair-trigger paranoia about any threat to their achievements. The discovery that for nearly twenty years the world's richest men had been covertly buying biotechnologies specifically designed for the manipulation and sexual oppression of womankind constituted a scandal such as the world of sexual politics had never known.

Giovanni Casanova, who had so far lived his life in secure obscurity, costly content with his unsung genius, found himself suddenly notorious. His name – that hideous curse of a name – suddenly became the progenitor of jokes and gibes displayed in screeching headlines, broadcast to every corner of the globe. It was constantly featured in news bulletins and tawdry comedy shows alike. Overnight, the new Casanova became a modern folk-devil: the man who had put the cause of sexual emancipation back three hundred years.

The divorce broke his mother's heart, and her sufferings were compounded when Marcantonio Casanova died suddenly of heart failure. She hinted to Giovanni in a reckless moment that his father had died of shame, and Giovanni took this so much to heart that he seriously contemplated suicide.

Denise, the victim of Giovanni's obscene machinations, achieved a temporary sainthood in the eyes of the women of the world. Melmoth, who had played Mephistopheles to Giovanni's Faust, was demonized alongside him. Thousands

of women filed copycat lawsuits against their rich paramours, against Giovanni, and against Cytotech. Giovanni
got sacks of hate-mail from tens of thousands of women
who believed (usually without any foundation in fact) that
his magic had been used to steal their souls.

As storms usually do, though, this hurricane of abuse
soon began to lose its fury. Marmaduke Melmoth began to
use his many resources to tell the world that the *real* issue
was simply a little attitude problem.

Melmoth was able to point out that there was nothing
inherently sexist about Giovanni's first discovery. He was
able to prove that Cytotech had several notable female
clients, who had been happily using the seductive sweat to
attract young men. He argued, with some justice, that the
cosmetics industry had for centuries been offering men and
women methods of enhancing their sexual attractiveness,
and that there had always been a powerful demand for
aphrodisiacs.

Giovanni's only 'crime', Melmoth suggested, was to have
produced an aphrodisiac which *worked*, and which was
absolutely safe, to replace thousands of products of fake
witchcraft and medical quackery which were at best useless
and at worst harmful. He argued that although Giovanni's
second discovery was, indeed, applicable only to male
physiology, its utility and its benefits were by no means
confined to the male sex.

This rhetoric was backed up by some bold promises,
which saved Cytotech's image and turned all the publicity
to the company's advantage. Melmoth guaranteed that Giov-

anni's first discovery would now become much cheaper, so that the tissue-transformation would be available even to those of moderate means, and to men and women equally. He also announced that Giovanni had already begun to work on an entire spectrum of new artificial hormones, which would give to women as well as to men vast new opportunities in the conscious generation and control of bodily pleasure.

These promises quickly displaced the scandal from the headlines. Cytotech's publicity machine did such a comprehensive job of image-building that Giovanni became a hero instead of a folk-devil.

The moral panic died, the lawsuits collapsed, and the hate-mail dried up.

On the downbeat side, however, Denise got her divorce, and custody of little Jenny. She did not get her thirty million dollars' compensation, but she was awarded sufficient alimony to keep her in relative luxury for the rest of her life. Giovanni was awarded the Nobel Prize for Biochemistry, but this did little to soothe his disappointment even though it helped his mother to recover from her broken heart and be proud of him again.

Giovanni launched himself obsessively into the work required to make good on Melmoth's promises. He became a virtual recluse, putting in such long hours at the laboratory that his staff and co-workers began to fear for his health and sanity. As he neared forty his mental faculties were in decline, but the increase in his knowledge and wisdom offset the loss of mental agility, and it is arguable that it was in this phase of his career that his genius was most powerful and most fertile.

He did indeed develop a new spectrum of hormones and enkephalins, which in combination gave people who underwent the relevant tissue-transformations far greater conscious control over the physiology of pleasure. As recipients gradually learned what they could do with their new biochemistry, and mastered its arts and skills, they became able to induce in themselves, without any necessary assistance at all, orgasms and kindred sensations more thrilling, more blissful and more luxurious than those which poor human nature, which had been crudely hewn by the hackwork of natural selection, had ever provided to anyone.

Giovanni created, almost single-handed, a vast new panorama of masturbatory enterprise.

For once, Giovanni's progress was the object of constant attention and constant debate. Cynics claimed that his work was hateful, because it would utterly destroy romance, devalue human feelings, obliterate sincere affection, and mechanize ecstasy. Critics argued that the value and mystique of sexual relationships would be fatally compromised by his transformations. Pessimists prophesied that if his new projects were to be brought to a successful conclusion, sexual intercourse might become a thing of the past, displaced from the arena of human experience by voluptuous self-abuse. Fortunately, these pessimists were unable to argue that this might lead to the end of the human race, because discoveries made by other biotechnologists had permitted the development of artificial wombs more efficient than real ones; sexual intercourse was no longer necessary for reproduction, which could be managed more competently *in vitro*. The cynics and the pessimists were therefore disregarded by the majority, who were hungry for joy, and eager to enter a promised land of illimitable delight.

As always, Giovanni was the first to try out his new discoveries; the pioneer spirit which forced him to seek out new solutions to his personal troubles was as strong as ever, and the prospect of combining celibacy with ecstasy appealed very much to his eremitic frame of mind.

In the early days of his experimentation, while he was still exploring the potential of his new hormonal instruments of self-control, he was rather pleased with the ways in which he could evoke rapture to illuminate his loneliness, but he quickly realized that this was no easy answer to his problems. Eight hundred thousand years of masturbation had not sufficed to blunt the human race's appetite for sexual intercourse, and Giovanni quickly found that the reason for this failure had nothing to do with the quality of the sensations produced. The cynics and pessimists were quite wrong; sexual intercourse could not and never would be made redundant by any mere enhancement of onanistic gratifications. Sex was more than pleasure; it was closeness, intimate involvement with another, empathy, compassion, and an outflowing of good feeling which needed a recipient.

Giovanni had found in the brief happiness of his marriage that sex was, in all the complex literal and metaphorical senses of the phrase, *making love*. However wonderful his new biochemical systems were, they were not doing that and were no substitute for it.

So Giovanni ceased to live as a recluse. He returned to the social world, with his attitude adjusted yet again, determined to make new relationships. After all, he still had the magic at his fingertips – or so he thought.

He looked around; found a grey-eyed journalist named Greta, a Junoesque plant physiologist named Jacqueline, and a sweetly smiling insurance salesperson named Morella, and went to work with his seductive touch.

Alas, the world had changed while he had lived apart from it. None of the three women yielded to his advances. It was not that he had lost his magic touch, but that Cytotech's marketing had given it to far too many others. When the relevant tissue-transformations had been the secret advantage of a favoured few, they had used it with care and discretion, but now that aphrodisiac sweat was commonplace, any reasonably attractive woman was likely to encounter it several times a week. Because women were continually sated with the feelings that it evoked they could no longer be conditioned to associate the sensation with the touch of a particular person. Greta, Jacqueline and Morella were quite conscious of what was happening when he touched them, and though they thanked him for the compliment, each one was utterly unimpressed.

Giovanni realized that promiscuity was fast destroying the aphrodisiac value of his first discovery. His quick mind made him sensitive to all kinds of possibilities that might be opened up by the more general release of this particular invention, and he began to look in the news for evidence of social change.

The logic of the situation was quite clear to him. As users found their seductive touch less effective, they would tend to use it more and more frequently, thus spreading satiation even further and destroying all prospect of the desired result. In addition, people would no longer use the device simply for the purpose of sexual conquest. Many men and women would be taken by the ambition to make *everybody* love them, in the hope of securing thereby the social and economic success that the original purchasers of the technology had already had. In consequence, he presumed, the world would suffer from a positive epidemic of good feeling. This plague would not set the entire world to making love, but it might set the entire world to making friends. The most unlikely people might soon be seen to be relaxing into the comfort of infinite benevolence.

Giovanni monitored the news very carefully, and realized long before it became generally known that he had wrought a more profound change in human affairs than he had intended or supposed.

Wars were gradually petering out.

Terrorism was on the decline.

Violent crime was becoming steadily rarer.

Oddly enough, these trends passed unnoticed for a while by the world at large, because the headlines, dutifully following time-honoured custom, carefully selected out whatever bad news remained to be communicated. The

271

majority of people did not begin to wake up to the significance of it all until a much-advertised contest to settle the
heavyweight boxing championship of the world was stopped
in the third round when the weeping combatants realized
that they could not bear to throw another punch, and left
the ring together with their arms around one another's
shoulders.

Because of these upheavals in the world's routines, the
clinical trials of Giovanni's new hormones and enkephalins
attracted a little less attention than they might have, but
their outstanding success was still a matter for widespread
celebration. In 2036 Giovanni was awarded a Nobel Peace
Prize to set beside his earlier award, and there was some
discussion about the possibility of making it the last prize of
its kind, given that the world no longer seemed to require
peacemakers. Giovanni became once again the darling of the
world's media. He was billed as a modern Prometheus,
sometimes even as a modern Dionysus, who had brought
into the world of men a divine fire more precious than any
vulgar power-source.

Giovanni was still embarrassed by these periodic waves of
media exposure. He still felt very self-conscious about his
physical appearance, and every time he saw his own picture
on newsscreen or in a videomag he blushed with the thought
that half a billion viewers were probably saying to themselves: 'He doesn't *look* like a Casanova!' He was probably
being oversensitive; nowadays it was his face and his
achievements which were called to the mind of the man in

the street by the mention of the name Casanova; his ancient namesake had been eclipsed in the public consciousness.

In addition, Giovanni no longer appeared to the unbiased eye to be as unprepossessing as he once had seemed. He was now bald, and his bare pate was by no means as freakish as the tangled black hair that once had sprouted there. He still wore spectacles for his myopia, but corneal surgery had corrected his astigmatism, and his eyes looked kind and soft behind his high-index lenses, not at all distorted. His complexion was still poor, but his skin had been roughened and toughened by age and exposure to the elements, and its appearance was no longer offensive. His paleness and frailness could now be seen as appealing rather than appalling.

He was startled the first time that he realized that a woman was using his own aphrodisiac technology upon him, and quickly jumped to the conclusion that she must be one of those people who used it on everyone, but he gradually became accustomed to the idea that he really was admired and desired.

In time, of course, the secretion of aphrodisiac sweat became subject to a new etiquette, whereby indiscriminate use was held to be in bad taste, and also to be unnecessary as it could now be taken for granted that everyone could love one another even without its aid. Politeness came to demand that a sophisticated and civilized person would use the Casanova secretion occasionally and discreetly, to signal a delicate expression of erotic interest with no offence to be taken if there was no response.

As this new code of behaviour evolved, Giovanni was surprised to find himself a frequent target for seduction, and for a while he revelled in sexual success. Many of the younger women, of course, were interested primarily in his wealth and status, but he did not mind – he could, after all, claim responsibility for his status and wealth, which he had won by effort.

Anyway, he loved them all. He loved *everybody*, and everybody loved him.

It was that kind of a world, now.

In this way, Giovanni Casanova succeeded at last in adapting to his name. He lived up to the reputation of his august namesake for a year or two, and then decided that the attractions of the lifestyle were overrated. He gladdened his mother's heart by marrying again, and this time he chose a woman who was very like the earliest memories which he had of his mother.

His new bride was named Janine. She had been born in Manchester, and she was embarked on a career in cosmetic cytogenics (which was the nearest thing to hairdressing that the world of 2036 could offer). She was much younger than Giovanni, but did not mind the age difference in the least.

Giovanni and Janine favoured one another constantly with the most delicate psychochemical strokings, and learned to play the most beautiful duets with all the ingenious hormonal instruments of Giovanni's invention. But they also had a special feeling for one another – and eventually for their children – which went beyond mere chemistry and physiology: an affection which was entirely a triumph of the will. This was a treasure which, they both believed, could never have come out of one of Giovanni's test-tubes.

With all these advantages, they were able to live happily ever after.

And so was everybody else.

RUTH FAINLIGHT

Dr Clock's Last Case

'Dr Clock Cures All Ills', read the card he gave her as soon as she crossed the threshold, and she put it in the side pocket of her handbag and believed what it said.

'Come to bed with me, and I'll make you better.' He began to undo the buttons of his greasy tweed jacket and trousers, grunting slightly as he strained over his paunch to reach them, long-haired grey head turned away as if never doubting for one moment that she would do whatever he ordered.

It wasn't really a bed, but a couch, upholstered in the same faded blue woven stuff that covered its pillows, standing against one wall of what he referred to as his consulting chamber. A tall narrow window, blurred by years of dirt, opened on to an inner courtyard, and that afternoon the room was even darker than usual as rain fell from an overcast, grey sky.

Lucy still wore her coat – a military-style black mackintosh. A slight fair woman of about thirty, she hesitated in the centre of the room, watching him undress. She felt satisfied but tired, as if after arriving at a destination sought for years. Everything she wore today was black or some other muted, sombre shade, except for her underpants, which were a vivid neon purple.

'Come on now, put that handbag down. Get your clothes off. You look like a prison visitor.' Dr Clock, shapely fat knees revealed between high socks and long green-and-white striped boxer shorts, tutted impatiently. 'You want me to cure you, don't you? Well, let's get on with it.'

'Can you really cure all ills?' she asked wonderingly, twisting round to unzip her skirt. Everything seemed so matter-of-fact that obviously he could. Otherwise, why would she be here?

'Headache, heartache, hernia, haemorrhoids, hopelessness, or any other letter you like. Just get undressed and believe what I tell you.' Dr Clock was naked now, but seemed no different than when he had opened the door fully clothed. His compact body looked as warm and healthy and unselfconscious as a rubber doll's. 'You'll be cold, I suppose,' he muttered, lighting the gas fire. 'I like that purple.' He picked up her nylon pants and draped them over the desk light. The room became a grotto. 'Now come here, next to me.' He sat on the couch and patted the grubby surface. 'Tell me what's the matter.'

There had been no chance to examine his face. An impresssion of paleness, of profuse greyish hair and rather bulging pale eyes was all she had taken in, and though sitting next to him now, she felt no urge to scrutinize him more closely.

'Come on, tell me what's the matter,' he repeated. 'That's

why you rang my bell and came here, isn't it? That's why you took my card and read it and put it somewhere safe. Lie back, and tell me everything.'

She stretched out on the rough fabric and he bent over and peered at the middle of her body, as if the truth would issue from there. 'I saw your advertisement on a noticeboard, and came here straight away, hoping you'd see me,' she began. 'Yes, yes,' he said encouragingly, placing one hand gently on her belly. 'And why did you think I could help you?' His head was bent so low he seemed to be more interested in how she smelt than what she said, yet Lucy was sure he was listening intently. 'I need someone to help me. Something is wrong with me, I know.'

The heat from the gas fire and its flickering light on the purpled ceiling made her drowsy. It seemed years since she'd been so comfortable. 'Open your legs,' Dr Clock said. 'I want you to talk to me, because I know that's what you want to do. You don't want to listen. I don't have to say anything. You know what's the matter.' Compliance was confirmation of his diagnosis. Of course she knew what was the matter with her and what she wanted. Hip-joints rolled flexed legs easily outwards as he bent even lower and fastened his mouth around the parted lips of her vagina and began a soft regular sucking like a baby at the nipple.

'I thought something was wrong with me when I was out there,' Lucy mused, watching the patterns on the walls and ceiling, distanced like all the complexities of her life outside this room. 'But in here there doesn't seem to be much wrong, after all.' She ended on an interrogatory note, but Dr Clock did not lift his head to reply, and after a short pause she continued. That gentle, rhythmic pumping was like a completion, as though if it could continue even after she left this room, if somehow it were possible to take his lips away and leave the rest of him behind, she would be invulnerable to every pain and uncertainty for the rest of her life. 'I'm not sick, am I?' The question did not need an answer. The knots in her joints and intestines were loosening like flaccid snakes after coupling. Dr Clock's mouth increased its grip, a hand moved under her hips and tilted her pelvis slightly.

'If I could feel like this all the time, nothing would hurt me, isn't that so?' Lucy asked. 'All the problems would go away.' She vaguely sensed a contradiction, but was beginning not to care whether she remained consistent with earlier statements, or even went on talking. But Dr Clock obviously would not tolerate silence. He lifted his head and ordered, 'Go on, you haven't said anything yet.'

'Leave me alone,' she gasped. 'Stop telling me what to do. Everyone tells me what to do, I can't stand it!' She half pulled herself up, but firmly, gently, he pressed her back down. 'Everyone bullies me,' she sobbed, in the grip of a tantrum such as dimly remembered from early childhood. She tried to fight him off, screaming, 'I hate you, you've always stopped me from doing what I want, you never let me have anything. I hate you. You're like everyone else, they're all against me.'

The purple light seemed glacial. 'I'm all alone and so unhappy!' Tears of self-pity softened her anger. If only he would comfort her she would forgive anything. 'Nobody has

ever loved me – never – nobody – and now you're the same.
I thought you'd cure me, but you're only making me even
sicker.' It was true – nodes of pain flared from every part of
her body. She was frightened by their clanging, grinding
intensity, and the conviction that she was about to die.
'Forgive me,' she pleaded, arms outstretched. 'I'll do whatever you say if only you'll forgive me and be kind to me. I
can't bear it otherwise.'

'Get up now,' Dr Clock said. 'I want you to beat me. Here.'
He pulled the leather belt from his trousers. 'Hit me. Take it
out on me. You don't want me to forgive you – it's just that
you're too frightened to punish me. Well, go ahead – hit
me.'

'No, no,' she begged. 'I do want you to forgive me, truly,
please. No one has ever forgiven me. I'm a great sinner.'

'All right, then. If you really want to be punished, I'll do
it for you.'

The first lash shocked, but the next blows infuriated her.
'Give that to me,' she shouted, trying to dodge the strap and
get it away from him. 'I do hate you, it's true. I do want to
beat you. I want to kill you. I want to kill everyone, because
nobody ever forgives me or loves me. Give me that strap,
you bastard.' Blinded by fury, she still could not see what he
looked like, but it did not matter; he had become father,
grandfathers, uncles, grown-up smirking cousins, every man
who'd ever teased and played with and rejected her.

'Hit me,' he said, surrendering the strap and waiting
passively, half turned away. She lashed at his back and

280

shoulders, but in that position he seemed androgynous, epicene, more like a plump middle-aged woman than a man. She stopped and frowned and blinked, shaking sweat-heavy hair from her eyes. Surely it was her mother standing there? In just that pose her mother had stood and stared into the gas fire at home when Lucy was a child, halted in her dressing by some reverie. Would it be possible to hit her mother? Did she want to?

'Are you my mother?' she asked in a low, nervous voice. 'Mother?' Whoever it was, the figure did not turn. 'For God's sake, tell me if you're my mother,' Lucy pleaded. 'Why don't you turn round? Don't you love me? Mother—' She fell on to her knees and began to beat her head on the floor. 'Mother, Mother, Mother,' she moaned. 'Do I want to hit my mother?' It was too terrible a dilemma to bear.

'You don't have to hit me if you don't want to,' Dr Clock said, and put a warm arm round her trembling shoulders.

'I can't kill my mother,' Lucy cried. 'It would be suicide.' He helped her on to the couch again and stroked her, and she immediately fell into an exhausted sleep.

A few minutes later she woke, alert and refreshed. He sat crosslegged in the armchair opposite, wearing a multicoloured silk kimono. 'Read this,' he said. It was another card, in the same style as the first, but with a different message: 'Dr Clock Never Stops'.

'Recite the alphabet for me,' he commanded, as she studied the cryptic inscription.

'The alphabet?' she repeated, confused.

'Come on, start saying it.' He didn't look at her, but pensively twirled a loose thread in the hem of the kimono.

'A-B-C—' Lucy began, barely able to believe that she was complying with his demands. 'D-E-F-G—' It was impossible to think about anything else while reciting these letters, saying these words which took over the entire mind like a meditation exercise. 'Aych, Eye, Jay, Kay—' She was aware of nothing except these letters, and his controlling power. 'M-N-O-P-Q-R-S—' Eyes fixed on the purple-tinged figure in the armchair, she crouched down and slowly began to crawl forward. 'T-U-V-W-X-Y-Z.' When she had reached the last letter her face was level with his knees. She sat on the floor at his feet and laid her head on his lap.

'Kiss my cock,' he said, shifting to open the kimono. Lucy closed her eyes and parted her lips and felt a thick, half-erect penis slide between them. It stiffened and enlarged in her mouth; she gagged as it pressed deeper into her throat. 'Kneel,' he said, pulling away, when she was about to suffocate. He knelt behind her, a breast clasped in each hand.

'Ah!' she groaned at his penetration.

'Now say the alphabet,' he ordered. 'But do it backwards.'

'I can't,' she moaned. 'Leave me alone.'

'Come on, begin.' He emphasized his words with a deep thrust.

'Z-Y-X-W—' With each letter she became more burning and open, fluttered and dragged him further inside her. By contrast, he barely moved, only to use his penis as a sort of prod when she stopped for too long, or began to droop towards the floor. There was no way to measure the duration of this alphabet. Between some letters aeons passed, as if she had sunk into the heart of a mountain of black basalt which would have to be eroded away by time and climate before she would be released to intone the next sound. She had never felt so content.

'Now stand up,' he said when she reached 'A', abruptly drawing back, wrapping the kimono close and sitting down again. Dazed, Lucy looked around the room. She could barely remember who or where she was, or why she knelt there, arms stiff and trembling, knees chafed by the rough carpeting. 'Tell me why you came to see me. What do you think I can do for you?'

She tried to break through this present moment and remember. 'Cure me, that's it,' she said at last. 'I want you to cure me. I want you to stop me from suffering. I want to escape from all the passions that torment me. I want my life.'

'Life?' he repeated.

'Maybe that's not exactly what I mean,' she amended uncertainly. Things seemed to be getting worse. 'I want to stop being affected by everything that happened in the past. And sometimes I think that future events are sending their influences back at me. How can I be kinder to anyone else than I am to myself?' She snorted with inappropriate, ironic laughter. 'Maybe I don't have the temperament for my beliefs.'

'I am not Dr Spock.'

'Who's Dr Spock?' she wondered. 'You're Dr Clock, aren't you?'

'Dr Clock, the lollipop,' he answered gleefully, and leaned forward to put one hand on each side of her head and clamp her startled face into his groin again. Roughly pushing his rigid penis into her mouth, he discharged a thick, hot, copious stream of semen. 'Swallow it,' he commanded sternly. 'It's your first dose of my medicine.'

Her throat convulsed, then as the viscous liquid mixed with her own saliva she tried to savour its faint saltiness. 'This is your medicine, is it?' she mumbled abstractedly when she could speak. 'I don't see how it's going to cure me.'

'It's life, my dear lady. You say you want life – that's the essence of life, or so I understand. What better medicine could I give you?'

'I don't see that things are any different in here than anywhere else,' Lucy said, petulant and bitter. She stood up and leaned against the mantelpiece to stare into the gas fire's incandescence. It wasn't the taste in her mouth making her feel sick, but intense disappointment. 'What's the difference between you and all the others? You've only made me feel worse. I thought there was some hope somewhere—' She turned away, but the tears would not hold back, and the gas fire flashed and sparkled through her lashes. She rushed towards the couch and pulled the heavy, square cushions on top of herself, howling with grief.

Such an outburst could not sustain itself against his uninvolvement. 'So I disappointed you, did I, Lucy? But

284

you didn't come to me for gratification, did you, but to be cured.'

It was difficult to say what she had expected. 'I thought it would be wonderful,' she murmured after a pause, ashamed by such an admission.

'You know better than that, or you wouldn't have come here,' he asserted. 'You didn't come just to be fucked. You said you wanted to escape from your passions.'

'I suppose so,' she concurred bleakly. She had not imagined that escape from passions would involve their re-enactment.

'Dr Clock unpicks the lock,' he stated in a confident tone of voice. 'Look up at the ceiling.' He stood behind his desk now, adjusting a small projector. By switching off the lamp, eliminating the purple glow of her underwear and leaving the orange light from the gas fire as the only illumination, he completely altered the atmosphere of the room.

'What are those things?' she asked, unable to decipher the mass of squirming, pullulating objects pushing blindly against each other.

'They could be cells, or bacteria, or they could be maggots in the earth or in a wound – or they could be larger animals, even people, I'm not sure. It's films of all those things, superimposed on each other. It doesn't seem to make any difference what the scale of life is or even what the motive is supposed to be. It looks the same from far enough away.'

'But what does that mean, what are you trying to say?'

'You decide what you want it to mean, and it will mean just that. You can't help but be right.'

The image covered the ceiling. Lucy looked upwards, held by the inexplicable activity. The colours flushed from cool to bloody, then back again, like a mass migration, the speeded-up view of a battlefield from high in space, or the changing pattern of seasons on another planet. It repelled and calmed her at the same time.

'I think this is cancer cells reproducing,' he remarked in an explanatory, schoolmasterly sort of voice.

'I suppose it could be.' She was beginning to feel bored and tired. 'I think I'll get dressed.'

'Yes, we've had enough for today,' he agreed, as she found her clothes and put them on by the light of the still-continuing film, which now might have been spores exploding open, or a distant view of land under heavy bombardment.

Searching through her handbag for lipstick and comb, Lucy saw the knife. She had bought it last summer on holiday, fascinated by the ornate handle and long blade, and it had lain forgotten in one of the bag's many compartments ever since. Without the transfiguring purple glow, the room had become as shabby as before. Dr Clock switched off the projector and moved round the desk until he stood in front of her.

For the first time she was looking directly at his face, which gave her the unnerving sensation of being transported into the future, studying the reflection of her own features as they would be in about twenty years. They both had the same anxious, staring blue eyes with puffy sockets, the same short nose and receding chin. Her hair would be as grey as his then, and float about her head in the same way. The differences were superficial: the effects of gender, weight and time which had dragged down his jowls and the corners of mouth and eyes. She was not merely frightened, but also deeply disillusioned by their resemblance. If she had looked at him properly, nothing would have happened, she was quite sure.

'When will you come again, dear lady?' the ridiculous old creature enquired in an unctuous voice. 'I'm sure we can make a lot of progress, in time. Don't forget, Dr Clock cures all ills!' he tittered, and stared calculatingly, boldly, into her eyes.

Lucy was closing the last button of her mackintosh. Pale hair tied severely back, insignificant body encased in the stiff garment, heavy black bag over one arm, she did look rather like a prison visitor, as he had commented when she arrived.

'Dr Clock gets a shock,' she hissed, furious with him but even more with herself, as she swooped her hand into the bag, brought out the knife, and pushed it into his chest where the kimono had fallen open. It sank between two ribs, up to the hilt. She had struck as accurately as a trained assassin.

His eyes opened even further. 'It is a shock,' he gasped, slumping slowly down and forward until he lay at her feet. She bent to pull the knife brutally out of his body, then wiped the blade clean on his kimonoed haunch and dropped it back into her bag. He had fallen between her and the door.

'Dr Clock, the stumbling block,' she said gleefully, stepping over him. There was no sign that she had ever been in the room, no one passed her in the long dark hall, and she met no one as she let herself out of the building and walked quickly away.

GEORGES BATAILLE

The Dead Man

Marie Remains Alone with the Dead Edward

When Edward fell back dead, a void opened in her, a long shudder ran down her, which lifted her up like an angel. Her naked breasts stood up in an imaginary church where the feeling of the irretrievable emptied her. Standing, near the dead man, absent, outside herself, in a slow ecstasy, overwhelmed. Edward, as he died, had begged her to strip herself naked.

She hadn't had the time to do it! She was there, in disarray: only her breasts jutted out of the ripped dress.

Marie Goes Out of the House Naked

The time had come to deny the laws to which fear subjects us. She pulled off her dress and put her coat on her arm. She was crazy and naked. She rushed outside and ran into the night in the downpour. Her shoes smacked in the mud and the rain eddied down her. She had to go very badly, but she held it in. In the softness of the woods, Marie stretched out on the ground. She pissed for a long time, urine covered her legs. On the ground she sang in a crazy impossible voice:

>   . . . there is some nudity
>   and some atrocity . . .

Then she got up, put her raincoat back on and ran through Quilly up to the door of the inn.

Marie Waits in Front of the Inn

Dazed, she remained in front of the door, lacking the courage to go in. She heard, coming from inside, screams, the songs of whores and drunks. She felt herself trembling, but she took pleasure in this trembling.

She thought, 'I'll go in, they'll see me naked.' She had to lean against the wall. She opened her coat and put her long fingers in her slit. She listened, fixed with anxiety, she breathed in the smell of her ill-washed sex. In the inn, they were screeching away, then everything went silent. It was raining: in a cellarlike darkness, a warmish wind slanted the rain. The voice of a whore sang a sad song about the working-class districts on the edge of town. Heard outside, in the night, the dark voice veiled by the walls was excruciating. It went silent. Applause and the stamping of feet followed, then clapping in rhythm.

Marie was sobbing in the darkness. She cried in her helplessness, the back of her hand against her teeth.

Marie Goes into the Inn

Knowing that she would be going in, Marie trembled. She opened the door, took three steps into the room: a gust of wind closed the door behind her. The farmboys, the woman who kept the bar, and the whores all stared at her. She stood motionless at the entrance; muddy, hair streaming with water, and just generally looking bad. She looked as if she had floated up on the squall of the night (they could hear the wind outside). Her coat covered her, but she pulled back the collar.

Marie Drinks with the Farmboys

She asked in a quiet voice:

– Got anything to drink?

The barkeeper answered from behind the bar:

– Calva?

She poured a shot at the bar.

Marie wouldn't take it.

– I want a bottle and some glasses, she said.

Her quiet voice was firm. She added:

291

– I'm drinking with them.

She paid.

One of the farmboys with dirt on his boots said timidly:

– You just dropped in for some entertainment?

– That's right, said Marie.

She tried to smile: the smile bored right through her.

She took a seat by the boy, rubbed her leg up against his, took his hand and placed it between her thighs.

When the boy touched the slit, he moaned:

– In the Name of God!

Excited, the others kept quiet.

One of the girls, getting up, lifted up one of her coattails.

– Take a look at this, she said, she's naked as the day she was born.

Marie let her go on and emptied a glass of liquor.

– She's used to milk, said the woman behind the bar.

Marie belched bitterly.

Marie Pulls out the Dick of a Drunkard

Marie said sadly:

– That's a fact.

Her wet black curls stuck to her face in ringlets. She shook her pretty head, got up, took off her coat.

A lout who had been drinking in the inn moved toward her. He staggered, beating the air with his arms. He screeched out:

– All naked ladies up for grabs!

The woman behind the bar warned him:

– I'll twist your ugly beak . . .

She grabbed his nose and twisted it.

He screeched.

– No, try there, said Marie, it works better.

She walked up to the drunk and unbuttoned his fly: she pulled out of his trousers his half-limp dick.

The dick raised a great burst of laughter.

In one gulp, Marie, bold as a beast, sucked down a second glass.

The barkeeper, eyes like searchlights, gently touched her behind near the cleft.

– Good enough to eat, she said.

Marie filled her glass again. The liquor gurgled out.

She slugged it down like she was dying. The glass fell from her hands. Her behind was flat and nicely cleft. Her softness lit up the room.

Marie Dances with Pierrot

One of the farmboys was standing over in the corner with a hateful look on his face.

He was just a little too good-looking a man, in high crepe rubber boots, that were just a little too new.

Marie came up to him with the bottle in her hand. She was feeling good and she was excited. Her legs swayed in her floating stockings. The boy took the bottle and took a slug. He screamed out in a fierce, unthinkable voice:

– Enough!

Slamming the empty bottle straight down on the table.

Marie asked him:

– Want another?

He answered with a smile: he was treating her like a conquest.

He started up the player piano. He pretended, when it began to play, to dance a little dance with his arms curved out in front of him.

He took Marie by the hand, they danced an obscene java.

Marie gave herself up to it completely, nauseated, her head thrown back.

Marie Falls Down Dead Drunk

The barkeeper all of a sudden jumped up screaming:

– Pierrot!

Marie was falling: she escaped from the arms of the beautiful boy who tripped.

The thin body, which had been gliding along, fell to the floor with the noise of a beast.

– The little whore! said Pierrot.

He wiped his mouth with the back of his sleeve.

The barkeeper rushed over. She knelt down and raised her head with care: saliva, or rather drool, was running from her lips.

One girl brought a moistened napkin.

In a short time, Marie came to. She asked weakly:

– Liquor!

– Give her a glass, said the barkeeper to one of the girls.

They gave her a glass. She drank and said:

– More!

The girl filled her glass. Marie lifted it out of her hands. She drank as if she was running out of time.

Nestling in the arms of one of the girls and the barkeeper, she lifted her head:

– More! she said.

Marie Tries to Speak

The farmboys, the girls and the barkeeper surrounded Marie waiting to see what she was going to say.

Marie murmured only one word.

. . . the dawn, she said.

Then her head fell back heavily. Sick, very sick . . .

The barkeeper asked:

– What'd she say?

No one knew what to answer.

Marie Is Sucked by Pierrot

Then the barkeeper said to pretty Pierrot:

– Suck her.

– Should we put her on a chair? said one girl.

Several of them grabbed her body at once and managed to get her ass onto the chair.

Pierrot, kneeling down, slipped her legs over his shoulders. The young stud had a smile of conquest and darted his tongue into her crotch hair.

Sick, lit-up, Marie seemed happy, she smiled without opening her eyes.

Marie Kisses the Barkeeper on the Mouth

She felt lit-up, frozen over, but endlessly emptying, emptying her life into the sewer.

A helpless desire maintained a tension in her: she would have liked to let that tension in her belly go. She imagined the horror of the others. She was no longer separated from Edward.

Her cunt and her ass naked: the smell of her ass and her wet cunt freed her heart and the tongue of Pierrot, which wet her, seemed as cold as death to her.

Drunk with liquor and with tears and not crying, she drank in this cold, her mouth open: she pulled over to her the head of the barkeeper, opening to the woman's decaying teeth the voluptuous abyss of her lips.

THE DEAD MAN

Marie Drinks in Huge Gulps

Marie pushed the woman away and she saw her head, hair dishevelled, twisted out of itself with joy. The face of the virago radiated drunken tenderness. She was drunk too, sentimental drunk: devoted tears came to her eyes.

Looking at these tears and seeing nothing, Marie was living bathed in the light of the dead man. She said:

– I'm thirsty.

Pierrot was sucking hard enough to take his breath away.

Hurriedly, the barkeeper gave her a bottle.

Marie drank in long gulps and emptied it.

Marie Comes

. . . Scuffling, a cry of terror, a confusion of broken bottles, Marie's thighs twitched like a frog's. The boys were screaming and shoving for position. The barkeeper helped Marie, laid her out on the bench.

Her eyes remained empty, ecstatic.

The wind, the squall, outside, were going crazy. In the night, the shutters banged away.

– Listen, said the barkeeper.

They heard the howling of the wind in the trees, long and moaning like the cry of a mad woman.

The door was wide open, a gust of wind blew into the room. Instantly, naked Marie found herself standing up.

She cried out:

– Edward!

And the anguish made her voice a prolonging of the wind.

Marie Encounters a Dwarf

From this bad night came a man, struggling to close an umbrella: his rat-like silhouette stood out in the doorway.

– Quickly, your lordship! come in, said the barkeeper.

She staggered.

The dwarf came forward without answering.

– You're soaked, the woman continued, closing the door.

The little man was possessed of a surprising gravity, enormous and hunchbacked, with a huge head crowning his shoulders.

He greeted Marie, then turned towards the farmboys.

– Good day, Pierrot, he said shaking his hand, take my coat if you would.

Pierrot helped the count to remove his overcoat. The count gave him a pinch on the ass.

Pierrot smiled. The count shook people's hands amicably.

– May I? he asked as he bowed.

He took a seat at Marie's table across from her.

– A few bottles, would you, said the count.

– I've drunk, said one girl, so much I could piss on my chair.

– Drink enough to shit, my child . . .

He stopped crisply, rubbing his hands.

Not without a certain detachment.

Marie Sees the Ghost of Edward

Marie remained motionless looking at the count and his head turned toward her.

– Pour, she said.

The count filled the glasses.

She said again, very wisely:

– I'm going to die at dawn . . .

The count's steely look moved up and down her.

His blond eyebrows went up, accentuating the wrinkles in his excessively wide forehead.

Marie lifted her glass and said:

– Drink!

The count also lifted his glass and drank: they greedily emptied their glasses in unison.

The barkeeper came and sat down near Marie.

– I'm afraid, Marie said to her. Her eyes never left the count. She made a kind of coughing: she murmured in a crazed voice into the ear of the old woman:

– It's the ghost of Edward.

– Edward? asked the woman quietly.

– He's dead, said Marie in the same voice.

She took the other woman's hand and bit it.

– You bitch, screamed the woman who'd been bitten.

But freeing her hand, she caressed Marie; kissing her on the shoulder, she said to the count:

– All the same, she's sweet.

Marie Gets up on Top of the Bench

The count in his turn asked:
  – Who is Edward?
  – You no longer know who you are, said Marie.
This time her voice broke.
  – Make him drink, she demanded of the barkeeper.
She seemed to be at the end of her rope.
The count snorted down his glass but admitted:
  – Liquor has very little effect on me.
The enormous little man with the excessively large head scanned Marie with a mournful eye, as if he had had the intention of annoying her.
He scanned everything in the same way, his head stiff between his shoulders.
He called out:
  – Pierrot!
The boy approached.
  – This young child, said the dwarf, has given me a hard-on. How about sitting yourself down here.
  – Be nice, Pierrot, jerk me off. I don't dare ask this child . . .
He smiled.
  – She isn't accustomed, as you are, to monsters.
At this point, Marie got up on top of the bench.

Marie Pisses on the Count

– I'm afraid, said Marie. You look like a fence post.

He didn't answer. Pierrot grabbed his prick.

He was in fact impassive as a fence post.

– Go away, Marie told him, or I'll piss on you . . .

She got up on the table and squatted down.

– I'd be only too delighted, responded the monster. His neck had no freedom of movement; if he spoke, his chin alone moved.

Marie pissed.

Pierrot vigorously jerked off the count who was struck in the face with urine.

The count turned red and urine drenched him. Pierrot was jerking him off like someone fucking and his prick spat cum on his waistcoat. The dwarf was emitting a death rattle, convulsing from head to foot.

Marie Sprinkles Herself with Urine

Marie kept pissing.

On the table amidst the bottles and the glasses, she sprinkled herself with urine with her hands.

She drenched her legs, her ass, her face.

– Look how pretty I am, she said.

Squatting down, with her cunt at the level of the monster's head, she made her lips open horribly.

Marie Falls onto the Monster

Marie had a bitter smile.

A vision of bad horror . . .

One of her legs slipped: her cunt struck the count in the head.

He lost his balance and fell.

The two of them crashed down screaming, in an incredible din.

Marie Bites the Dwarf on the Dick

On the ground there was a horrible scuffle.

Marie broke loose, bit the dwarf on the dick and he screeched. Pierrot knocked her to the ground. He spread out her arms to form a cross: the others held her legs.

Marie wailed:

– Leave me alone.

Then she fell silent.

By the end she was panting, her eyes closed.

She opened her eyes. Pierrot, red, sweaty, was on top of her.

– Fuck me, she said.

Marie Is Poked by Pierrot

– Fuck her, Pierrot, said the barkeeper.

The others moved excitedly around the victim.

Marie let her head fall back, annoyed by these preparations.

The others laid her out, opened her legs. She was breathing quickly, her breath was burning.

The scene in its slowness evoked the slaughter of a pig, or the burial of a god.

Pierrot had his pants off, the count required that he be naked.

The delicate young man stamped like a bull: the count facilitated the entrance of his cock. The victim quivered and struggled: bodies locked with incredible hatred.

The others watched, their lips dry, stunned by this frenzy.

The bodies knotted together by Pierrot's prick rolled on the ground struggling. At the end, arching forward to the breaking point, completely out of breath, the farmboy howled, slobbering all over himself. Marie responded with a death spasm.

Marie Listens to the Birds in the Woods

. . . Marie came to.

She heard the songs of birds on the branch of a tree.

The songs, of an incredible delicacy, flitted whistling from tree to tree. Stretched out on the moist grass she saw the sky was light: the day was being born at that very moment.

She was cold, seized by a frozen happiness, suspended in an unintelligible emptiness. However much she would have liked to gently lift up her head, and in spite of the fact that she fell back in exhaustion on the ground, she remained faithful to the light, to the foliage, to the birds that peopled the woods. For an instant, occasions of childhood shyness brushed lightly over her, in memory. She recognized, bent over her, the great and massive head of the count.

Marie Vomits

What Marie read in the eyes of the dwarf was the insistence of death . . . this face expressed only an infinite disillusionment, that a frightful obsession made cynical. Hate leapt up in her, and death approaching, she got very frightened.

She raised herself up, clenching her teeth in front of the kneeling monster.

Standing, she trembled.

She took a step back, looked at the count and vomited.

– You see, she said.

– Relieved? asked the count.

– No, she said.

She saw the vomit in front of her. Her torn coat barely covered her.

– Where are we going? she said.

– Your place, answered the count.

Marie Shits on the Vomit

– My place, groaned Marie. Once again his head turned toward her.

– Are you the devil himself to want to go to my place? she asked.

– Yes, the dwarf came back, they've sometimes told me I was the devil himself.

– The devil? said Marie, I'd shit in the devil's face!

– Just a moment ago you vomited.

– I'd shit.

She squatted down and shit on the vomit.

The monster was still kneeling.

Marie leaned against an oak. She was sweating, in a trance. She said:

– All that, it's just nothing. But *at my place* you'll be scared . . . Too late . . .

She shook her head and, wild, marched roughly up to the dwarf, pulled him by the collar and screamed:

– You coming?

– My pleasure, said the count.

He added, almost quietly:

– She's worth it to me.

Marie Leads off the Count

Marie, who heard him, looked directly at the count. He got up:

— No one, he murmured, ever speaks to me that way.

— You can leave, she said. But if you come . . .

The count interrupted her curtly.

— I follow. You're going to give yourself to me.

She remained violent.

— It's time, she said. Come.

The Gnome Enters the House

They walked swiftly.

Day was breaking when they arrived. Marie pushed on the gate. They took a path lined with old trees: the sun made their heads golden.

Marie in all her surliness knew she was in accord with the sun. She led the count into the room.

— It's over, she said to herself. She was at once weak, full of hatred, indifferent.

— Undress yourself, she said, I'll wait in the next room.

The count undressed unhurriedly.

The sun through a clump of leaves speckled the wall and the speckles of light were dancing.

Marie Dies

The count got a hard-on.

His dick was long and reddish.

His naked body and his dick had a devilish deformity. His head in his angular shoulders, which were raised too far up, was pale and mocking.

He desired Marie and limited his thoughts to his desire.

He pushed open the door. Sadly naked, she waited for him in front of a bed, provocative and ugly: drunkenness and fatigue had beaten her down.

– What's wrong? said Marie.

The dead man, in disorder, filled the room . . .

The count stammered gently.

– . . . I didn't know.

He had to steady himself on a piece of furniture: *he lost his hard-on.*

Marie had a hideous smile.

– *It is accomplished!* she said.

She looked stupid, holding out a broken phial in her right hand. Finally, she fell.

Marie Follows the Dead Man into the Earth

. . . Finally *the count noticed the two hearses in a row, heading slowly toward the cemetery.*

The dwarf hissed between his teeth:

– *I was had . . .*

307

He didn't see the canal and let himself slip.

A loud noise, for an instant, disturbed the silence of the water.

The sun remained.

Translated by Austryn Wainhouse

Notes on the Authors

MARGARET ATWOOD (b. 1939) is the dominant figure of Canadian literature, whose writing explores the lives and emotions of women and has received worldwide acclaim. Her work includes the short-story collections *Dancing Girls* (1977) and *Bluebeard's Egg* (1983), poetry collections such as *Two-Headed Poems* (1978) and *Interlunar* (1988), children's books such as *Up in a Tree* (1978) and novels which include *Lady Oracle* (1976), *The Handmaid's Tale* (1986, filmed in 1990), *Cat's Eye* (1988) and, most recently, *Alias Grace* (1996).

NICOLA BARKER (b. 1966) won the David Higham Prize for Fiction and (jointly) the Macmillan Silver Pen Award for Fiction with her first collection of short stories, *Love Your Enemies* (1993). She has also written two novels, *Reversed Forecast* (1994) and *Small Holding* (1995); 'Bendy-Linda' comes from her second story collection, *Heading Inland* (1996). She lives and works in East London.

309

GEORGES BATAILLE (1897–1962) has been described as 'the true inheritor of the Marquis de Sade'. A philosopher, novelist and acute critic, Bataille was the first French writer to undergo Freudian analysis – an experience that he utilized in his writings, which played an important part in the Surrealist movement and pioneered the use of such imagery in erotic fictions such as *Story of the Eye* (1928), *Blue of the Sky* (1935), *Madame Edwarda* (1941) and *My Mother* (1966), most of which have been banned at various times and in various countries. His works of literary criticism include *Literature and Evil* (1949), *Eroticism* (1958) and *Tears of Eros* (1961).

STEVEN BERKOFF (b. 1937), 'the rottweiler of the British theatre' with 'a gift for releasing the four-letter-ridden lower-fifth delinquents lurking in almost everybody' (*Sunday Times*) is an actor, director and playwright. He formed the London Theatre Group in 1968, which put on adaptations of Kafka and Poe, then went on to write and present original works such as *Decadence*, *Kvetch*, *Sink the Belgrano!* and, most recently, *Massage*. As an actor he has appeared in such films as *A Clockwork Orange*, *Beverly Hills Cop*, *Gorky Park* and (portraying a James Bond villain) *Octopussy*. His first volume of autobiography, *Free Association*, was published in 1996, and he has recently been reading some of his stories (though not 'Gross Intrusion') on BBC Radio 4.

T. CORAGHESSAN BOYLE (b. 1948) made an immediate impact with his first hilarious collection of stories, *The*

Descent of Man (1979), and is much in demand as a performer of his own work; the *Sunday Times* has described him as 'the Frank Zappa of the short story'. Alternating with story collections, his novels have also been enthusiastically received, and they include *Water Music* (1981), *East is East* (1991) and The *Road to Wellville* (1993, filmed by Alan Parker in 1995). Born in Peeskill, New York, he now lives in Southern California where he is an associate professor at USCA; his stories still appear regularly in magazines.

POPPY Z. BRITE (b. 1967), now resident in her native New Orleans, has lived most of her life in the Southern states of the USA, where she worked variously as a cook, a mouse caretaker and an exotic dancer before finding success as a writer. She is now one of the stars of the new horror fiction, and her books to date include the novels *Lost Souls* (1992), *Drawing Blood* (1993) and *Exquisite Corpse* (1995), plus a story collection, *Swamp Foetus* (1994).

CHARLES BUKOWSKI (1920–1994) was born in Germany but moved with his family to the USA at the age of two. During the 1960s he began to acquire a cult reputation with stories and poems published in the underground press, but his heavy drinking led to the charity ward of Los Angeles County General Hospital, where he nearly died. After this he worked as a clerk for the Post Office and began writing again, his stories achieving wider fame when collected as *Erections, Ejaculations, Exhibitions and General Tales of Ordinary Madness* (1972), which was adapted into a biographical movie, *Tales of Ordinary Madness*, in 1981. 'The Copulating Mermaid of Venice, California', included in this anthology, together with some of Bukowski's poems, has been adapted into a seldom-seen erotic movie in Belgium: *Love is a Dog from Hell*.

ANGELA CARTER (1940–1992) grew up in the working-class north of England and went on to work as a journalist, academic and writer in Britain, the USA and Japan. An early exponent of what has come to be called Magic Realism, her novels include *The Magic Toyshop* (1967), *Heroes and Villains* (1969), *The Infernal Desire Machines of Doctor Hoffman* (1972) and *Nights at the Circus* (1984). Her short stories are collected in *Fireworks* (1974), *The Bloody Chamber* (1979, including the famous story 'The Company of Wolves', successfully filmed in 1984) and *Black Venus* (1985). Among her non-fiction works are *The Sadean Woman* (1979) and *Nothing Sacred* (1982). She also edited the extremely popular anthology *Wayward Girls and Wicked Women* (1986).

LUCY ELLMANN (b. 1956) was born in Evanston, Illinois, and came to England as an uncooperative teenager. Her first novel, *Sweet Desserts* (1989), won the Guardian Fiction Prize, and it was followed by *Varying Degrees of Hopelessness* (1991), which received high praise. She currently lives in Hampshire with her daughter. Her keenly awaited third novel, *Man or Mango?*, is imminent as this book goes to press.

RUTH FAINLIGHT (b. 1931) is best known as a poet with thirteen collections to date, but she has also published short stories, translations, plays and opera libretti. Her poetry, collected in such volumes as *A Forecast, A Fable* (1958), *Sibyls and Others* (1980) and *Fifteen to Infinity* (1983), is technically accomplished and expresses 'a specifically female anger'. Her short fiction has been collected in *Daylife and Nightlife* (1971) and *Dr Clock's Last Case* (1994). American by birth and citizenship, she has lived mostly in England since the age of fifteen, with long stays in France and Spain, and is currently resident in London with her husband, the author Allan Sillitoe.

HAROLD JAFFE No information has been made available for this author.

YASUNARI KAWABATA (1899–1972) was one of Japan's leading twentieth-century writers, whose short stories began to attract attention soon after he graduated from Tokyo Imperial University. His novels include *The Izu Dancer* (1927), *Snow Country* (1948), *The Lake* (1954) and *The Master of Go* (1954), and his erotic shorter fiction was collected in *The House of Sleeping Beauties* (1960). He won the Nobel Prize for Literature in 1968, but committed suicide in 1972.

MILAN KUNDERA (b. 1929) was born in Brno, Czechoslovakia. He was Professor of Advanced Cinematographic Studies (and a jazz musician) in Prague until the Russian invasion of 1968, when he lost his position and his works were banned. Since 1975 he has lived in exile in Paris, and his books have been acclaimed in the West; his novels include *The Book of Laughter and Forgetting* (1979), *The Unbearable Lightness of Being* (1984, memorably filmed in 1988 with Daniel Day-Lewis in the principal role) and *Immortality* (1991), while his short stories have been collected as *Laughable Loves* (1984).

TANITH LEE (b. 1947) began writing children's fantasies in the early seventies, starting with *The Dragon Hoard* (1971), but since *The Birthgrave* (1975, subsequently developed into a trilogy) has written primarily for adults and become a prolific leading name in both fantasy and science fiction, taking as her primary theme 'the ethical and sexual initiation of an adolescent character into a volatile world s/he herself will shape . . .' (John Clute). She also excels in the short-story form, her collections including *Dreams of Light and Dark* (1986) and *Women as Demons* (1989). She has also written erotic novels such as *Volkhavaar* (1977) and *Night's Master* (1978).

CLARICE LISPECTOR (1925–1977) is regarded as Brazil's most important female writer although she was born in the Ukraine, her family emigrating when she was an infant. She took up writing after training as a lawyer and published seven novels, including *Uma Aprendizagem ou O Livre dos Prazeres* (1969, translated as *An Apprenticeship or The Book of Delights*, 1986) and *A hora da estrela* (1977, translated as *The Hour of the Star*, 1986), as well as nine story collections and four children's books. Translations of these have gained her an international reputation.

CLIVE SINCLAIR (b. 1948) has had stories, interviews and travel pieces published in *Encounter*, *London Magazine*, *Penthouse*, *Lillit* and *Transatlantic Review*. His novels include *Bibliosexuality* (1973), *Blood Libels* (1985), *Cosmetic Effects* (1987) and *Augustus Rex* (1991). His first short-story collection, *Hearts of Gold* (1979), won the Somerset Maugham Award and was followed in 1982 by *Bed Bugs*.

BRIAN STABLEFORD (b. 1948), one of Britain's leading science fiction writers, has a degree in biology and a doctorate in sociology, which he taught for some years before turning to writing full time. If his early novels had been rather formulaic, a spell away from fiction in the early 1980s when he concentrated on criticism led to his transformation into 'a writer whose fiction befitted his intelligence' (*The Encyclopedia of Science Fiction*) with novels such as *The Empire of Fear* (1988), *The Werewolves of London* (1990) and *The Angel of Pain* (1991). Some of his sharpest short stories are in *Sexual Chemistry: Sardonic Tales of the Genetic Revolution* (1991).

LISA TUTTLE (b. 1952), an American writer of fantasy, horror and science fiction excelling in the short-story form, has long been a UK resident: she currently lives with her husband in a remote part of Scotland. Her stories appear regularly in the leading generic magazines and have been collected in *A Nest of Nightmares* (1986), *A Spaceship Built of Stone* (1987) and *Memories of the Body: Tales of Desire and Transformation* (1992). With Rosalind Ashe she wrote *The Encyclopedia of Feminism* (1986), and her most recent novel, *The Pillow Friend* (1996), shows a new command of the longer form.

Acknowledgements

'In Love with Raymond Chandler' by Margaret Atwood, from *Good Bones* (London: Bloomsbury, 1992), copyright © 1992 by O. W. Toad Ltd, reprinted by permission of Bloomsbury Publishing Ltd and the author's agent Phoebe Larmore.

'Bendy-Linda' by Nicola Barker, first published in *Critical Quarterly*, collected in *Heading Inland* (London: Faber and Faber, 1996), copyright © 1996 by Nicola Barker, reprinted by permission of Faber and Faber Ltd.

'The Dead Man' by Georges Bataille, from *My Mother, Madame Edwarda and the Dead Man*, translated by Austryn Wainhouse (London: Marion Boyars, 1989), copyright © 1989 by Marion Boyars Publishers Ltd, New York and London, and reprinted with their permission.

'Gross Intrusion' by Steven Berkoff, from *Gross Intrusion and Other Stories* (London: John Calder Ltd, 1979), copyright ©

317

1979, 1993 by Steven Berkoff, reprinted by permission of the author and the author's agents, Rosica Colin Limited.

'Descent of Man' by T. Coraghessan Boyle, first published in *Iowa Review*, collected in *Descent of Man* (London: Victor Gollancz Ltd, 1980) and *The Collected Stories of T. Coraghessan Boyle* (London: Granta Books, 1993), copyright © 1974 by T. Coraghessan Boyle, reprinted by permission of Richard Scott Simon Ltd.

'The Sixth Sentinel' by Poppy Z. Brite, first published in *Borderlands 3*, ed. Thomas F. Monteleone (Baltimore: Borderlands Press, 1993), copyright © 1993 by Poppy Z. Brite, reprinted by permission of the author and the author's agents, Richard Curtis Associates, Inc.

'The Copulating Mermaid of Venice, California' by Charles Bukowski, from *The Most Beautiful Woman in Town & Other Stories*, ed. Gail Chiarrello (San Francisco: City Lights, 1988), copyright © 1983 by Charles Bukowski, reprinted by permission of City Lights Books.

'The Loves of Lady Purple' by Angela Carter, first published in *Fireworks: Nine Stories in Various Disguises* (London: Quartet, 1974), copyright © 1974, 1987, 1992 by Angela Carter, reprinted by permission of the Estate of Angela Carter c/o Rogers Coleridge & White Ltd, 20 Powis Mews, London W11 I JN.

ACKNOWLEDGEMENTS

'Love: The World's Oldest Profession' by Lucy Ellmann, first published in *Cosmopolitan*, July 1990, copyright © 1990, 1998 by Lucy Ellmann, reprinted (with some revisions by the author) by kind permission of Serpent's Tail, London.

'Dr Clock's Last Case' by Ruth Fainlight, first published in *Bananas*, collected in *Dr Clock's Last Case and Other Stories* (London: Virago, 1994), copyright © 1977 by Ruth Fainlight, reprinted by permission of Virago Press/Little Brown.

'Sex Guerrillas' by Harold Jaffe, first published in *Avant-Pop: Fiction for a Daydream Nation*, ed. Larry McCaffery (Illinois State University: Black Ice Books, 1993), copyright © 1993 by Harold Jaffe, reprinted by permission of Fiction Collective Inc.

'One Arm' by Yasunari Kawabata, first published in English in *The House of Sleeping Beauties*, translated by Edward Seidensticker (Quadriga Press Ltd, 1969), copyright © 1969 by Yasunari Kawabata, reprinted by permission of Kodansha International Ltd.

'The Hitchhiking Game' by Milan Kundera, from *Smesne lasky*, first published in English as *Laughable Loves*, translated by Suzanne Rappaport (New York: Knopf, 1974), copyright © 1974 by Milan Kundera, reprinted by permission of Faber and Faber Ltd.

'The Beautiful Biting Machine' by Tanith Lee, first published in a limited edition by Cheap Street (1984), first published in the UK in *Arrows of Eros: Unearthly Tales of Love and Death*, ed. Alex Stewart (London: New English Library, 1989), copyright © 1984 by Tanith Lee, reprinted by permission of the author.

'Plaza Mauá' by Clarice Lispector, translated by Alexis Levitin, from *Soulstorm* (New York: New Directions, 1989), copyright © 1974 by Clarice Lispector, © 1989 by Alexis Levitin, reprinted by permission of New Directions Publishing Corp.

'Titillatio' by Clive Sinclair, from *Hearts of Gold* (London: Allison & Busby, 1979), copyright © 1979 by Clive Sinclair, reprinted by permission of the author c/o Rogers Coleridge & White Ltd, 20 Powis Mews, London W11 1JN.

'A Career in Sexual Chemistry' by Brian Stableford, first published as 'Sexual Chemistry' in *Interzone 20*, collected in *Sexual Chemistry: Sardonic Tales of the Genetic Revolution* (London: Simon & Schuster Ltd, 1991), copyright © 1987 by Brian Stableford, reprinted by permission of the author.

'Manskin, Womanskin' by Lisa Tuttle, first published in *By the Light of the Silvery Moon*, ed. Ruth Petrie (London: Virago, 1994), copyright © 1994 by Lisa Tuttle, reprinted by permission of the author.